DIANA'S PHILO~~...~~ : **Sex is. Money** ~~...~~ **comes only to t**~~...~~ **usually by taking** ~~...~~

Meet some of Diana's ~~HAPPY Friends.~~

'PUTZI DA SILVA: Fabulously wealthy Brazilian aristocrat who rides like a goucho – but not on a horse.

SYLVIA DA SILVA: Putzi's gorgeous sister with her own well-deserved reputation as 'the world's most successful lesbian.'

MAXEY VON FUCHS: Prussian stud of magnificent proportions. But as Diana says, 'You can't eat filet mignon every night.'

DICK SCHLONGA, MD: Lustful doctor with a fantastic bedside manner who has been known to give his patients intensive care.

HUGO BATTISTA: Impassioned Latin bellhop. 'Finally," cooed Diana, 'the room service that really delivers.'

Hungry for the fruit of passion, their ravenous appetites will soon be served when they enter DIANA'S PARADISE

Books by
LYTTON SINCLAIR

Diana's Debut
Diana's Paradise

LYTTON SINCLAIR

Diana's Paradise

Futura

A Futura Book

Copyright © 1983 by Warner Books Inc

First published in the US by
Warner Books Inc,
666 Fifth Avenue, New York, New York 10103

This edition published in 1988 by
Futura Publications, a Division of
Macdonald & Co (Publishers) Ltd
London & Sydney

ISBN 0 7088 4033 7

Photoset in North Wales by
Derek Doyle & Associates, Mold, Clwyd.
Reproduced, printed and bound in Great Britain by
Hazell Watson & Viney Limited
Member of BPCC plc
Aylesbury, Bucks, England

Futura Publications
A Division of
Macdonald & Co (Publishers) Ltd
3rd Floor, Greater London House
Hampstead Road
London NW1 7QX
A Maxwell Pergamon Publishing Company plc

For
Melissa,
who is famous for sex

Diana's Paradise

Prologue

In my last account, *Diana's Debut*, I detailed the extraordinary story of my maiden voyage to Rome for my first fashion show, an occasion which signaled my successful debut as an international designer of women's clothes. My rise to fame and fortune had been absolutely phenomenal; in less than a year, I had gone from a 'career' as a Howard Johnson's hostess in Beavertown, Pennsylvania, to a newsworthy position as widow of one of the world's great couturiers, my late, great, beloved husband, Adolfo Adoro. Unfortunately for Adolfo, his massive wrestler's chest with its matted black fleece could not compensate for his fragile, damaged heart beating within. Adolfo's heart gave out with a bang at the very moment his thick Sicilian cock was spurting its last load of creamy white come deep into my ravenous cunt. Oh well, what is there to say about stark and bitter tragedy? In order to survive, I have had to adopt a positive philosophical attitude. The megabucks Adolfo left me have helped, too. So has my business manager and financial adviser, Maxey von Fuchs, that Teutonic god, whose constant affection, hot mouth, and grappling, exploring hands, forever desperate to finger my vulva, have kept me from going over the edge of despair. It was Maxey who originally suggested we rent the Roman Colosseum to display my first collection of clothes. My Roman holiday, as celebrated in *Diana's Debut*, turned out to be the most valuable learning experience of my short life.

And when I say 'learning,' I mean sex, the one inexhaustible subject in the *Book of Knowledge*.

In the Eternal City, I discovered that there are Catholic priests, deep within the confines of the Vatican itself, who are starving for pussy. There is even a certain Pope with secret appetites, desperate to be stroked and fondled. I also discovered from firsthand experience the constant self-sacrifices of the everyday Roman prostitute, and, although I do not approve of homosexuality, I experienced a dramatic breakthrough in my love-hate relationship with my archrival Glorianna Bronx. I also fell face first into the bittersweet chocolate cunt of a black American whore. All in all, however, my crowning achievement in Rome was my innovation of using hookers as fashion models in my Colossseum show. My strategy was simple enough: the audience got to see each outfit twice, once on a willowy, scarecrow, fashion-model type, then on my big-breasted, full-hipped beauties who followed the fashion models close behind. Needless to say, it was quite a contrast. And, in a word, it worked. I became known as the designer who cares about the average woman with her average woman's body that breathes sex and sensuality. Luckily for the House of Adoro payroll, it seems that almost every American house-wife, way down deep in her secret fantasies, wants to be a Roman whore with her dishevelled hair a little too wild, her bloodshot eyes a little too thickly outlined with black mascara, her overfed tummy a little too round with ripe, come-hither flesh. I encouraged such fantasies. Weren't we all sick of dieting and running to the hairdressers to have every stray lock clipped and shaped like a boxwood hedge? Weren't we tired of dressing for angry nuns and angrier feminists? Weren't we all weary of trying to retain the bodies of fifteen-year-old virgins?

Unlike his American counterpart, the Roman male appreciated the mature woman in her middle twenties. What normal American woman didn't crave one of those Latin love gods? Those paragons of almost professional masculinity loved to parade with jutting erections pressing against their tight silk pants, especially when I walked by with my clinging Spandex dresses, half silk, half elastic, that sucked my body, revealing every inch of nipple and slit. I learned such wisdom from my new-found friends, those wonderful Roman whores. They became a pervasive, lifelong influence on my uptight, small-town American ways.

So, given my stunning, although admittedly controversial success in using Roman prostitutes, I hatched another idea: I would visit Rio de Janeiro, where the House of Adoro contracted knitting mills; I would return with Brazilian call girls to model my summer wear line at my spring fashion show. This latest account, *Diana's Paradise*, tells the story of my visit to Brazil and what happened afterward. In the first place, my big idea backfired; I hit Rio during Carnival week, a time of orgy and abandon, and I found myself asking every sexy stranger on the street, man and woman alike, to come back to Manhattan with me. Some of them took me up on my offer; the subsequent 'goings-on' were considerably more than I had bargained for. I found myself yearning for the good ol' days of the Roman prostitutes.

My one impression of Brazil had been from a documentary travel film which made the Rio Carnival look like a Connecticut beach club follies. I had not counted on the raw truth of the pre-Lenten festivities; pulsating flesh, dark and sweet, throbbing to jungle drums. Yes, Rio with its predominantly black population is the heart and soul of Africa. I can still feel the rhythm of hot blood pumping through ebony limbs, the beating of the South Atlantic surf on Copacabana Beach, the incessant salsa, the unending chanting of the voodoo priestesses, and the sexual pounding which does not stop.

The Carnival frenzy proved to be too much for New York. Manhattan's fabled energy is mostly mental; the famous career drive is at root a constant push to excellence in finance, publishing, theatre, fashion. New York is basically mercurial, intellectual, of quicksilver mind. When Manhattan gets physical, that means another skyscraper, a real estate deal, open-heart surgery at Columbia Presbyterian. Yes, New Yorkers talk about sex, and it's true, many New York men naturally gravitate to a sexually healthy woman like me, but it's in Rio, and not New York, where you can actually smell the sex in the midnight air. You can smell the woman's secretions: her musk, her cheap French perfume, her lover's come drying between her thighs. In New York, you can smell only the money and the power, which, for many people, is more of a turn-on than mere flesh. In Brazil, to the contrary, nothing is more powerful than sex. For centuries, the Brazilians have been open to the mixing of races and the crossing over from one social class to another; the principal religion in Brazil is a mixture of Catholicism, voodoo, and sex; it has never heard of birth control. Even I, with my ever-present Protestant IUD, gasp when I think of the women of Rio who experience sex as the open channel to a never-ending stream of life which began fifty billion years ago. No wonder Brazil has the highest birth rate in the world. By the end of the century, Brazil is expected to have quadrupled its population; it has been predicted that, by the year 2000, Portuguese, the language of Brazil, will be the most widely spoken language in the Western Hemisphere. Not Spanish. Not English. Portuguese. I will go further than that. After spending Carnival in Rio, I predict that sex, Brazilian style, will someday overtake the present sad situation of the European and American middle classes, millions of men and women, who, if given half a chance, could be lusty and sex-obsessed. Now, these people are so constrained by background and education that they waste their lives being well-behaved and never 'get it on,' as my black friends say, with people from different races, and markedly different incomes.

Diana's Paradise is, at root, the story of my Brazilian Big Idea, or 'How To Overload Manhattan's Sexual Circuits by Arriving With a Boatload of Brazilians.' But, like I say, how do you sell bathing suits when you've got hard-driving career women seated at your summer wear fashion show, order blanks in hand, and a coffee-coloured Afro-Hispanic god with black hair and ice-blue eyes struts out in a peacock headdress, carrying a six-foot spear, wearing a khaki bathing suit with the fly unzipped and his cock sticking out? What do you do when a copper-skinned Inca goddess parades in front of the editor-in-chief of *Womens Wear Daily* in a white pleated tennis skirt with nothing underneath but her silky black beaver with its bright coral gash? What do you do when the editor in question cannot see the clothes on the runway, he's so busy trying to hide his hard-on? I mean, how do you sell clothes? What do you do about impassioned Latin revolutionaries who follow the cruise ships with their terrorist bombs in the hopes of starting World War Three. This, too, is *Diana's Paradise*. Life in the fast lane. Too fast. I never thought the day would come when I would feel like a virgin among men and women who really knew how to use their cocks and their pussies. I never thought I'd feel deformed and deprived for not having at least one African ancestor. In Brazil, among the 'old money' aristocratic families, there are always a few mahogany-colored progenitors to make their nostrils flare, and their skin shine like gold, and their lips become, well, that much more sensual.

And what the famous Brazilian passions with their roots in the surrounding jungles can do for the development of juicy pussy flesh, oversized clits, and cocks that are the marvel of the Western Hemisphere, is too much to get into here. In *Diana's Paradise*, however, I talk about my sexual reawakening with the Brazilians, who frankly overpower the North Americans with their passion, their sensuality, their driving samba rhythms, their nudity, their voodoo, their lust for lust, their overspiced food, their extravagant spending, their ongoing revolution.

The previous summer, Rome had almost defeated this simple girl from the wilds of Pennsylvania; if it hadn't been for a humpy Holy Father, I'd be back in the Beavertown Howard Johnson's. Brazil gave me a new lease on lust, and taught me there is only one basis for guilt, and that is not having fucked enough. And I never thought I'd be so attracted to one man, in this case, the international playboy 'Putzi' Da Silva, that I'd be willing to abandon my career and my native land to devote the rest of my life to him; he was that good in bed. His all-consuming passion for a certain European princess with fantastic tits, no names mentioned, came between us, and I faced the all-time crisis of my life. How could I compete with a girl who had a palace and a second language to offer him? Then, there was 'Putzi's' sister, Sylvia Da Silva, the world's most successful lesbian, who had the hots for me. Of course, like I say, I do not approve of homosexuality, but the day I saw Sylvia masturbating on her private beach, I lost control of my senses. I could not help it, I had to eat her out. She provoked me with her extreme sensuality; I found it disgusting the way she stroked and pinched her own nipples with such obvious enjoyment. Nothing is worse than a narcissistic, masturbating lesbian, but my lips and tongue still tingle when I recall my first mouthful of her raw meat. She possessed me. Clearly, she was a witch; she perverted my normal sexual appetites into a sweet desire for her. Such is the power of Brazil.

When my personal Carnival arrived in New York, the city was divided in its reaction. Normally staid people seemed to be suddenly given permission to become Latin heathens carousing in the spangled dark. Maxey von Fuchs was one. I never expected to find that Prussian penny-pincher in a glittering jockstrap, fucking a man and a woman at the same time to a pulsing salsa beat, with the odor of marijuana in the darkened room strong enough to choke a horse. I never expected to see my archrival Glorianna, the object of my intense love-hate, with her obvious passion for women, who's kidding who, running stark naked down Park Avenue, chasing after a great black stud who had just taken my breath away, literally. She is so jealous.

Then, there is the chapter in *Diana's Paradise* where preteen Brazilian girls are deflowered. I cannot reveal the erotic details at this time, but the subject matter is handled in good taste. To the contrary, in how much bad taste can it be to describe human beings of whatever age who are having a terrific time?

For reasons beyond my control, my summer wear fashion show turned out to be the scandal of the season, and I had to go to extraordinary lengths to salvage my reputation. But, thank God, wherever I turned for help, the most wonderful people welcomed me with open arms – and legs. I'm so grateful to the human race. *Diana's Paradise* promises to be my best account yet.

Chapter One

New York in February. What a dull month. The fog floats in like a dead eel. The previous August, I'd had a triumphant debut in Rome with my Colosseum show. My new friends, the fat whores from Mrs Boothby's, had created a sensation. As a result, I was now a world figure, or so they told me. I could have cared less. I had never wanted to be a celebrity in the first place, and when the flash bulbs exploded in my frightened face every time I went out to buy a pack of cigarettes, or a pair of pantyhose, or some vaginal deodorant, it meant nothing. Nothing meant nothing, and I didn't know why. I was twenty-three and gorgeous, with a terrific pair of tits and an ass that stopped traffic, but I didn't care. When I was fifty, I knew I'd wonder how I could have looked so great so effortlessly, and been so miserable.

The truth was, I felt tough and masculine. Total strangers kept calling me, asking me to design interiors for sports cars, handles for luggage, toothbrush holders, and leather belts. Totally boring. Wait, it gets worse. For me, as with many women, happiness begins in bed, and, during those dreary days in February, I was stuck in a serious sexual rut. Night after night, I found myself taking the same people home to bed. The same people, for the sake of the record, were Maxey von Fuchs, that Prussian stud I normally adored, but you can't eat filet mignon every night, and the House of Adoro's top model, Glorianna Bronx, with whom I had suffered intermittent breakthroughs in an intense love-hate relationship. Although I am not a lesbian, and was usually not sexually attracted to Glorianna, there were times when I accidentally caught her naked in the models' dressing room, and the ripeness of her full breasts, so unusual in a woman of her height, made me gasp for breath; I just couldn't help myself. Surely, there is a level of sexuality that transcends the male-female axis. Surely, there are some people of either sex, who, at a certain age, are possessed of such excruciating beauty that their ripe skin and full sexual organs cry out for my sucking mouth and my hungry hands. From time to time, that's how I felt about Glorianna. But not that February in New York. No, in February, something happened that made me think I must be bored, that I should get away from it all, that I needed a change of scenery; sexual scenery, that is.

For pious people with religious scruples, or Ph.D.'s in English literature who believe that sexually explicit literature is trash, read no further. For feminists who imagine that my so-called promiscuity means I possess no real sense of self-worth, there is no need to turn another page. Read *The Remembrance of Things Past*, Shakespeare's sonnets, or St. John of the Cross, where the depth and complexity of the human soul is explored and celebrated, where good taste and breeding counts, where language is a central event.

Anyway, getting back to me, there we were, the three of us, Maxey, Glorianna, and I, on the top floor of the House of Adoro in that glorious suite of paneled mahogany rooms, in bed. We lay snug inside a rosy box of a cherry, eight-foot square, tightly paneled compartment; an island of pink silk sheets and crimson velvet quilts under a Chinese red, lacquered awning. Some bed. I had tightly shut the brocaded, wine-colored draperies around us. The thick, wall-to-wall carpet of burgundy pile muffled every sound, natural or otherwise. All incoming phone calls were rerouted automatically to the main switchboard in the basement. All entrances to the House of Adoro were guarded by an omnipresent electric eye. One strange foot on the stairs, any stairs, and loud bells went off in my local precinct house. Maxey, Glorianna, and I were an island of love in the middle of the world's busiest city, where there is usually no time for anything but 'Slam bam, thank you Ma'am.' Glorianna's magnificent twin mounds of delectable flesh, with those mocha, cone-shaped aureolas and coffee-colored nipples, rose and fell on her chest as she lay snarled in a knot of pink silk sheets, frustrated at her failed attempts to pleasure me.

'What have I done wrong?' she moaned.

'It's not you, my darling,' I reassured her, kissing the golden valley that sloped down from her bellybutton into a black silk thatch, where I knew her coral gash lay waiting for the touch of my warm, wet lips.

'Please kiss my pussy,' she begged. 'Pulleese, Diana!' Her black Cherokee eyes mirrored depths of untold pain. Glorianna seemed so tragic and so lost.

For my part, I was absolutely bored. It was only out of the deepest friendship and the most profound professional courtesy that I yielded to her anguished request for human contact and bent over to run the pointed tip of my well-practiced tongue up and down the orchid-petal edges of her outer labia. Normally, I would have been ravenous by now, since her labia, those hot pink lips, smelled of the jungle and rank animal desire. Maxey, who I thought was fast asleep, apparently never slept too soundly when there was the remotest possibility of 'putting it in me.' I should never have stuck my ass six inches from his nose. Dead, he could smell my cunt. Asleep, his erection was immediate, and, like a programmed robot, while still half-conscious, his mouth was eating me out from behind, his precome ooze glistening on the pink marble head of his rampant Teutonic cock. Germans seem to be the one civilized race who have retained their barbaric appetites. Fucking is as natural to them as sleeping or eating. It's true that the Latins have transformed sex into the major art form of the twentieth century (well, maybe not major art, but certainly folk-art, or, as Maxey says, 'fuck-art'), but sex-as-art presupposes some distance between the genitals and the brain. With Maxey, there was no mental distance. Using his sizeable cock was as natural to him as using his right hand.

'Oh Diana,' he moaned, as he woke, 'I want you. I can't live apart from you. Please let me eat you out every hour of every day.' In his half-conscious delirium, Maxey was still flattering, but I was still bored.

'Maxey,' I said, finally. 'do what you want with me, but don't expect me to respond with much enthusiasm. I don't know what's wrong with me, but nothing excites me anymore. Maybe I should see a shrink.'

Predictably, Maxey was too busy eating me out to listen to my complaint, and the third person in our triumverate, the self-absorbed Glorianna, had a mind (and a cunt) of her own.

Glorianna's already heavy breathing became louder and huskier. With her elegant hands, she grasped my blonde head, as I, half-aroused, continued to mechanically mouth her ripe labia, letting my tongue occasionally light on her choice oyster of a clitoris which throbbed under my almost professional touch. It's too bad the United States is so puritanical. Truly, Glorianna's open cunt should have been on the covers of leading magazines. It far outclassed her face, which was flawless, perfect, and fine-boned, but hardly exciting. Her cunt was absolutely spectacular; it possessed mystery; it retreated into its own sensuous recesses; it was soft, yielding, vulnerable, in a woman who did not suggest such qualities. Her lean, prima ballerina's limbs, with thighs as smooth and firm as molded butter that led directly to that black triangle of pubic hair, did not fully prepare the half-awake lover

20

for the forbidden treasures she revealed when she spread her legs. Believe me, if I hadn't been so bored, I probably would have gone berserk. Her coral gash suggested bejeweled tropical fish, and when she ran her long fingers up and down that slit and parted her vaginal lips, the raw meat she exposed in that wonderfully obscene gesture normally made my poor heart beat to the point of hyperventilation. I became a cannibal, slurping, devouring, coming up for air only when absolutely necessary to gasp for breath before diving into her flesh once more to feast and forget the outside world.

But not that dreary February day. I ate her out for friendship's sake, and enjoyed what pleasure I could. At least, she was a warm body. In the meantime, Maxey, rock-hard at fifty-five, had mounted me from behind, doggie-style. I could feel his taut nipples tracing lines on my back as he held me. I could feel his heavy balls slapping against that handful of dark-meat fuckflesh that seems to hang between my thighs when I crouch on all fours, that special view of my golden-furred vagina that drives men like Maxey wild. His bush, a nest of copper wires, scratched and tickled me as that thick, engorged cock of his, big as a baby's fist, rammed back and forth, deeper and deeper, into my vaginal maw. Don't get me wrong; any woman within a two-hundred-mile radius of New York would have gladly sacrificed a year's pay to spend a night with that deep-voiced, barrel-chested Thor whose computer brain helped the House of Adoro gross fifty million dollars a year, but I couldn't have cared less as I came in torrential waves of orgasm on that pink-sheeted bed. My orgasms were automatic. My soul was not engaged. My imagination was dead. I suppose it seemed like I was acting like a spoiled rotten princess, but nothing, not even two of New York's hottest numbers, could solve my emotional problem. When Maxey came, he shuddered and bolted, screaming animal sounds of pleasure and release. I could feel his

21

thick, warm come oozing out of my electrified but noncaring vulva and down my silky thighs.

By now, Glorianna had bucked her tasty pubes into my mouth, where she had several writhing orgasms in succession. My lips were sore from accommodating her. Eventually, I pushed her away from me. She seemed stunned at my rejection, but I needed time to breathe. My rise to fame and fortune had been too quick and too complete. My widowhood had come too soon. Now, my daily routine as a leading international designer was cluttered up with successful go-getters who were too rich and too sophisticated.

I was, after all, only twenty-three. I had always drawn my strength from my humble beginnings; my people back in Beavertown were pastry chefs and waitresses and traffic cops and seamstresses. But, every time I tried to talk to one of our Adoro seamstresses, she'd blush and clam up. If I let the cop on the corner feel me up, we'd both end up in *The National Enquirer*. My trouble was, I'd lost touch with ordinary people.

There was a long silence. Finally, Maxey spoke. In retrospect, I realize now that his wisdom saved my life, or at least salvaged my sanity. 'My darling Diana,' he began, 'I can see the tears in your lovely eyes and I want you to know there is absolutely nothing wrong with you ... '

'Oh, Maxey,' I blurted out, 'there *is* something wrong. I feel absolutely dead!'

'No, no, no,' he countered. 'Stop that talk. Your problem is you're bored.'

'Yes, I'm bored,' I replied. 'I'm an ironing board, straight and wooden, I think I need a psychiatrist.'

'Stop it, Diana,' he insisted, stroking my nipples with his finely chiseled fingers. 'You don't need a psychiatrist, you need a change of scenery. After all, genius that you are, you're still a young woman who's only been out of the United States once, for a two-week trip to Rome. New York is an electric city, certainly, but your batteries are overcharged. You're beginning to short-circuit.'

Glorianna, that self-absorbed cunt, was listening to none of Maxey's sensitive analysis of my emotional trauma. She was fast asleep, her dark, chocolate nipples like two staring eyes floating in the custard of her creamy breasts. It was just as well. She would have turned lizard green from jealousy if she had heard Dr von Fuch's ingenious prescription for my malady.

'Diana, I think you should spend a week or two in Rio de Janeiro,' said Maxey.

'Is Rio de Janeiro near Acapulco?' I asked, completely ignorant of geography, which I flunked after my First Big Affair in high school with my geography teacher, Mr Rivera, had turned to bitterness and hysteria when I discovered he was also dating my mother.

'Rio de Janeiro is in Brazil,' Maxey answered, cutting through my fantasy with his razor-sharp intelligence. 'It's summer there now,' he continued. 'Rio is completely different from New York and, of course, the knitwear factories there manufacture a lot of our Adoro summer wear. Maybe we could introduce Brazilian swimsuit and beach wear designs to our American and European customers. I want you to spend some time on the beach there and see what you think.' Little did Maxey or even I suspect that, by the time I got to that dazzling two-and-one-half mile stretch of white sand called Copacabana, I would be stark naked, with swimwear designs the last thing on my ever-designing mind.

In any case, Maxey had made his mind up, and by midnight I was on Pan American Flight #69 and booked into Rio's latest luxury hotel, the Rio Palace on Avenue Atlantica overlooking Copacabana Beach on the Atlantic Ocean. No, I did not travel alone. (What kind of a woman do you think I am?) Maxey's choice of a travelling companion for me, Lulu Touché, couldn't have been more ingenious. Lulu was head of the House of Adoro's workroom; it was Lulu who had first shepherded and guided me when I arrived there as a lowly seamstress less than two years before; it was Lulu who first pushed me under the nose (and mouth and cock) of my beloved Adolfo.

Lulu knew intimately every possible stitch, pleat, hem, panel, lining, zipper of every possible garment, from crotch-less pantyhose to strapless wedding dress, both house specialities, in every possible fabric from peek-a-boo lace to see-through gauze. Lulu knew cost; Lulu knew workmanship.

Fortunately, or unfortunately, Lulu was also a hot-blooded Sicilian in her middle years. Let's just say that businessmen did not exactly drop to their knees in front of her, begging to unbutton her dress and pull down her panties as they did to me. She was short and dynamic in her movements; her pixie haircut dyed brick red made her interesting, but fearsome. I could tell that she had invented a tough facade to disguise the whore-house within, and I knew that if she ever let down her guard, something she was reluctant to do for the sake of her own survival, she could outmatch any two-dollar hooker for pure, unadulterated raunch.

For the moment, however, Lulu was the perfect companion for me; she taught me the rags business and she looked the other way when I wanted to wallow in pussy and cock. Did I say pussy? I mean to say pectoral muscles – or something. I never think about pussy unless it's staring me straight in the face, which happens more often than you might think. Women are so brazen these days.

Our leave-taking from Kennedy Airport and the ensuing flight to Rio de Janeiro were without incident except for the flight attendant, male, who served me a Bloody Mary with his cock as a stirrer. Apparently, he thought that was funny. I made him take it back and start over. I told him I was a lady. He looked me straight in the face with penetrating blue eyes and said, 'Sure.' Lulu muttered something about the decline and fall of Civilization. I was too depressed to pursue the matter or the flight attendant.

When we arrived at the new International Airport in Rio, the most strikingly modern in South America, it was very late. I was half asleep. I thought I smelled a tropical sea, warm and salty, full of pink-fleshed fish and rotting vegetation, but I was too tired to notice. Was that a samba or a rhumba I overheard on somebody's radio? It made no distinct impression. Then, we checked in at the Rio Palace. Our separate bedrooms were joined by a shared bath. I was too exhausted to care. I expected nothing. I hoped for nothing. I had visions of sweltering days spent in a steamy factory arguing with egomaniacal Latins over the various designs for swimming suits, real or imagined. That, and discussing hems with Lulu.

Little did I realize, as I laid my weary head on the hotel pillow, that the next day, Sunday, was the beginning of Carnival. How could I have known that, soon after the sun rose at six A.M., the full force of Rio would hit me like a tropical hurricane? How could I begin to suspect that Brazil would forever change my boring, self-centered life? Yes, thank you, my Maxey, for your incredible surprise. Before the week was out, I was to be completely transformed.

Chapter Two

The sun rose ten minutes before I awoke. It was an orange sun, a sun in flames. The heat rose up from the street four floors below. The ocean, on the other side of the hotel, seemed a mile away. That's what happens when you make last-minute reservations.

Without warning, the samba beat began. 'One, two, three, four – one two!' 'One, two, three, four – one two!' Not one samba beat, not one samba drum, but samba everywhere, samba coming from the beach, from the fishing boats, samba from the shacks in the hillside slums, the favelas that crowd the hills like jungle flowers. Hundreds of layers of 'One, two, three, four – one two!', an intoxicating beat that echoed in my pulse. As I slept, I could feel the beat in my temples, behind my eyes, in the veins in my breasts, in the arteries that course around the cunt. 'One, two, three, four – one two!' The word is 'Samba!' If samba sounds African in origin, it's not. The samba is an invention of Brazil, more specifically of Rio, and Rio is an invention all its own. No parent culture can claim Brazil, not Spain, not Portugal, not Africa. Brazil is unique, and Rio de Janeiro, 'the River of January,' is to Brazil what the crotch is to a healthy, functioning human being. It is the seat of pleasure, the locus of regeneration and reproduction. Rio is sex as sex was meant to be, and, at Carnival time, sex is center stage.

I awoke with a start and ran to the window, searching for the source of this new and delicious sound, completely forgetting I was stark naked. When I looked out the window, I could scarcely believe my eyes! Nothing Maxey had said prepared me for what I witnessed on the streets below. Carnival!

Some background notes: in Europe, during the Middle Ages, when every human being was beholden to the Pope, the forty days before Easter were called Lent. Lent was a time of prayer and penance – and fasting. No animal dietary products were allowed; no milk, no eggs, no cheese, and most importantly, no meat. That's what Carnival means – 'farewell to meat.' So, as the legend goes, the European peasantry, knowing they were in for a grim forty days, celebrated and partied and used up all their animal products during the week before Ash Wednesday, the first day of Lent. In the Mediterranean countries, in those days before Club Med and Pan Am, people began to wear costumes and kick up their heels in what was called 'Mardi Gras,' or 'Fat Tuesday,' the day before Ash Wednesday. In Beavertown, where I grew up, Mardi Gras was, at best, a street parade in New Orleans that usually got about two minutes coverage on the CBS News. The New Orleans Mardi Gras looked like a half-time rally at our local high school football stadium. A Catholic family next to my grandmother, the Durochers, deep-fried donuts and passed them around, the only catch being that Mrs Durocher, who was particularly devout, insisted on explaining the origins of Mardi Gras, telling how, in the Middle Ages, people used up their fat by deep-frying donuts. Her son, Timmy, insisted I know this. Timmy had a big, sausage-shaped cock with a curve in it; very sexy, except he wanted to marry me when I was seventeen and have five kids immediately.

My point is, Mardi Gras never made much sense to me until I got to Rio, where Mardi Gras is Christmas, Easter, and Life After Death rolled up into a festival that starts the day after Christmas, and then, the week before Ash Wednesday, bursts into an orgy of spectacle, samba, and – well, sex. Mind you, below the equator, the seasons are reversed; February in Brazil is like August in Georgia. Hot. Steamy. Sizzling.

Another crucial point to remember: for almost four hundred years, the tropical sun has worked itself into the bones of the Afro-Hispanic melting pot. The difference between Brazilian culture and its Euro-African roots is the difference between a torrid love affair and masturbating under the covers at age ten. All the anger and resentment that keeps blacks and whites apart in North America, Europe, and Africa has melted in the Rio de Janeiro sun. The release of energy from the mingling of the races has given rise to a unique culture; vibrant, free, sexually liberated. In Rio, Mardi Gras is no longer a Catholic feast in the cold European night; it is a primal release of love in the passionate summer of the south. In Rio de Janeiro during Carnival, Jesus, Mary, and Joseph make love in the streets, and then pay homage to Oxala, the supreme god of Umbanda, and to Yemanjá, the ruling divinity of the sea. On the warm beaches of Copacabana, in the navy-blue tropical night, revelers wearing the cone-shaped hat of the Roman pontiff and the dove-winged headdresses of the Sisters of Charity roll their hot tongues around the pulsating labia and meaty glandes of black-haired, golden-hued boys and girls dressed as Saravá, Nana, Xangó, Oxóssi, and Oxumaré, the spirit gods of the African slaves.

In Rio, during Carnival, there is no more Catholic, no more Jew, no more tribal worshipper; the angry sects of the religious past break down into a new Garden of Eden where new gods are found in the samba, and in every possible variety of sex. The oncoming Lent provides an excuse for something more basic than Western Civilization. The rhythm that connects every human being with the swell of the tides and the regular passing of day into night erupts once a year into an ocean of glittering flesh. The Cariocas (that is what the citizens of Rio call themselves) draw

28

strength from their common humanity and their common heritage. They also fill each other's hunger with music, with dance, and with mouthfuls of each other's sexual flesh. *M'mm m'mm good.*

As I watched from my fourth-floor hotel window, the samba hypnotized Rio de Janeiro. Drum hypnosis. Steel drums. 'Bom, bam, bom, bam – bom bam.' The samba, snakelike, sinuous, like a Medieval plague, stalked the city and crept into the gray matter of the human brain. Without thinking, my feet began to beat in time to the big steel drums. My knees bobbed; my tummy swayed. My hips gave way to the beat. Without resistance, I was carried away into incantation and ecstasy.

Then, as I looked down at the street celebration below my window, I saw, standing by a wrought-iron lamppost, a swarthy man with the headdress of an Amazon Indian, all purple and black feathers, the tail of a psychedelic peacock. I watched, in utter fascination, as he lifted out of his red nylon bikini a leaden cock throbbing with blood. Spitting on his hand, he began to work his prime piece of sexual pork, jerking its thick, dark outer muscles over what looked like a rod of steel inside. And all the while, oblivious to the lecherous remarks of his fellow Cariocas, he was staring up at me, his black, Indian eyes glinting like live coals in the glare of the hot tropical sun.

He must have been a witch doctor from the upper headwaters of the Amazon, because I stood there absolutely hypnotized, completely unconscious of the fact that my index finger was already inside my vagina, smearing my sticky lubricant over blood-marshaled labia. Soon, a small crowd gathered, and I watched in fascination as a few businessmen in black, fitted suits and bowler hats, surely an odd upper-class minority for Rio, and certainly super-repressed – they'd have to be to wear those black suits in the midday Brazilian sun joined them. But no, I was wrong about their being repressed, I mean – where was I? They stood there, those black-suited businessmen, at least eight of them, with cocks in hand; white cocks, tan cocks, black cocks, long, skinny cocks with bulbous heads, fat slugs of cocks that ballooned in the middle, bright red cocks shaped like cupid's arrows, inflamed with lust. The cocks were a sea of tropical fish, a species which feeds on heat and desire. There were street vendors, too, sizzling fat slices of marinated pork on iron grills over glowing charcoal fires. There were schoolboys in soccer uniforms. There were men in late middle age, most of them in Carnival costumes, their bodies slashed with warpaint; vermilion, crimson, lavender, silver, gold. All of them were masturbating in front of my window. Was this a joke? Were they serious? I did not know, and I did not care. I only knew that, after one hour in Rio, I was no longer quite as bored as I'd been the day before.

I was gasping in my self-induced orgasm as the men below my window began to ejaculate in different styles, each one more erotic than the next; wide arcs of shimmering globules, streams of egg-white albumen, short bursts of freshwater pearls, gushes of buttermilk, bursts of *creme anglaise*. At that point, my long-standing depression must have lifted completely, because I collapsed on the thick, brown carpet, heaving and moaning in total orgasm. I found myself transported far beyond my imagination, far deeper than my most erotic dreams both in and out of bed. As the full force of the orgasm hit the center of my brain, I must have blacked out, because I lay on the floor asleep for at least an hour. It was not until I awoke that I realised I was naked, that, somehow, I must have provoked the men in the street below. Tired, I crept back into bed for a short nap.

Since I had forgotten to turn on the room air conditioning, forgetting I was no longer in cold New York, the air in my room was now as hot and heavy as an open-mouthed kiss. I guess I must have fallen asleep, because I did not notice the little maid enter my room. When, with a start, I awoke – she must have been humming too loudly, but who cares? – I saw a vision of absolute black beauty staring down at me. This child, she could have been no more than sixteen, had, as I later found out, come to Rio from Bahia, a city in the north, when she was about twelve. She had been inaugurated into prostitution by one of her cousins, and, for several years, she rented her body to visiting sailors. Eventually, one of the sailors, the younger son of a German hotel family, introduced her to a better way of making a living. Let's just say that, in American terms, she worked for tips.

This girl was that fabled blue-black color that only the purest Africans can boast of. There are few blue-blacks in the United States, since so many slave masters took their pleasure with the slave women. In Brazil, apparently, there were absentee landlords; my morning visitor was carved out of the finest ebony. Her hair was the soft, black cashmere of the rarest Persian lamb. Her eyes, gray-yellow, suggested an Egyptian temple cat. Her lips, full and bold, seemed chiseled out of precious onyx. The body, in true African fashion, was half art, half animal. The muscles under her midnight skin were as lithe as an Anaconda. There was no flab, no wrinkling, no blotching of the skin. She was of one piece.

Did I forget to say that as she stood there peering down at me, some ancient psychic powers informed her that I was naked under the covers? On the other hand, not to denigrate psychic powers, but given the state of my reawakened desire, surely this girl could smell my cunt, one sure giveaway that I was not likely a nun on leave of absence. With barely a flick of her wrist, she untied her white organdy apron and let it drop to the floor. Then, she lifted her black taffeta maid's uniform over her head like she was taking off a sweater. Underneath was an ebony goddess, her pointed tits perfect in all respects, with their licorice nipples already erect – Christ! – I caught a glimpse of

31

her labia and the flesh prepuce over her clitoris that promised to be at least a full inch long when erect. She had twice the fuckflesh of a white girl. Her vaginal muscles clearly had a life of their own; they undulated like a coiled snake. What I would have given for a big black cock at that moment. Praise the Lord, I had hands and a tongue!

I felt sharp pain in the pit of my stomach, pain of urgent hunger, pain of bottomless desire, the pain that comes from thinking I'd be rejected by such a treasure as she. Of course, she spoke no English, and at that moment I did not know her name, although later I found out she was 'Tia Maria' like the liquer, whose nectar, as I was to discover, was no match for her intoxicating cunt juice.

I decided I'd give her what money I had. Oh yes, I forgot; she did know the English words, 'dollar bill.' I gave her five twenties, which, in time, when all was said and done, she accepted with gratitude.

In the meantime, I wasn't sure how I'd proposition her. I didn't want to be crude about it; she seemed much too refined for that. Of course, if I were a lesbian instead of just a little bisexual, I would have ripped the clothes right off her and sunk my hungry mouth into her pussy without asking permission. But, as it turned out, I had nothing to worry about. Fate intervened; it always does. When I got out of bed to get my purse, Tia Maria took one look at me, and her Egyptian temple-cat eyes practically popped right out of her pretty head. I guess some black women like white girls like me. This one's smile of all-knowing sexual authority shrank to a look of shock and then to an expression of indescribable pleasure, as she lunged for my ass, rubbing her black hands up and down, up and down, stroking my thighs of liquid gold, then darting into my already wet cunt with her clever pink tongue. The girl was ravenous. I guess she was used to the typically underexercised bodies of middle-class American tourist women; I do make it a point to keep in

32

shape. Sex is certainly no substitute for the gymnasium. I must confess that, out of false modesty, I am avoiding describing the almost indescribable excitement that followed.

Obviously I could not stand idly in the middle of my hotel room allowing my black jungle cat to devour me from behind. I, too, wanted a piece of the action – and the action of the piece! Within a minute, we were sixty-nining it, with me on top, my face buried in her delicious fuckflesh, my tongue lapping up the sweet cunt tartare, raw meat, my body on fire from the odor of her musk. We were like cannibals or fish eating each other out as the obscenely suffocating air of the equatorial summer slowly anesthetized us, blotting out our ordinary concerns for the details of daily living. We drowned in each other's flesh and, for a long time, we did not come up for air.

Tia Maria and I had other early morning encounters during my long week in Rio. Often, she moved silently into my room like a dark specter, a ghostly visitor from the shades of the preceding night. Maybe she was really an African goddess, a ruling deity in that Afro-Latin metropolis. Who knows? We spoke the simple sign language of suck and fuck; and when we touched we were strictly flesh and blood.

After she'd gone, I looked at my bedside alarm clock. It said ten o'clock. My God, I'd been fucking for hours! I must say that, for the first time in weeks, I felt elated. Clearly, Maxey's instincts had been right on target. Then again, my own feelings about keeping in touch with ordinary people seemed to be equally correct, although I'm not sure I'd classify Tia Maria as 'ordinary people.'

With a start, I realized I'd told Lulu Touché I'd knock on her door when I wanted to go downstairs for breakfast. Poor Lulu, that poor, dear, stocky, middle-aged Sicilian. I pictured her sitting on the edge of her bed, absolutely famished, gnawing her fingers and waiting for yours truly.

Wrapping a sheet around me, I ran through our intervening bathroom to her bedroom door, which, as it so happened, was slightly ajar. I am here to tell you I could not believe what was going on in that bedroom. In the two years that I had known her, Lulu, a war widow and a devout convert to Presbyterianism, had been on public record as being disgusted and fed up with what she termed 'the pornographic American culture.' Now, there she was, stark naked, lying on her back, her chunky legs wrapped around the perfect ass of a prime stud, a six-and-a-half-foot-tall German-Afro-Hispanic athlete with burnished copper skin.

I had never seen anyone fuck like him. As he pumped in and out, his strongly muscled ass seemed to be moving sinuously, in a circular fashion, snakelike. 'Snake' was definitely the operative word. The man was half snake between his legs, where a huge, slippery cylinder as thick as a half-grown python was sliding in and out of her slit in a white heat, the juice of her pussy mingling with his sweat and his precome ooze. The two of them glistened and shone. His shaft seemed to have a powerful effect on Lulu, who, I had always imagined, was as middle-aged in bed as she looked in our New York workroom where the fluorescent lights cast unhealthy purple shadows under her tired, dark eyes, telling so much about the pain of the Second World War from which she had barely escaped.

So, like I say, as I barged into her bedroom, half-expecting to find her asleep, I was not prepared for the sight that greeted me. I especially did not expect to discover that Lulu, undressed, had the firm body of a peasant girl. Her labia looked positively virginal. The prepuce around her clitoris was a choice, pink oyster, so fresh, so meaty, it seemed to be begging for my lips. Or his lips. Why not? She was enjoying the greatest fuck of her life with a gentleman, who, as she explained later, was originally Room Service sent up with some french toast and a soft-boiled egg. She explained that when he arrived she found him very

34

distracting. Here he was, with African features, but his eyes were ice-blue – his German heritage.

Then, it turned out, he'd forgotten to zip up his fly and he wasn't wearing underpants. A simple oversight. Then, what a coincidence! It turned out that she, without realizing it, had answered the door stark naked! Apparently, without either one of them intending anything the least bit unseemly, he began to be aroused. She found herself staring at a very large, half-erect cock, and he – Hugo was his name, Hugo Battista – was so monumentally embarrassed that, right then and there, he dropped his tray of french toast. Lulu explained later that she decided on the spot that she could spend the next half hour consoling him about the dropped tray, or she could follow her instincts, which is what she did. She instinctively lay on her back and spread her legs apart, as if to say 'Fuck me, fuck me.'

Hugo got the hint. In a flash, his clothes were on the floor, and he was inside her. Lulu said it happened so quickly she never even got time to introduce herself, but she didn't have time for formalities. Nothing like Hugo Battista had ever happened to her before, certainly not in New York, city of uncertain survival, where men tend to look before they leap.

Watching my one-time mentor, this mother figure grappling in lust with a neo-Nubian prince, I found my body temperature rising. I felt like I was being sucked, almost against my will, into a vortex of sexual appetite. I was shocked to find myself whimpering involuntarily, but what choice did I have? My body responses were clear enough; my genitals became suffused with blood; that warm, familiar ache overtook my brain; my vagina was the center of my consciousness and it led me like a dumb animal to the edge of Lulu's bed. Somewhere, deep within the recesses of my brain, a voice kept telling me I'd just had four hours of early morning sex with a person I'd never met, a young woman, and now I was about to join a couple who were in the middle of intercourse for the first time; she my employee, he a man neither of us had ever known existed a half hour before!

This very judgmental, narrow-minded voice inside me kept taunting me with 'Diana, you slut! You grimy little slut! Enough already!' I don't like judgmental voices. I never have. Maybe it comes from my background in Beavertown as an unwilling Tabernacle Witness. I told the voice to shut up. Miraculously, it obeyed my order. I fell onto the bed as if I'd been shot by a sniper, and, without being able to control myself, I placed my tongue in Lulu's twat, right at the spot where Hugo's flesh pole was humping her. Her clitoris clearly was not getting the attention it deserved, and I owed Lulu so much for her overtime in my downstairs workrooms.

Apparently it did not occur to me, egomaniac that I seem to be, that I had received no invitation to join my devoted employee and her new-found friend. My intentions, however, were the best, and that's all that counts. Besides, Hugo's muscles rippled like a race horse's, and his ice-blue eyes in that dark face devastated me. Unfortunately, I keep forgetting that, at this time in my life, I cannot nonchalantly fall into orgies because the men, invariably, all want me, and the women go berserk with jealousy. If I sound conceited, I'm sorry. The truth is, at twenty-three, I am cursed not so much with classical beauty, God forbid, but with incredible golden skin that I had absolutely nothing to do with – I just came that way. My muscle tone is perfect; my tits amaze even me: golden mounds of firm flesh that, with the technological genius of a world-class suspension bridge, waft out into midair, peaking in toffee-colored aureolas, little inverted cones of silky flesh that end in what I call my caramel nipples. Amazing. When I walk naked across a room, my breasts bounce like molds of Jell-O and drive men wild. When I was eighteen, in my final year at Beavertown Central, my girlfriends in the locker room loved to tell me that my tits would sag by the time I was twenty-one. Well, I'm here to say that, so far, the good ol' Girl Scouts were wrong. So far, there has been no sag, and I doubt that there ever will be; my tits are too round and fully packed. This condition got me into trouble when I first came to Manhattan to become a fashion model. Agents laughed at me. They said that no leading designer ever designed a dress for women with tits like mine. I was built too much like a dairymaid. All that's true, but when a man wants a roll in the hay, who does he look for, a high-fashion model?

My ass is another thing. As I've explained in my other books, I possess a black woman's ass. Even when I was little, some of my flat-assed playmates called me 'Fanny.' Today, those same flat-assed girls, now flat-assed women, are in absolute sexual turmoil, having discovered at a late age that, 'Yes, Virginia, there is a clitoris and, despite what you may have heard in church, most people are at all times on the make!' My ass, like my tits, rises up into mid-air and stays there. There is no sag on this sister. My ass is like a ripe peach that's been split down the middle, ready to be mouthed and sucked for all its sweet juice.

Have I missed something? There's no point in pulling back now. I hate to brag, but my cunt is one of nature's golden wonders. First of all, my thatch is a lion's mane of golden fur; I am truly blessed there. It draws immediate attention to my greatest talent, yes, the one between my legs. Again, most women have to be content with a slit. Don't ask me how I lucked out, but I arrived with super-deluxe equipment, a pussy that purrs, and labia that can grab ahold of an engorged cock and suck it deep into my love canal.

The first morning in Brazil, I was so selfish I surrendered to my own egotistical appetites, completely forgetting that Lulu, however firm and fully packed she seemed, was after all, fifty-two, and grateful for anything she could get. When I fell onto her bed, hoping for nothing more than a warm body to rub against, something in Hugo Battista, 'The Room Service That Delivers,' stirred. Within seconds, his black hands were placed firmly on the inside of my thighs, pushing them apart as his pink and muscular tongue tasted my sweet meat, his hawklike nose nuzzling my clitoral bud. Sensational.

I guess Lulu just snapped. Let's just say she forgot her place. She forgot who was paying her salary. She forgot that she was fifty-two. She forgot she was a tragic survivor of the world's most horrendous war to date. She forgot that 'beggars can't be choosers.' Besides, face facts, she and Hugo were not exactly dear old friends who happened, by coincidence, to meet in a hotel room where he was now Room Service, and where she had just, by coincidence, written a chapter about him in her autobiography. No, I'm afraid that, just as I was greedily pulling Hugo's sizeable member into me with both hands, my impeccable seamstress Lulu went berserk. At first, I didn't notice her extreme discomfort. The plum-sized knob on the end of his crowbar cock was driving me wild with delights as my outer labia gave way to the force of its battering ram. Hugo was panting, not from fatigue, but from pure lust. Can I help it if I turned him on?

Lulu started shrieking, gouging his neck with her well-manicured fingernails, screaming, 'No, no, you animal! You animal!' She was crying and sobbing, 'Diana, I hate-a you! You take-a all my men! You leave-a nothing for me!' Then, she squeezed my left tit and pinched it sharply; then, she twisted it, causing me great, excruciating pain.

'Ow!' I shrieked. 'Lulu, how can you be so mean to me?'

Lulu could stand it no longer. She had been under too much strain; the long trip, the many years of overwork, her confusion at being in her mid-fifties, the guilt of having tried to mutilate me, and, I guess, too, the fear of losing her job – it was all too much. She broke down and started sobbing, 'Oh Diana, forgive me. Forgive me. I forgot how truly special you are.' And with that, absolutely contrite, she began to slaver me with kisses, paying special attention to my tender nipples, her silky cheeks rubbing sensitively against my stiffening flesh. She ran the tip of her surprisingly adept tongue around my tits making me wonder where she had learned the art of rimming and sucking. In any case, I thought it was a perfect apology for her unto-ward outburst. Huge was, by now, well, pile-driving me, his black steel cylinder sending shock waves of pleasure throughout my system. What's more, he was moving to the samba beat in the outside streets. 'One, two, three, four – one two! One, two, three, four – one two!'

I met his member with my own undulating hips. Were we dancing or making love? Who knew? Who cared? It was too much fun to analyze. We began to laugh in low, gutteral outbursts at the joy of it. Carnival was wonder-ful; it gave permission for everything, especially to be low-down dirty.

Ever-earnest Lulu groped for our genitals. She was trying so hard to please. With one hand she squeezed Hugo's thudding balls, then traced circles around the base of his humongous cock. With the other, she ran her finger up and down my satin slit, her fingers finally settling on my clitoris. She knew just where to rub, just where to suck, just how far to go with her teeth, scraping gently as I screamed out in excruciating pleasure. I couldn't have been happier. My bone-racking depress-ion was finally over. I was no longer bored out of my fucking mind. When I came, the weeks of repression which had been bottled up inside every cell of my body exploded in the kind of orgasm that is in every sense of the word religious. I felt cleansed. I felt renewed. I felt like God had left his calling card. My vagina was a tidal wave of orgasmic flesh. It blotted out my sense of where I was. All reality was reduced to the samba beat and the overwhelming heat. I was swept away on the raging tide.

'Oh God!' I screamed. 'I'm coming!' Then, I couldn't

speak. I couldn't get my breath. Hugo kept ramming his licorice stick in and out, in and out. My spasms held me in a shattering climax while Hugo the Huge sank deep into me. He began to jerk and writhe in his own orgasm. He buried his cock deeper and deeper as burst after burst of jism spewed out of his cock and coursed up my juicy pussy.

'Aaaggrhhh!' he moaned in the international language of sex, a language which requires no translation.

Lulu just about went crazy as Hugo and I climaxed together because she couldn't get her mouth around his shuddering blackjack and my sunset-pink cunt lips at the same time. She wanted to contain us both; she wanted us both to come in her mouth. She was famished for the salty sweetness of sperm and pussy juice perfectly blended into an intoxicating brew. Finally, my Italian perfectionist, Lulu Touché, God bless her, went hog wild. She climbed onto Hugo and me like a little girl climbing a pile of rocks. She masturbated by rubbing her blood-engorged cooze over every inch of our genitals she could manage, grinding her clitoris into the steel wool of Hugo's black African bush, an exercise that made her squeal with an insane delight.

The lady was out of control for the first time in her life, and she loved it. The Italians, you see, are the most civilized people who have ever existed. They cook pasta with the precision of atomic scientists. Their renowned sensuality has always been more of a perfectionist's love of detail in food, furniture, clothing and art than the hedonist's wallowing in appetite, an unqualified love of nature in the raw. The Italian style of making love is, at root, their greatest art form. I should know; my beloved Adolfo, my dearly departed, was the best Italian lover of this century, according to informed sources, and Adolfo, above all, never lost control. Nor had Lulu Touché, my seamstress queen, until now. It takes the heat of the equator and the nearness of the jungle to transform an Italian. It takes a black African cock during Carnival in Rio de Janeiro to reach all the way down to the control button buried deep in the European cunt. Oh sure, a white cock could do it, too, but how many white white men base their lives on being in control, and how many white cocks are still waiting, some without knowing it, for the crimson gash gleaming in an ebony cunt, for the taste of chocolate ooze, and, for some white men, the special deliverance that comes from a big black cock up their tight white ass?

Message to Hugo Battista: 'Dear Hugo, ever since you came back with me to New York to model bathing suits for my summer wear show, and then disappeared shortly thereafter, an illegal alien, into the black masses of Manhattan, are you still a Brazilian, Hugo, in our cold, northern clime? Can you function in bed without the samba beat? Can your splendid black ass still move in two directions at once as you pump hot pink pussies full of your southern seed? I have seen Lulu sitting on the front stoop of the House of Adoro scanning the street, looking for Hugo in the crowd, her sad little expression brightening when she sees a proud black face on a tall Nubian warrior like you, only to sink into an immediate depression the second she sees he is somebody else. For who, after all, Hugo, has your majestic bearing and your cocksure sense of yourself? Hugo Battista, a patriarch with eight children and two different wives, your role of busboy in the Rio Palace is God's way of keeping you humble to protect you from the jealousy of other men, especially husbands who would surely seek to destroy you for your sexual supremacy, if your surface role seemed any more grand. Instead, seeing only the blue-eyed, black busboy, they pay no more attention to you. They allow you to deliver poached eggs and chilled mango juice to their wives, never imagining their wives are lingering in their beds fantasizing about hot cock sausages between their legs, a gourmet treat that you, Hugo, deliver best of all. Hugo the Huge, you are the king of Latin-American love, and love is all that matters. By the time my little Lulu saw the last of you, she was a different woman. Gone was the intense, workaholic immigrant woman who had weathered a terrible war; gone was the middle-aged survivor who kept her knees locked in the presence of men, and crossed in the company of women. Now, she regularly sits, legs akimbo, the city air blowing its mischievous drafts up her thighs, blowing hot and cold on her friendly pussy. Miaow. Miaow. And for myself, Hugo, thank you for, more than anyone, restoring me to mental health. Maybe someday we will speak the same language, and we will be able to sit down over a carafe of wine and discuss our common future, if we have one. Hugo, please, if you read this, if you know how to read, or if a friend of yours can read, please don't be an illegal alien. Please come back to us. Please, Maxey von Fuchs is a wonderful lawyer. He can help you. Hugo, whatever you do, come back to the House of Adoro. We need you.'

Chapter Three

After our vigorous pleasure marathon, Lulu and I decided to take a half-hour's nap to the beat of the samba, which I pretended was the rain, so I could sleep. While visiting Winken, Blinken and Nod, I dreamed that Carnival was an ocean of confetti which carried me out on the tide, then bore me down into the ocean depths, where I nested in the arms of a maternal octopus. Her suction cups kissed my nipples and aroused me. Schools of brightly colored little fish swam into my cunt and nibbled at my clitoris, causing me to have such orgasmic convulsions that I drowned, except that death was not the end for me. In my dream, I fell through the black night of the sea into a blazing white light that did not burn. I had fallen through a hole on the ocean floor that led directly to the center of the sun. The light there was incandescent, yet I remained comfortable and cool.

When I awoke from my dream, it was noon, one-hundred-two degrees outside, hot even for Rio. Inside, we had air conditioning. Outside, the revelers samba'd to the ever-present drums. Most of them were half-naked. I counted many naked breasts, although I will admit that most of the women had pasted on a few sequins in striking designs around their nipples with bright-hued grease paints. Where I come from, that's called naked. I mean, be it red, white, or blue, if you can see the naked nipple, that's called naked, period.

I, for one, was in no way emotionally equipped to

display my nipples on the street. Where I come from, sex is something done indoors. I confess I'm incredibly puritanical that way; one of the salutary results of my trip to Rio was to get over my block about outdoor sex, but, for the moment, for the sake of the story, let's take one thing at a time.

The next 'thing' for me, a huge crisis, was my trip to the knitwear factory. Despite Lulu yelling at me in a Sicilian accent that I was an asshole, I tried to do it right. I wore a typically Brazilian brassiere; little red triangles of fabric just big enough to cover my aureolas, ingeniously connected to two pairs of tie-strings, one tied around my neck, the other around my broad back, which was made to be exposed. My bottom garment was equally brief; a larger red triangle, this one inverted, just big enough to cover my pubic hair (and yes, my labia, although the fabric was so sheer you could see the outline of my slit – very sexy). My ass, in the authentic Brazilian style, was covered by a couple of tie-strings. To be honest, my ass was, and is, pure ass, and, like I say, my distinctly African bee-hind with its high-rising cheeks of gold Anglo-Saxon skin is such a turn-on for so many men, I decided to be super modest, just to be safe. To this end, I wore an unbuttoned man's white shirt over my Brazilian bikini, with a lot of gold chains around my neck. In addition, I wore my red alligator high heels and matching purse. This way, my ass was covered by the back of the shirt, and my gold-spangled front offered some distraction from my perfect twin mounds of liquid gold. I figured if any really good-looking Brazilian superstud tried to stick his hand down into my bikini, I could always unbutton my shirt.

Lulu's jaw dropped when she saw my sexy outfit. 'Diana, you're a businesswoman; we have an important apppointment at the knitwear factory at three o'clock; why are you dressed like that?'

'You don't like it?' I asked, a tear of rejection forming in the corner of my eye.

Lulu, who was herself dressed in a white silk wraparound dress, saw how desperately sensitive I was, a stranger in a foreign land, and, within seconds, she was kneeling at my feet, kissing the upper reaches of my thighs, begging my forgiveness in her sweet Italian accent. 'Can't I stick-a my tongue in between-a your vagina? I could better apologize-a for making you feel like a slut.'

'No, no, Lulu,' I replied. '*I* know that *you* know that *I'm* paying your salary!' (Phew! It takes a while to learn to be assertive.) 'And, right or wrong, Lulu,' I continued in my executive style, 'this is the New World. I have to take my cues from the society around me. I mean, I don't want to hurt your feelings, Lulu, I know you mean well, but who the fuck wants to dress like an Italian countess in 1933?'

Lulu looked stunned. Her complexion went from olive to tomato-sauce red in the space of ten seconds. She momentarily forgot her thirty-five years' worth of English. 'Do you want-a me to continue-a working for you?' she asked. All I needed was for Lulu to quit; without Lulu, there'd be pandemonium in the ranks. I mean, not to knock yours truly, but how much can a twenty-three-year-old ex-Howard Johnson's hostess know about running a fashion empire? Without my ability to hold on to the best experts in the business, I'm nothing. Fortunately, Lulu's deal with the House of Adoro, made before I arrived on the scene, included a good deal of Adoro stock, so the prospect of her leaving the company was unlikely. I really had no choice but to show her how much I really cared for her.

I knelt down and faced her, looked squarely into her dazzling emerald-green Italian eyes and gently whispered, 'Lulu, I'm so grateful to you for caring.' As a token of my appreciation, I kissed her squarely on the lips – everybody likes that – unwrapped her wrap dress and stuck my hand down her sheer panties, searching for her fat slug of a clitoris. 'I didn't mean to steal Hugo,' I lied again, 'but I was just overwhelmed with lust. I am so sorry.'

Lulu was so grateful that I cared about pleasuring her (e.g. clitoral stimulation), that she began to kiss the sides and back of my neck. She was already sopping wet when I wedged the side of my hand into her vulva and began to rub up and down to open her up; her vaginal flesh sucked at my fingers as I coaxed open the flesh petals, my thumb shielding her clitoral jewel. When the tip of my index finger was lubricated with her juices, I began to make circles around the distended nub, first clockwise and then counter-clockwise, subtly pressured strokes that ignited the dynamite buried deep within her overcivilized Italian cunt. And all the while, I felt guilt because I really wanted to push her backward and go down on her, using the tip of my tongue instead of my fingers to bring her to orgasm. I stayed with the fingers; there was only so much time in the day for sex. I had already spent the morning, first masturbating in my window, then fucking the blue-black jewel of a chambermaid, then getting humped by a magnificent blue-eyed, black stallion of a stud, during which time I allowed Lulu to do with me as she pleased. Try as I might to transform my image of her, she was a fifty-two-year old woman employee of mine; there are limits to my sexual activity. I must make that clear, in light of what followed during the rest of my stay in Brazil. I do not fuck everyone whose hot breath raises my tempera-ture. I respected Lulu. I cared for her, but I decided that, since we were late for our afternoon appointment at the knitwear factory, finger-fucking was all she was going to get.

'Oh, Diana, Diana,' she moaned. 'You are so gorgeous. Let me kiss-a your pussy. Pulleas-a! *Carissima mia, bella* Diana!'

I must say, Lulu's pussy felt like the ripe, oversexed cunt of a fifteen-year-old girl, trapped in a convent school. I wished we could walk through Rio with our hands in each other's warm, wet cunts, but, of course, society would never approve. Even in supersexual Rio we'd be labeled homosexual in every language under the sun, when, of couse, we were just two normal women sharing each other's company. Why should people have to walk alone? Why can't normal, pussy-loving men walk down the street, flies open, stroking each other's cocks? Are cocks and cunts opposites? Are men and women opposites? Maybe so. I don't have the final answer. I do, however, feel that we could all be generally more sexually oriented to everyone we know, but I realized that, all the same, Lulu and I would probably have to walk through Rio looking as chaste as nuns, deliberately giving the impression that we had never entertained sexual thoughts about each other. '*Quel dommage*,' as the French say. 'What a shame!'

We left the Rio Palace Hotel and walked north through ever-deepening crowds toward the Dom Pedro knitwear factory near the new cathedral in the center of Rio. From the reaction I was getting from the men in the crowd, maybe Lulu was right about the way I was dressed. I wish I could report some of the remarks the guys made, but I don't speak Portuguese. The bulging eyes and the slavering lips spoke for themselves, as did the constant bumping up against me. I suppose it was my own fault. There I was, my man's shirt open to the breeze, while the best golden globes in the Western Hemisphere were bouncing along with only virtual postage stamps holding them up. Plus, in the bright silver sunlight, it was obvious to one and all that my golden pubic hair was not entirely covered over. Originally, I had fancied that I was starting a new style. It didn't bother me to see those wiry hairs glinting between my legs, but some Cariocas almost went berserk. I guess they don't see enough blondes down there.

Before long, Lulu and I were right in the shadow of Babilônia Hill, a vast hillside slum ghetto or favela just south of Botafogo Bay and the Rio de Janeiro Yacht Club. As a matter of fact, Babilônia Hill was used for the movie *Black Orpheus*. In a word, it is green and mean. The slums of Rio have no zoning regulations, are not attached to regular gas, electric, or water lines, and have no real schools or hospitals. Most of the inhabitants are lucky to receive two or three years' education. Makeshift cardboard and tin shacks sprawl up and down the hillsides with no sense of planning. The squatters help each other hook up pirate lines to the city utilities. Whenever possible, the inhabitants install concrete stairways and dig gutters for obvious purposes. Some industrious slum dwellers even plant flowers and shrubs in and around their hovels, which gives them a touch of beauty, however insubstantial. I was told that some of the worst-looking slums boast indoor plumbing, plus fine carpets and furniture.

Anyway, there I was in my one-hundred-two degrees Carnival finery, parading along in the heat, wearing what, by Brazilian standards, would be considered modest apparel, when suddenly, from out of nowhere, a gang of boys, maybe eight in all, and none older then eighteen, began to stalk me like savage dogs. The wolf whistles were my first clue. Lulu told me to walk faster. I walked faster, but how could I walk faster than the dogs, I mean the boys? I was wearing four-inch high heels – and, what's worse, my bikini strings kept coming undone. Every time I turned around to see who was whistling, they froze. We had at least a ten-block walk north to Dom Pedro Knitwear. It was a definite walk; most of the taxicab drivers were out on the streets in costume, dancing. The savage boys were now making obscene gestures, giving me the finger and the devil's horns.

Finally, I decided to face them head on. I turned around, smiling, looking supremely confident, and began to chase them. They shrieked, and ran back in the general direction of Babilônia Hill. One little boy, a mulatto, or mixed-blood youngster of about fourteen

(I later found out he was sixteen, almost seventeen) tripped on a curbstone and fell flat on his face. He was crying. I arrived just in time to wipe a trail of blood off his scraped nose. His knee was also bruised. Thank goodness, I always carry a supply of Band-Aids in my purse. Considering this beautiful boy had about the same complexion as Harry Belafonte, the beige stripe across his dusky face became a badge of honor, a favelado's (slum dweller's) Purple Heart.

'My poor wounded boy!' I cried. Lulu was decidedly less compassionate.

'Two minutes ago, he was a dog; now he's a poor-a wounded boy. Diana, whats-a the matter wid you?'

'The poor wounded boy,' I soon realized, was rapidly recovering from his wounds. His angelic face was staring up at the inverted red triangle of my bikini bottom. His chocolate-brown eyes blazed with a familiar masculine flame, unusual in one so young, but not exactly what I'd label 'perverted,' either.

I guess I was so taken with his precocious masculinity that I began to smile one of my 'fuck me' smiles. I couldn't help it. A woman is a woman. Then, as I looked down at my crotch to more or less confirm to both of us that, yes, wasn't I wearing a darling little Carnival costume, I saw, to my horror, that, without knowing it, I had lost my bikini bottom! My thick, blonde bush was dazzling in the fierce tropical light which reflected off the walls of the white skyscrapers on either side of us. As I looked down at myself to make sure that, yes, it was really my cunt, I caught a glimpse of my luscious, hot pink gash. With lightning-quick reflexes, both my hands went to – you guessed it – my tits. Yes, thank God, my bikini top was still in place! (Even though one side had slipped half an inch, and that nipple was completely visible.) My wounded boy was now laughing. For my part, I didn't know whether to laugh or cry.

Lulu, who was once again securely wrapped in her dress, was furious. 'What's-a the matter wid you, Diana? We late for the factoria.'

'Lulu, I lost my bottom!' I cried, adjusting my legs so that the little fellow could get a better glimpse of some very precious real estate. I figured that his life was already so hard, why deny him his manhood – right? I mean, if a man's life has to be hard, let it be hard in every department, especially between the legs.

'Button your shirt!' Lulu ordered. I really had no choice but to obey her. As puritanical as Lulu was, she had a point. How could I possibly attend a business meeting stark naked from the waist down? I buttoned the bottom button; I looked a hell of a lot more respectable, but clearly the Brazilian heat was affecting my brain. The day before, I'd been bored to death; now, my libido was running away with me. What was I to do?

'Give me one of our business cards, Lulu,' I said. She produced the card. I wrote 'Diana Adoro, Hotel Rio Palace, Room 69.' Then, I wrote, 'Wednesday.' (Ash Wednesday, the day after Carnival.) I wanted to write 'Come Wednesday,' but I wasn't sure if the word 'come' in Portuguese functioned the way it did in English. When I think of the word 'come,' I immediately imagine a big sperm-gushing cock, not 'come' as in 'come and go.' I hoped the simple word 'Wednesday' said it all. Like I say, since I wasn't sure how the word worked in Portuguese, I didn't want to write 'Come Wednesday' and then have the boy or his translator think I wanted him to come on me. Of course, there was a sick part of me that really did not want him to come on me, that is, if he was old enough to have an erection. I had a perverted impulse to draw a picture of the big sperm-gushing cock as an international symbol of the word 'come,' but how could I be sure he'd get the pun?

At this point, no pun intended, I was not only complicating my life and his, but I was also behaving like a total hypocrite. I would not blame a normal American housewife for not buying my clothes. As a matter of public record, I would like to apologize to the readers of this account for the hypocrisy in question. I would also like to say that, in a later chapter of this account, I describe my Wednesday with the boy in question. His name turned out to be Remo, and Remo turned out to be more than I could have possibly hoped for when I first dropped, I mean lost, my bikini bottom in front of him.

Dom Pedro Knitwear, named after the first emperor of Brazil, was on Avenida Infante Dom Henrique right off of Flamengo Bay. Like most small factories, it rented space on several floors of a larger building, and used the cheap labor of hard-working folk, usually immigrants right off the boat, ambitious souls who could not easily find jobs in the mainstream marketplace. Any fool who talked unions or strikes got the sack immediately. There were no benefits, no health insurance, no social security, no sick leave, no pension. Workers, usually women, worked ten hours a day to make a living wage, and often they brought piecework home with them and continued sewing until midnight. Why am I talking in the past tense? These practices are still going on. But please, I didn't invent the injustices. Furthermore, if it weren't for the sweatshops all over the world, no one but the very rich would be able to afford new clothes. We'd have to return to homemade tailoring and hand-me-downs.

Che Miranda, self-styled labor leader and champion of the oppressed, did not agree. He wanted a revolution. He wanted the House of Adoro to burn to the ground. His intention was to begin by staging a strike during the week of Carnival, when so many members of the foreign press were in Rio. Except that Mr Karl Marx, Jr., underestimated the hold that Carnival has on the poor, most of whom regularly skipped the work the week before Ash Wednesday, and who, in any case, had no intention of parading up and down in front of their building with signs telling the revelers not to buy Adoro clothes.

So, when Lulu and I arrived at Dom Pedro Knitwear

thinking we were going to discuss new designs and a possible wage increase of a few cents an hour, we found the place closed down and Senhor Miranda outside in a rage. It seems that most of his 'strikers' were still sleeping it off from the night before. Miranda had succeeded in closing down at least thirty sweatshops in the Rio area. All the major design houses were affected, but it was Carnival, and the heat was deadening, so who cared? The House of Adoro had most of its clothes manufactured in Taiwan, Puerto Rico, and the United States, anyway; I wasn't about to go into a tailspin over losing Rio.

Che later told me that when he first saw me, he saw another rich bitch with blue eyes and a fantastic ass who probably wanted something for nothing like all rich bitches who inherit companies from their dead fathers or dead husbands. I later discovered he had an American mother, an Irish-Italian Ziegfeld beauty. Her Brooklyn-Irish father, Che's beloved grandpa, had been a dockside labor leader who idolized – you guessed it – Karl Marx himself. 'Che' (his real name was Patrick Joseph) was clearly oblivious to the Carnival that was swirling around his head. The samba made no impression whatsoever.

What can I say about the afternoon? It was steaming hot, the few strikers who showed up were miserable, and it was impossible for anyone to work. Che Miranda had hired a goon squad to shoot anyone who tried to cross the picket line. Lulu and I, once we had sized up the situation, agreed that we did not want to end up on slabs at the city morgue.

I had not counted on Che Miranda being one-quarter American-Irish, and Brooklyn-Irish at that. That particular genetic inheritance was most evident; he looked like a brawnier version of Jimmy Cagney in one of his 1930's gangster movies, except that Miranda, unlike Cagney, was an absolute fanatic about the rights and privileges of the working classes.

'You know what Carnival's purpose is?' he bellowed

in what sounded like the Portuguese version of a Brooklyn accent. 'I'll tell you what it's for – to keep ordinary people from taking hold of their lives, that's what. It's the big distraction engineered by the people that own this fuckin' country to keep the vast majority from figuring out what's going on. It's the Roman emperors providin' bread and circuses to keep the people focused on anything but changin' the system.' And then, this Portuguese Mick landed into yours truly for supporting 'the system.'

'Mr Miranda,' I began, trying to look dignified by crossing my legs and buttoning another button on my shirt because I didn't want my golden pubic hairs to show at a time like this. 'Mr Miranda,' I said again, 'I have factories all over the world. We deal with available labor rates. We take what prices are offered to us. You'd do the same if you were in my position.' It was not until circumstances brought us together in Manhattan two weeks later that I found out he really did want to be in my position; actually, right on top of me, to be exact, fucking his brains out. And, yes, even in Rio during our first meeting, his work shirt, casually hanging over his jeans, disguised a humongous hard-on, a direct response to my casual bourgeoisie attitude he claimed he had absolutely no use for.

For the moment, however, to continue this strange tale of an even stranger holiday, it was now late in the afternoon on the Monday before Fat Tuesday, and I was extremely uncomfortable discussing labor problems with a self-proclaimed Latin-American revolutionary in what seemed like one-hundred-ten-degree weather; a closet stud, yet, who did not have the simple honesty to let me know he wanted to hump me.

Lulu Touché saved the day for me. She said to him that she didn't know a revolution from a radish, and that after living through World War Two in Italy she hated wars and men with guns, and that she just wanted to make dresses. Miranda couldn't have cared less; he said he wouldn't let Lulu inspect Adoro swimwear as long as the strike was on. He said he wanted another dollar an hour for the garment workers, and that the two of us could rot in hell until we learned the meaning of a living wage.

Finally, I had had enough of this claptrap. I had no choice but to faint dead away. It was the only honorable way out.

Some people are here for justice, revolution, radical politics, and the Rights of Man. I applaud their efforts, but me, frankly, I'm just here for a good time. When it comes to giving my workers higher wages and a shorter working day, I send my lawyers to work it out. As far as the so-called spiritual dimension goes, I have never been reborn, have not personally met Jesus, and do not completely understand Karl Marx. I don't even completely understand Groucho Marx. Frankly, I'm not all that bright. My idea of the good life is a good lay. I have always felt sorry for multimillion-dollar industrialists who can't get it up. Most of them would spend every penny they have to be reborn as Hugo Battista, with a black anaconda swinging beneath chiseled, ebony legs, looking for pussy to devour and finding it at every turn, pussy after pussy, begging to be consumed.

Chapter Four

My next six hours took place in Los Invalides Hospital, about five blocks from Copacabana Beach. After I fainted, I was rushed there by a hysterical Lulu, a guilt-stricken Che Miranda, and three utterly bored strikers looking for a way out of the picket line. According to Lulu, they made a point of holding me between my legs at the top of my thighs, and their hands kept slipping accidentally onto my vulva, which was visible most of the time, since my shirt kept riding up. Lulu said I created a sensation. The crowds, according to my Italian, must have imagined I was a dead saint being carried in a religious procession, since strange men and women kept touching me. Lulu maintained that her function was to protect me from being molested. Of course, she told me all this two days after the incident. By the time I had revived, in a private room, under strange and questionable circumstances, Lulu was nowhere to be seen. When I threatened to fire her for abandoning me, she protested that once the doctors had assured her I was fine, she went downstairs to get something to eat and suffered complete and total amnesia. She completely forgot who she was, she claimed, and did not recover her sense of identity until two days later, when she woke up in Babilônia Hill in a tarpaper shack, sandwiched between two young men, both of them very drunk and very sexy.

'Until that-a moment, I think I'm a twenty-year-old

girl again. Then I realize I'm-a old enough to be their *mamá*,' explained Lulu.

How judgmental can I be? Lulu's experience was not altogether different from mine. When I awoke four hours later, after having been sedated by injection, I found myself having sex in the missionary position – no, not with a missionary, but with a young staff physician (with quite a staff) who turned out to be an American from Cleveland. Dick Schlonga, M.D. I must say I was shocked. If I had not been dreaming about having sex with someone who looked exactly like Dick, I would have pressed rape charges. It was an incredible coincidence. In my dream, the man had thick, sandy hair, horn-rimmed glasses, crinkly blue eyes, and the large, thick body of a wrestler. I woke up smiling to find a man of that exact description making love to me. I couldn't believe it; even though I'm not a religious person, I decided that he must be a gift from God. I mean, this doctor could really heal. Talk about a bedside manner!

As it turned out, there was no impropriety. We were in a private room, the door was locked, and the curtains around my bed were drawn. Most of the available staff was downstairs in the emergency room dealing with the dead-on-arrivals. The dark side of Carnival can be frightening. The year I was there, a hundred and twenty-five Cariocas ended up in the morgue. The death toll included fifteen people who were murdered, seven who were drowned, and thirty-four who were killed in car crashes. Over fifteen thousand people went to the hospital, many suffering from what is politely termed 'alcohol poisoning.' In Beavertown, we'd call it 'drunk'; then, again, Beavertown never had Carnival.

Dick told me later he had come to Rio to study tropical diseases. He didn't have the stomach for gunshot wounds in Cleveland. On the particular day he discovered me, he said he'd been asked to work in the emergency room for a few hours. He said he felt like he was back in Cleveland. When he needed a break, the last place he wanted to be was out on the streets, so he found himself wandering the hospital corridors. On impulse, he stuck his head in my room and was shocked by what he saw. Let me explain.

Because it was so hot, the hospital staff had undressed me, placed cold compresses on my head, and left me lying naked on my bed. Lulu Touché, as I said, had developed a case of amnesia, and disappeared for the next two days. Che Miranda and the goon squad had deposited me, then returned to the cause of world revolution. By the time Dr Schlonga stuck his head in my door, a little orderly named José, normally a mild-mannered fellow with a head of black curls and a hot muscular tongue, had wedged his freckled face between my legs and was lapping up my cunt juices with loud slurping and sucking noises, while he jerked himself off. Appalled by such a breach of ethical conduct, Dr Schlonga threw the man out, threatening to report him. Then he called the head nurse and said he was not to be disturbed for the next hour; he was going to be conducting tests on me to see if I was suffering from a rare, undiagnosed, and totally contagious tropical disease. Within two minutes he had drawn the curtains around my bed, stripped off all his clothes and stood in front of me with a steel-hard erection, ready to conduct his examination, and, if necessary, begin the proper treatment. While Dr Dick Schlonga was trying to decide what to do, I was still half-unconscious, half-asleep, and dreaming. Obviously, I had nothing to be concerned about, I was in the best of medical hands.

In my dream, I was an African princess in an ancient kingdom on the northeast coast of the Dark Continent, my favorite land of dreams, a place where the blood of three distinct peoples, the black Africans, the tan Egyptians, and the olive-skinned Arabs had intermingled over the centuries to produce a fine-boned race of chocolate-brown beauties. At fifteen, I was the most beautiful maiden in my tribe. As the dream began, I was standing under a date palm examining my aureolae, which seemed like milk chocolate cones attached to the ends of my silky young breasts. I loved my breasts. At first, they had been little folds of delectable flesh, then pointy cones, until finally, almost overnight, twin masses of soft flesh seemed to be hanging off the front of me with the milk-chocolate cones I mentioned coming to points of inch-long nipples. As I looked at my body, the same gorgeous excess seemed to be present everywhere. My vagina was not like most women's, who, at best, could boast of slits and holes and little mounds of fuckflesh between their legs. I had thick, fleshy cunt lips swollen with desire set under my legs, the midpoint between my high-riding ass cheeks and my thick, black bush. My clitoris, an inch-and-a-half long and fat as a sea slug, seemed to hang off the front of my labia like a baby's cock, stiffening when sucked or stroked or when a loving face nuzzled it with warm lips. My underlying cunt gash, in contrast to my mahogany skin, was ruby-red and glistening wet in the summer light. In my dream, I was truly a princess of love desired by all the lusty men of my tribe, with a reputation from Egypt to Zanzibar. Despite what you have read about the strict, puritanical sexual practices of Africa, my tribe was an exception. According to tribal legend, Jesus appeared a week after his famous Resurrection and announced he was sorry, he'd made a mistake in not talking about sex. He wanted us to know that sexiness was next to godliness, and to get on with it. 'In your fucking, you shall possess your souls.' As the story goes, he appeared a second time a week later, announced that every time he intended to appear in the Holy Land, God the Father sent him to our village instead, and that it was up to us to pass on the word about sex. Could we do that, please? In a nutshell, we tried, but nobody believed us, especially the Christians, many of whom believed that sex was intended for married couples only, and for one reason, to produce children. Like I say, this was only a dream in a Rio hospital.

As the dream continued, my African girlhood came to an abrupt end as tall, blonde men from the north, men with big muscular chests and straight yellow hair, invaded my kingdom with long sticks that spat fire. The 'sticks' were Winchester 73's. The year was 1906. Again, this was only a dream. Diana Adoro does not go back that far. I, the African princess, watched in horror as they enslaved my people, especially the men and boys, and sent them in chains to the lands of the west, especially to the Americas, north and south. My young husband, a prince of Ethiopia, was garroted, beheaded, drawn, and quartered. At that moment, I realized my world had changed forever. In any case, I was not absolutely wrecked by the experience of becoming a widow; in fact, I was intrigued by these tall, blonde, hairy men who seemed infinitely powerful. Their leader, a man about six-foot-five, dragged me into a tent as soon as he saw me, and, with his lieutenants standing guard, stripped in front of me. Everything but the horn-rimmed glasses. I lay there in amazement. I had been used to carved, chiseled, black bodies with foot-long penises savoring me like a gourmet treat. This man was different. Definitely more serious. More predatory. He looked straight into my soul. His body was a wonder to behold, a square build with a broad chest, matted with red-gold hair. His cock was thick, almost as wide as it was long, and, at the sight of my juicy pink clitoris, it began to grow. He grabbed me by the buttocks, squeezing me like fresh bread, finger-fucking me in my hot pink gash, bringing me to such a pitch of excitement that I lost control of my bladder. My urine mixed with my lubricating pussy juices; thick fluid ran down my smooth, dark thighs. Without further hesitation, the massive blonde foreigner burrowed his ramrod deep into my sucking cunt hole; the copper wires of his chest hairs entangled in the supersensitive nerve endings of my nipples, causing my vaginal muscles to convulse in orgasm. That's when I woke up, and I'm here to say that if Dr Dick Schlonga, also massively built, his broad wrestler's chest also matted with thick, golden hair, had not been fucking me when I awoke, I would have completely gone over the edge.

Let me explain. I have never been able to separate waking reality from my dream life. My Nordic lover in my dream was inutterably real to me, as real as my own intoxicating, dusky body. It was hard enough to wake up and discover that my inch-long nipples had shrunk, and my clitoris was no longer the size of a baby's cock, and my mahogany skin was bleached out to pale gold – what a shock – but to lose my rapacious, destroyer male at the height of my orgasm would have been an excruciating, horrendous loss. That's why I say God sent me Dick. When it comes to orgasms, I really don't care how I get them; on that score, no pun intended, I would sooner take advice from a nun than from a feminist. No, I was not raped; let's not be silly. Dr Schlonga was doing me a favor. If it were not for him, I would have awakened from my dream in a hot, deserted hospital room in a strange city, having completely lost the blonde lover who comes alive only in my dreams. Am I making myself clear? When it comes to my fantasy lovers, I suppose I should shut up. I could easily be committed. In this case, I would have run down the halls babbling away. But God sent me Dick Schlonga, M.D., to heal my anxiety.

One thing keeps me alive during times of stress, and that is a man's overpowering desire for me. It goes without saying that Dick desired me. Once I awoke, and he informed me that, medically speaking, I was okay, he withdrew his driving pole from my cunt meat with a sucking sound that was loud and hungry – an animal sound, really, or are all sexual noises animal sounds?

'Baby, baby, you're driving me crazy,' I screamed. 'Oh God, thank God, I got big tits!' I couldn't stop my idiotic ravings, this man so excited me. 'I really love to tit-fuck your thick tool, baby, your big blonde cock, baby, yes, yes, yes!' I ran his flesh weapon over my erect nipples, engaging the rim of his purple glans with my own engorged tissue. He couldn't talk. He sucked on air. His throat made strange involuntary sounds. I pressed my tits around his sexual member as he fucked the smooth channel between my ripe melon mounds. I snugly wrapped my long legs around his waist. With my right heel, I stroked his backbone up and down, up and down, causing him to shiver with pleasure. Simultaneously, I tweaked his tiny nipples, pinching them sharply; most men prefer a little pain now and then. It has something to do with their having thicker skin than women. They need more than a casual caressing to arouse their secondary centers of sexual pleasure. 'Fuck me! Fuck me!' I screamed, now fully awake. Dick lifted his heavy tool out of my tit channel and began to run it up and down my pussy slit without entering my vaginal canal. The fragile ridge of skin running down the center of his undershaft ripped me apart with its delicacy as it engaged my clitoris, a push button of unrestrained lust.

Imagine! This aggressive young doctor, so idealistic he was willing to forsake his own native country and live in a strange exotic land, so unselfish he was willing to forsake Carnival to pinch-hit in the emergency room, so sensitive to human pain he had to forsake the emergency room and wander the understaffed corridors in existential torment, as Maxey von Fuchs describes his own depressions, so absolutely a man of self-giving was willing to overlook the fact I was unconscious, out cold when he began to make love to me! We fucked all afternoon, as the hot sun shone through the gold hairs on his chest, creating a halo effect, a haze of light blessing the baby-white skin underneath. I could see the almost imperceptible bones of his rib cage under his milk-white skin. Strange, how the most aggressive men seem like the most vulnerable. Take his testicles, for instance; why do people call them balls, and mean by that proof of manhood? Nothing has ever seemed more fragile to me than two superdelicate plum-sized testicles, one slightly larger than the other, connected to the man's body by only a few fragile threads; testicles liable to so much pain, to so much easy injury, and to the possibility of almost instant castration; the lightest blow can be almost fatal. In the strongest men, they often seem larger and more vulnerable, hanging loose in a dark, wrinkled sack, which, when I see it up close, often swings back and forth, thudding against my lower lips, two areas of almost indescribable softness meeting in the dark. Dick's testicles, needless to say, were oversized and especially sensitive as they softly banged against me – I'm talking about while he was fucking – I mean, making love to me, of course. His bush, more reddish than mine, was thick and cushiony, and when we rubbed our bushes together, it felt light and tickly; in a word, wonderful. Everything about Dr Schlonga was wonderful. Even the way he came was wonderful. I could fee his sperm bullets volleying into me like spring rain. When he came, he sucked on my lips and my tongue; when he came, he fell into me, cleaving into me, dissolving into me, genitals, eyes, mouth, hands, brain. Flesh of my flesh. And then, it was back to the emergency room. The crippled and the maimed were waiting for the genius of the man, waiting for his healing touch, waiting for his love. That's it. End of story. No prolonged good-byes. Take it or leave it. Yes, of course I wanted a prolonged good-bye. Yes, I wanted Dr Schlonga. I even thought about maiming myself so I could remain at Los Invalides Hospital. That's when I knew I had to get up and leave. Immediately.

When I left the hospital, it was pushing midnight. The streets of Rio were predictably flowing with waves of spangled travelers intoxicated by the samba beat. I was now wearing a nurse's uniform, the only garment available to me. My white shirt had long since disappeared. Of course, since I am a leading dress designer, and the public has certain expectations, I did what I could to improve the nurse's uniform. Actually, what I did was simplicity itself. I just cut the top off the dress and fashioned a bandeau brassiere out of surgical gauze, attaching it to my back with adhesive tape. Then, with a surgical scissors, I cut the skirt, from the mid-thighs down, into long, narrow strips. And then, faced with clunky, white nurse's shoes, I had no choice but to dye them bright red with Mercurochrome. What the hell, it was Carnival! I didn't want to step out into one of the world's most glamorous cities looking like I'd just been cleaning corpses in the morgue!

I had not gone a block from the Los Invalides Hospital when I had a strong hunch I was being followed. Turning around, I could not believe my eyes! Che Miranda and two of his bullyboys were gaining on me!

'You think you're gonna play sick on me, Adoro?' Miranda snapped.

'For chrissake, Miranda, I was unconscious for three hours!' I shouted back, appalled at his insensitivity.

'Yeah! Well, get this, cunt, I hear you're planning a summer wear show in New York in two weeks, and you're planning to bring Brazilians back with you … '

'Yeah?' I interjected, wondering what Lulu had told him. She was the only one who knew my plans.

'Well, ya ain't gonna have your swimsuits on time,' he added, ' 'cause no Brazilian seamstress will be able to work for slave wages!'

'Guess what, Miranda?' I said, lying through my teeth, 'Lulu was here six months ago to do sketches; you see, I'm introducing her as a new designer. Half of her clothes are already in New York. Brazil won't make my clothes, I won't pay; tit for tat, I'll cancel the order and give it to Taiwan, and we'll do another summer wear show next fall. We'll start a trend; summer wear in January.'

To put it plainly, the man's mouth was agape. He

couldn't believe I had half a brain between my ears. He couldn't believe I had figured out a strategy. He also didn't know I was lying. The truth is, I think pretty quick both on and off my feet. I still wasn't sure what I was going to do about my summer wear show, except that, somewhere, I'd find some sexy Cariocas and bring them back to New York for a couple of weeks. What the hell, I wasn't going to lose sleep over a relatively minor fashion show. I also wasn't going to be bullied by Senhor Big Shot Miranda. 'Furthermore, Miranda,' I went on, 'I ain't taking no seamstresses to N.Y.C.; I'm taking real live flesh and blood Brazilians off the streets. The green cards are being arranged through the American Embassy (this much was true, if Maxey was doing his job). You want to come, I'll arrange for you. You can make sure everyone gets fed properly. If I exploit "the workers", you can hold a press conference and start an international incident.' The truth was, I wanted the satisfaction of seeing the look on Senhor Miranda's face when he saw for himself how happy the House of Adoro really is. I also wondered how he and I would get along at a quiet dinner at an intimate New York restaurant away from the hassle of world poverty and hired goon squads. For the moment, however, he was still foaming at the mouth.

He said, 'Are you denying American unemployment is pushing ten percent, that factory workers are being exploited while the rich get richer and sales of Rolls Royce's Silver Clouds are up sixty-five percent over last year?'

'Che,' I said, licking my lips with my tongue, valiantly attempting to restore what vestiges of femininity were left to me, 'I'm only one person, I do what I do; if I go out of business, unemployment will get worse; so I don't intend to go out of business, you dig?'

'You capitalistic slut!' he screamed. 'You're a prostitute working for the multinational con-glomerates!'

Well, with that cheap-shot remark I was nonplussed. I had no idea what the man was talking about. I didn't know a multinational conglomerate from a cocoanut creme pie. I was sick of this constant barrage of insults from a person who had never been to a fashion show!

Chapter Five

Vowing never to have anything further to do with class struggle and world revolution, my eyes still blinded by hot, stinging tears, I ran toward the smell of the ocean. I needed to be free of serious people, free of endless talk about finance, salaries, workers' compensation; in short, I needed to be rid of the cares of the business world.

I remembered how much I had loved the Jersey shore when I was sixteen and seventeen and eighteen, visiting my mother's half-sister Rose, a bedridden arthritic, and her truck-driver husband, Stanley. Stanley used to take me for walks on the beach after the sun went down and Rose finally went to sleep. Stanley showed me the dunes. The year I was sixteen, we had many, many private conversations in the dunes. The summer I was seventeen, I'd just begun to really blossom as the gorgeous woman I was destined to be. Rose was sicker than ever, and one night Stanley whispered, 'God forgive me!' lifted up my shirt, and put his whole mouth over my budding breasts, sucking and slurping on my tender, growing nipples. I felt such an indescribable glow of pleasure, that, after that, I let him do whatever he wanted. The very first night, he placed my small, teen-age hand around his thick erection; it was the first time I had ever held a cock. Then, I let him fuck my outer vaginal lips, using my slit as a channel for the fleshy, supersensitive underside of his penis, which lay like a warm, leaden pipe on me, slowly moving up and down until his warm, sticky 'lotion' flowed onto my skin. It was all very innocent. He never penetrated me. Uncle Stanley told me later, before his death, that the very thought of me, in my girlhood years, gave him the courage to continue with his marriage. I told him that I had felt privileged to be part of his private life.

And so, thinking of my Uncle Stanley, and feeling warmly toward the possibilities of the Brazilian dunes, I headed in the direction of Copacabana Beach, where, as it turned out, there were no dunes, but endless possibilities.

Have I discussed Copacabana? It is a two-and-a-half mile long crescent of sugar-white sand. Don't tell me it's dirty; that's not the way I want to remember it.

In the hot night of the Brazilian summer, in February, in the land where so many natural elements are reversed: where our frozen winter becomes their time for sizzling fun; where our summer is their cool season of rain; where Cariocas work in order to play, and not as we do, play in order to work; where the pitch black night is the high time of the twenty-four-hour cycle, noon is a curse to be slept through, and midnight the passageway to the gods. Yes, midnight on the Copacabana Beach is a technicolor descent into dreams.

I crossed one avenue after another in my flight to Copacabana; Rua Tonelelros, Rua Barata Ribeiro, Rua Copacabana, past white concrete luxury hotels, ghostly specters which loomed above me in the night. Occasionally, a drunken reveler staggered toward me, stretching out an uncertain hand to innocently stroke my breasts, although, in one case, the man in question, clearly starving for human contact, reached under my skirt to caress my silky bush. Another man, with a silly, endearing grin, leaned against me, half-kneeling, rubbing his erection against my thighs, which glowed golden in the light of the crescent moon. It was nice to know there were still men preoccupied with the eternal truth of Man and Woman in an overly-intellectual world increasingly given over to theories about the meaning of the world and how it should be organized and run. It was also nice to reflect that, in the city of sex, I was a sexual magnet. I hate to brag, but face facts – I was young, blonde-all-over, American; my bank account was overflowing with money due to the tragic and untimely death of my beloved Adolfo, and my pussy had, it seemed, an inexhaustible supply of pussy juice. Yes, there were other women in Rio that night, many more desirable than I, but none more obsessed with sex, none more willing to let go of little-girl fantasies about Prince Charming, none more anxious to stop being a lady and start becoming a flesh-and-blood creature of love. For these reasons, I suppose, I was drawn to the warm, salty sea, the eternal mother of us all. Perhaps I was insane. Who can say? I do know that I could not stop my race to Copacabana. It was as inevitable as death.

As I crossed Avenida Atlantica, I saw it, Copacabana, lying in front of me. It shimmered in the moonlight like living flesh, the flesh of a woman lying on the edge of the waves, a white Nordic woman like me, who cannot bear to return to the cold wind and freezing water of the Northern Hemisphere. Iridescent butterflies, purple, black, and gold, fluttered in front of me. Huge, white birds, with seven-foot wing spans and long, forked tails, circled and swooped on the edges of the sea. Restless men and women streamed on and off the sands, most of them minimally dressed, most of them wandering, looking. So much was a blur that night. I wanted only to lie down at the water's edge, take off my clothes, and let the sea make love to me. I had no particular fantasies about meeting anyone. The ocean was enough fantasy for me. Strangers on the beach seemed to be touching more than talking, but, of course, that was their business. I'm not a voyeur. I never stare. I just look. One swarthy man in a jockstrap was rubbing cocoanut oil on his woman's breasts, her rampant little points silhouetted against the white moon. I saw them when I sat down on the beach to rest for a moment, when I was halfway down to the water's edge. Of course, Copacabana is almost three miles long, and on a steamy Sunday can hold a hundred thousand people. That night, there were maybe a thousand bodies randomly scattered up and down the length of the beach, some singles, some in pairs, most in casual groups. Like I say, I wasn't paying much attention; I was transfixed by smells; the salt smell of the incoming tide and the sharp odor of fish blood as savage birds of a species yet unknown in America plummeted into the sea and speared their prey with razor beaks.

Then, I smelled the pungent odor of human sperm and the cunt musk of a hundred loins open to love and sensuality. Where was it coming from? The samba drumbeat continued on the beach, only it was softer and slower. More languid. I smelled incense, too, where the worshippers of Yemanjá, Brazilian goddess of the sea, lingered on the beach, scattering white roses into the waves in homage and supplication. Pork meat roasted on braziers, sending pungent, tantalizing smells across the sand. Tropical melon smells mingled with the scent of jasmine, mustard, allspice, chutney, and homemade beer. Cariocas had come down to the beach that night to feast and to sleep. I heard the sweet voices singing plaintive ballads in counterpoint with samba. Clouds moved in front of distant stars. I saw the twinkling lights of distant ships on the navy-blue horizon. The warm drafts of air, wafting southward from the equator, lulled me and comforted me. I kicked off my shoes and dug my bare feet into the warm sand and walked smiling toward the salt soup of the Atlantic. When I got to the water's edge, I was transported by the magic incantations of the voodoo worshippers far to my right. There was nothing left for me to do but to remove the gauze brassiere and my tattered skirt and let them drop into the surf. I then faced the incoming sea, stretched out my arms, and embraced the night. I lay down at the water's edge with its quiet, lapping foam and stretched open my legs for the ocean to make love to me. I was finally home, at the exact place where my slimy, reptilian, far-distant ancestors had first crawled onto land; where, in time, they would stand upright and grow breasts and labia and penises and testicles; where, eventually, they would begin to experience sexual desire, and to crave the pleasure of making love, whenever possible.

I must have fallen asleep into my primeval dreams. They tell me the incoming tide had reached the top of my rib cage, and that, whenever a wave came in, my breasts would begin to float. I only know that I was rescued from death by drowning by – who else; – a wonderful man! If it had not been for him, my anonymous saviour, I would have slid down into the briny deep and forever held my peace. Instead what happened was, I held his piece.

I woke up in a canvas tent, actually a large cabana, a few hundred yards from the water's edge. The front of the tent was open to the sea, which stroked and caressed the Copacabana sand in front of me. I discovered I was lying on silken pillows, all colors of the Arabian nights – eggplant, water-melon, hot pink, cinnamon, orange-red, coral, lilac, navy blue. A metal, filigreed brazier lamp, ten feet above my head, cast patterned light cut out in diamond shapes. I felt so groggy, and yet absolutely secure. An extra-large pillow had been positioned under my ass. It seems I was lying with my legs akimbo, my vaginal lips open to the world. Then again, what's wrong with that? Men sleep that way, sexually active men, that is. No one condemns them; no one considers them cheap or loose. I have to confess I am so culturally brainwashed that, yes, I began to close my legs out of modesty.

I opened my eyes a little bit wider. Who was standing in front of me? At first, he looked blurry, I was still half asleep. Then, he became clearer, a tall, well-built, red-headed male, strong shoulders, a wrestler's chest matted with golden wires. His square pectorals narrowed down to a trim waist and flat stomach with a line of dark hair right down the middle of it. He was wearing kelly-green boxer trunks. I noticed a familiar bulge in his kelly-green crotch. Was I still dreaming?

'I know you don't speak English, Miss Brazilian blonde,' he whispered, 'and that's good, because I can't make it with girls who speak English.'

What was I to do? His eyes were the softest shade of blue I had ever seen, baby-blanket blue. I knew he had probably spent half his life's savings flying from Cedar Rapids or Salt Lake City to find fresh pussymeat to fuck, without risking intimate involvement. The man had been hurt by someone, somewhere. I resolved right then and there he was never know the truth. As long as I was with him, I would be Diana Deafmute. So, communicating the only way I knew how, I spread my thighs and stroked the insides of them, cupping my vulva in both hands, inserting my middle finger into my cunt hole, as if to say in sign language, 'Fuck me! Fuck me!'

The man straddled me, and then pulled down his trunks, which I helped him to struggle out of, working the inner support over and around his blood-stiffened tool. My God! He was a work of art. I guess red-hot is my favorite color, anyway. It reminds me of the setting summer sun, and of gold itself, the most precious metal we poor humans have. His bush was luxuriant. I grabbed two handfuls of it. Thick, rich hair smelling of spice. His egg shaped testicles swung loosely in a dark sack. The cock was thick, straight, and topped by a pink-white glans. He was so erect, so rampant; his strong organ visibly throbbed with his blood's pulse. He knelt down on top of me, his kneeling legs gripping my sides. I rubbed my hands along the tops of his thighs, explored the red-gold jungle of his chest, and finally stroked his back, grabbing his ass in handfuls. He was so white, so pink and white, I called out

71

'Angelo!' He *was* Angelo to me. My angel. My deliverance. He was on top of me now.

'Jesus! Fuck!' he screamed. 'I want you! I've been watching you lying in the waves for the last half hour! Now it's my turn!'

I so wanted to shout out, 'I'm here! Fuck me!' Somehow, through extrasensory perception or something, he understood what I wanted. He moved his head down onto my breasts, and ran his hot tongue around my nipples, pressing down hard as he drew circles in my flesh, his teeth lightly biting me, scraping me, tasting me. My breasts were on fire. I wanted to scream out, 'Tit-fuck me! Tit-fuck me! My angel, use your cock!' But again, I dared not. I would lose him forever. Then, without warning, his flame-coloured head was between my legs. He was eating me out. His clever tongue was already drawing those same excruciatingly delicious circles around my stiffening clitoris, while his nimble fingers made love to my tits. I held his head and stroked his ears, while he brought me to orgasm. My cunt was bucking right in his face with unrestrained abandon.

Then, it happened. He knelt up straight, that flagpole cock sticking out of him; with his own singular sense of command, he took my two hands and clasped them around his sexual staff in a praying position. 'To hell with prayer!' I thought. 'I have my own way of invoking the gods!' With both hands, I grabbed his throbbing cock and pushed my pelvis up to impale myself on it. I shrieked out loud as that big, fat, peppermint stick split my sucking fuckflesh in two and found the center of my vaginal whirlpool. He invaded my inner passageway. He ravished me. I took him to the hilt.

Now, it was his turn to scream, 'Jesus, fucking Christ! You sucking cunt! You fucking, sucking … !' He grabbed me up with both arms, embracing me as he bucked like a stallion, back and forth, in and out, up and down and around. His muscular fingers with their strong, knotted joints took hold of me, kneading me (and needing me, too). My brain dissolved into my breath and I breathed all intelligence away. What mind remained was inside my cunt. I was an appendage attached to a cunt. He was a giant cock.

'Fuck Women's Liberation! Fuck NATO! Fuck the Pope!' he shouted, thinking no one understood or cared.

But I understood. And I cared. My dumb act was driving me to the breaking point. I needed to cry out to him that I loved him and I understood. He came in shuddering bursts, his wet, glistening pole burst forth globs of smooth, whipped *crème de come*, which coated the insides of my vagina.

'You're the greatest fuck I ever had, you fuckin' blonde Brazilian!' he exclaimed. I could no longer contain myself. He was too perfect, too sculptured, too absolutely dear not to know who I was.

'I love you!' I shouted out. I know. I blew it. I couldn't help myself. His cock felt so fucking fantastic. The man went pale.

'What did you say?' he whispered.

'I said, I love you,' I replied, already beginning to cry, knowing full well I had blown what could have been a storybook romance. He was devastated.

'I can't believe you understood what I was saying to you,' he muttered, looking ashen. Well, what could I say in my defense? I had broken the rule of our particular game. His cock was shrinking to human proportions. He turned sadly away from me. My Angelo. I knew I'd never see him again.

'I think you're a great fuck!' I called out after him. But it was too late. He'd already put his trunks back on and had disappeared into the night. I felt lonely and abandoned. It's a terrible thing to have a great sexual partner turn tail on you and disappear two minutes after what seemed like the greatest orgasm of your life. But something happened. That's what I like about life; something always happens. Like they say. 'The Lord giveth and the Lord taketh away.' What happened to me next was a prime case of the Lord giving back again.

It seems that while my golden wrestler was fucking my buns off, a line had formed outside my cabana. The sad truth is, for all the talk about Brazilian culture and Christian religion being grounded in black African culture and tribal gods, black African women are even more proper than their Spanish counterparts. Sure, Brazilian women wear string bikinis to market and nurse their babies in full view of the business world; the truth is, they don't necessarily 'put out' as we used to say at the Beavertown Drive-In. Like women everywhere else, moreover, Brazilian women spend ninety-nine percent of their time talking to other women. For every hour of sex with the men in their lives, there must then be a hundred hours of discussion about it. The sad truth is, that once the woman has found the man, married or unmarried, that she's been desperately searching for, she's not likely to lie down on Copacabana Beach during Carnival and spread her legs. I was unique in this respect. The local Brazilian men, evidently, appreciated just how unique I was. I cannot tell you how grateful I was, a lonely woman in a strange city, to be afforded such overwhelming attention and affection.

The next 'visitor' turned out to be two men together. They could have been brothers. They could have been buddies. Who knows? Who cares? They walked into my cabana tent stark naked, grinning like apes. They were dark men, and hairy, but the skin below their bathing suit lines was pale olive. When these stallions saw me lying with my great golden mounds of tit floating like molded custard on my chest, and my dark blonde pussy purring away between my legs, the flesh appendages hanging down in front of them began to stiffen and lengthen into stout poles. I felt so lonely for the sun god who had just deserted me for no other reason than his own selfish neurosis, I thought, 'Oh well, God must be sending me two to make up for the loss of him.'

These young men did not waste time. In a flash, they were beside me, nuzzling me, sucking my flesh in mouthfuls. Without warning, there were dark hands all over me, inside my thighs, stroking me, exploring me. One's lips rubbed the base of my throat, while the other one kept sucking my nipples and my aureolas into his mouth, where the soft sides of his inner cheeks played havoc with the hair-trigger nerves in that part of my anatomy. But my breasts did not satisfy him. He was ravenous. His hands were all over me. Then, he was where he wanted, between my legs, eating me out. He was ravenous. He kept pulling my clitoris and its surrounding flesh into his hot mouth, the same way he had sucked on my nipples. I was used to my clitoris being tongued, but never before had I felt a whole portion of my delicate fuckflesh disappearing and reappearing, the sides of his mouth squeezing hard on both sides of my pleasure bud while his tongue met it head on, pummeling wet muscle with wet muscle, relaxing it, then devouring it all over again. I felt like my whole pussy was rising into the almost genital flesh of his mouth. I had help: the other brute was rimming me from behind. The tip of his strong peasant tongue encircled the supersensitive nerve ends of my anal hole, until, at last, he began to plunge his tongue deeper into me, sending my blood-engorged vulva smack into the other animal's face. The man behind me had a head of hair like a Persian lamb – black, tightly curled, and soft as dark fog. As he drove deeper into me, his hair engaged every nerve ending between my anal hole and my clitoris. I held onto the man in front of me with both hands, stroking his ears, as he feasted on fresh cunt.

'Fuck me,' I said.

'Fuck me, you mother-fucking animal!' I knew he couldn't understand me, but I could hear the tone of my voice getting louder and louder and raunchier.

'You fucking goddamn animal!' I shouted again. 'Put your mother-fucking pork-pole up my twat!' Fuck! I never felt better in my life. I loved to talk dirty; it made me feel clean all over. I can't explain why, but my gentlemen callers must have understood. Within minutes, I had two dark, hairy Latin gods sandwich-fucking me. I helped my rear guard smear K-Y jelly on his vein-wrapped passion pole with its hot pink head. (Even though both men had entered my tent buck naked, one of them had brought his knapsack along with all the supplies a fella might need for an impromptu sex life.) The gentleman at my front entrance needed no lubricant; I had enough pussy juice for several studs, which turned out to be a good thing, considering the rest of the evening. Before I knew it, the man facing me had turned me on my side, had lifted my leg and guided his thick rod through my sweet, sucking labia into my channel of love, where we began to move back and forth to the pervading samba rhythms of the tropical beach. My other guy entered me, too, groaning with pleasure as my tight ass muscles pressed hard on every nerve fiber in his penile tissue. His cock felt like a crowbar pressing against the column of flesh in my vagina; the two magnificent organs, separated by a thin veil of membrane, set up indescribable vibrations within me. I cannot explain the biological process, but I had orgasms inside me crashing into one another. My ass was shaking and tingling. The men's hairy chests and abdomens tickled me, continuously arousing my nipples and causing my spine to shiver. They had such thick bushes, I was getting brushed and buffed with every stroke. With one hand, I reached down between my legs to fondle their soft, vulnerable scrotums. They felt so delicate there, their big balls almost free-floating in down-covered sacks. I tried to intermingle the two hanging sacks, touching one man's balls to the other's. That touch of homosexuality seemed to increase their pleasure. No doubt, with the scrotal intercourse, one man's testicles stroking another's, I had allowed them to experience the violation of a sacred taboo, something which is always exciting and wonderful when it happens.

Some people think two men sandwich-fucking a woman in itself reveals marked homosexual tendencies; that is, the woman serves as a medium for the two men to relate to one another sexually. I am here to deny such allegations. My two Brazilian beasts were simply enjoying sexual collaboration, the shared adventure of common lust. When are people going to get off of kindergarten Freud? I never felt so wanted and so secure as I did that night between my two teddy bears. Four restless hands, stroking my sides, six legs entangled, thighs rubbing thighs, two mouths nibbling my neck, sucking my shoulders, two red hot rods setting up orgasmic vibrations that threatened to explode into flames. Just before they came, my two pillars of Hercules withdrew their cocks. At the last instant, for about thirty seconds, the two men cock-fucked, running the undersides of their long poles against one another, the delicate ridges of flesh just under their glandes, connecting the most sensitive, more erotic zones of two male bodies and sending immediate shivers of delight up their spines and down their cocks. In no time they came, almost simultaneously, splattering a cloud of come, mostly over me. Then, they lovingly massaged their fresh come all over my body, paying special attention to my caramel nipples. At least two hands continued to pet my pussy, finger-fucking me and kneading my labia. Then, in no time, the visitors were gone, back out on the beach, probably lost in the tropical night between the stars and the pounding surf. What a strange and lovely night this was turning out to be.

There were men waiting in line, sex partners who kept me royally entertained throughout most of the night. Modesty constrains me to mention but a few. The truth is, it has been only a few months now since my Brazilian journey, and already, faces have begun to fade. My memory of my night at Copacabana Beach was of several hours in paradise with the gods. The memory of warmth remains. The memory of being held. The memory of the eternal sea caressing the edges of our human landscape. What more do I have to remember? Faces? What are faces? My grandmother's religion, the Tabernacle Witnesses, say there are no faces in heaven, only the feeling of absolute love. That's exactly what happened to me that night at Copacabana Beach. Yes, I was being totally physical, but my body was but a vehicle for something more, for a sustained ecstasy. I have no one but the wonderful young men in Brazil to thank for that. Not one of them that night mentioned politics or revolution. There were few words of Portuguese exchanged, even fewer of English. I guess the Portuguese for 'I love you' must be *'Et tu amo,'* because I kept hearing that phrase all night. *'Et tu amo, et tu amo.'* I began to say it, too, hoping it meant everything it suggested.

The next man I remember was an older man of about fifty-five, a patriarchal type who spoke English. He was tall and lean, with a long, craggy face and a thatch of snow-white hair. He entered my tent wearing white tennis shorts and a white cotton alligator shirt.

'How do you do?' he said politely, in almost perfect English. His chalk-white complexion was washed with the ruddy flush of a man who doesn't belong in the sun. 'I usually swim and play tennis at night so I won't get sunburned,' he explained. He removed his shirt and pants, revealing a hard, white body with knotted muscles, and a broad, flat chest, the body of a full-blooded European, most rare for a Carioca. 'My ancestors came from northern Portugal,' he explained. 'We're Celts, cousins to the Bretons in France, and the Welsh, and the Irish, and the Scots.'

'But your eyes are so black,' I remarked. Indeed the man's eyes were coals – hard, flinty, and gleaming in what little moonlight shone into our canvas-enclosed space.

'We're what's known as Black Celts,' he told me. 'Every Celtic land contains some of us. We seem to be the troublemakers wherever we go.'

'What are Black Celts?' I asked, thinking that, except for his eyes, he wasn't very black, and wondering what kind of trouble he had in mind.

'We are descended not only from the blue-eyed Celts, who originally came out of the steppes of Russia, but from the peoples of Atlantis,' he explained, stroking my forearm, 'the peoples who settled in Spain and Portugal and northern Africa before the continent finally sank forever into the Atlantic Ocean.'

'When was this?' I asked, looking at that rigorously disciplined body standing above me, giving me his ancestral history.

'About ten thousand years ago,' he explained, fondling the side of my face. He had a terrific body for an older man. I love men who keep in shape. I had forgotten my question. It had something to do with a lost continent. Something about sinking, somewhere. The man kept staring at my cooze. In no time, his long, white pole stuck straight out and turned red with hot blood, a red-hot handle waving in front of my face. He still hadn't laid a finger on my sexual parts, although I have to admit he seemed interested. What was he waiting for? He paraded around with his magic wand waving up and down in front of me. 'There are men in line out there waiting to see you,' he exclaimed. 'They think I'm a crazy old man.'

'No, no,' I replied. 'Not you. You're not crazy. You're in terrific shape.'

'They were joking that I came to give you spiritual guidance,' he continued.

'Spiritual guidance?' I asked, wondering if he was talking about some variety of sado-masochism I hadn't heard about.

Suddenly, he was kneeling in front of me. 'You see,

young lady,' he exclaimed, breathlessly, 'the truth is, I don't know who I am. I was the Bishop of Rio, and for twenty years I was celibate. I never had sexual fantasies. I never looked at a woman except to see her soul. I thought continuously of our Blessed Lord dying on the cross, and that image successfully stifled all thoughts of sex. And now I am allowed to do nothing except travel and play tennis. They gave me a small pension, but I have been stripped of my title, and am no longer allowed to say Mass or to hear confessions.'

'But wait a minute, sir,' I interrupted, realizing he had skipped the best part of the story. 'What happened to you that caused you to lose your job?'

'My episcopate, yes,' he answered, not making much more sense than before. 'All right, I'll tell you. You may as well know.' His nipples were hard and pink, like pencil erasers. I wanted to bite down hard on them. I was tired of talk. I wanted to know what his mouth tasted like. But something about him made me shut up and listen. Something hard and masculine. Maybe it was the red-hot cock. Maybe it was the accent. Maybe it was his black eyes galvanized on my cunt as he continued his strange and compelling tale.

He said, 'You see, there was this young woman in the Cathedral parish, about your age, who declared her love for me through notes and letters. She was, as it so happened, the most luscious girl in all of Rio. I paid no attention. All flesh is grass, they used to tell us. I decided she was what we call a hysteric. The clergy are frequently called in to deal with such types. This girl's this woman's notes continued. She sent me gifts, at first, china figurines of bulls and goats, then, pornographic magazines, artificial vaginas, aphrodesiacs, athletic supporters. She was crazed. Naturally, I avoided her like the plague. What should I have done, I thought, invited her to Christmas dinner at the chancery? Then, one day, fate intervened. At the time, I did not believe in fate. I had just celebrated, or I should say, *mourned* my fiftieth birthday. My mother had died during the previous year, my saintly mother who never remarried after my poor father accidentally fell down an elevator shaft. There were, to be sure, nasty rumors about that terrible incident. The concierge claimed she saw my mother push my father into the elevator shaft, but I was never able to believe that. Anyway, when my dear mother finally died her tragic death in the sanatorium, I was all alone. My mother had lived with me, you see, at least until her final years. Anyway, the luscious young lady who was in love with me must have put some drug into my altar wine. In any case, after I had said three Masses that particular Sunday, too many Masses, and too much altar wine, I staggered back into the sacristy, where the priests dress for religious services; there she was, lying stark naked on the vestment case, stark naked and masturbating. She had lit incense candles and plain candles. She must have bathed in perfume. The effect quite overwhelmed me. Something in me snapped. I couldn't help myself. From what they tell me, because I remember nothing, they had to pull me off her. I'd been fucking her for forty-five minutes straight, apparently. Three orgasms. My cock was still so red-hot, I shocked the other two priests and the three nuns who pulled me off the woman, who was, by now, quite out of her mind. She was ranting that she was Mary, the Blessed Virgin, and that she was pregnant by the Holy Ghost, namely me, and that she was going to give birth to the savior of mankind, who would rescue Brazil from the influence of the United States.'

'They were jealous of your cock!' I snapped.

'Who?' he asked.

'The other priests and the nuns!' I replied, angry that this noble sexual aristocrat had languished so long in abject celibacy. You see, my great and good friend, Monseigneur Giovanni 'Vanni' Caro, that sweet northern Italian ex-hockey player, with that massive, white hulk of a body, who had officiated at my beloved Adolfo's funeral at St Patrick's, and who had worked so

81

long and so arduously in the Vatican itself, where it was excruciatingly difficult for a single gentleman to entertain a woman, explained to me in great detail about the Catholic Church's militant attitude about sex outside of marriage, a point of view that seems to grow more rigid with each generation. There had been a time, Vanni had explained to me, when most of the priests in Latin America had common-law wives. There had been a time when a bishop of Rio fucking a woman who got him drunk on altar wine and then shoved her pussy in his face, would have been seen for what it was – a terrific opportunity – but, alas, no longer. With the rise of rules and regulations in the military and the multinational corporations, a lot of the bawdy fun was being lost. How much longer before there would be a tax on Carnival, and the military police would be arresting people for fornicating in the streets, just like they'd do in New York?

I remembered how Vanni had sneaked me into his splendid quarters in the Vatican, where we had fucked like rabbits, an adventure I relate in great detail in *Diana's Debut*. I remembered how the magnificent medieval screen in Vanni's bedroom came crashing down to reveal a hidden chamber where a naked man in a white skullcap was watching us through peep-holes, and whacking off. Who else? The dear man, no names mentioned, was so embarrassed he began blurting out that at least he didn't use birth control, and, to comfort him, I had to place that lovely, tumescent organ of his in my hot, young mouth and bring him off. So you see, I fully understood the hypocrisy of organized religion.

My heart went out to my defrocked visitor, who had lost the best years of his life keeping it in his pants. I lay him down on my blanket, cupped his firm buttocks in my hands, and lowered my hungry mouth over his organ. I was more than pleased to have the opportunity to experiment with my 'deep throat' technique, which Maxey had taught me just a few weeks before. 'Deep Throat,' from the movie of the same name, refers to the art of controlling the gag reflex in the back of the throat; the head is bent in a certain way so that the throat is one straight channel and can accommodate dorks of any size. I could tell that my defrocked Don Juan had not had enough head. He went absolutely wild with excitement.

'Yes! Yes!' he squealed. 'I love you! You wonderful whore.' How could I spoil his fun, and tell him that I wasn't a whore, that I was just an all-American girl on holiday? I loved his big glans, shining like a ripe plum and oozing precome. It hit the corrugated roof at the front of my mouth with a shudder, and, when the soft meat at the back of my throat gave resistance to the spongy undershaft of his erect cock, the friction created by rubbing two ultrasensitive surfaces together drove my man wild. He was experiencing at sixty what he should have first enjoyed at eighteen.

But there was definitely a hitch. Like I said, I was relatively new to the deep throat technique, myself. I realized I was going to suffocate if I didn't assume a more natural position. I pivoted my body around so that my cooze was right over his gaping mouth. It was the only natural way to do it; good ol' sixty-nine, one of life's magic numbers. I was thrilled and relieved when he grabbed my ass with his two strong hands and brought my cunt down straight onto his mouth. I guess that no matter what some professional sexologists say, some men come by eating pussy naturally. The Bishop, as it turned out, was the cunnilingus expert of Rio. Maybe it came from twenty-five years of hearing confessions. I must say that my fantasies about those confessions began to take over my imagination:

'Bless me Father, for I have sinned. I cheated on my wife.'

'How did you cheat on your wife, my son?'

'I picked up this fantastic piece of ass on Rua Do Ouvidor.'

'And what did you do with her, my son?'

'I ate her out, Father, and then I fucked her.'

'You ate her out, my son? What exactly does that mean?'

'That means I reached down her pants and finger-fucked her until she was wet, and then I stripped her, and then I went down on her.'

'Went down on her, my son?'

'Yes, Father, I stuck my face in her cunt, my mouth to be exact, spreading her outer cunt lips with my thumbs, opening the prepuce over her clitoris with my hot tongue, licking it open till her fat, little slug was exposed. Christ, I could smell the perfume on her, Father; she smelled like Paris and New York and all those fucking places I dream about; she smelled warm and wet and salty. She smelled of the fresh-turned earth and the ocean, and she clasped her legs around my shoulders, and locked her ankles around the back of my neck, and I devoured her. I made her squeal like a pig; I made her scream "Fuck me! Fuck me! I worship you, my stud! I worship you; don't ever leave me! More! More!" I drew circles around her clit with my tongue, Father, pressed down hard with the tip of my hot mouth muscle, and drew deep circles, and licked the clit, and licked the cunt, and slurped the juices, until, finally, she bucked and heaved and lost control. And then I fucked her.'

'How many times did you do this, my son?'

'Every day for a week, and then my wife was coming back from her visit to Bahia, so I had to stop, and for these and all the sins of my life, I am heartily sorry.'

'Bless you, my son. For your penance, say five Hail Marys and make a good Act of Contrition.'

I mean, fuck, sooner or later, if you'll excuse the expression, the world made itself known to the Bishop of Rio. Sooner or later, his God-given cock was bound to rise.

And so it did. The man went sexually berserk. He visited every whorehouse in the city, got the clap three times, started fucking nurses, and doctors' wives, and then, inevitably, turned his attention to the nuns. The nuns wanted it bad, but had profound guilt complexes, which they resolved by talking to the superiors. My night visitor's career as a bishop ended abruptly when anonymous sources began writing to the Vatican.

But who cared? He was in my mouth, and I was in his. He ate with all-consuming desire, like a starving man with a feast in front of him. Nothing turns me on more than a man's desire. Nothing makes my blood rush faster to my cunt. Nothing makes my heart feel warmer, more attached to the world, more anxious to fill my mouth and my throat with a man's appetite; with his, how can I put this, his big meat, his dork, his dong, his sausage, dick, prick, pork, putz, cock, rod, prod.

'Give it to me! Stuff me with your mother-fucking night-stick! Ram me! Jam me! Baby, just fuck my brains out!'

Some stud with a hairy chest and a heavy, hanging cock kept peeking in to check our progress. Being basically a monogamist, I refused to entertain fantasies of any other man while I was with the man of my choice for that magic moment. It's not that my tendencies toward monogamy rule out occasional orgies or gang-bangs, but those activities are not really serious. They belong in a separate category called 'fun and games.' With my bishop, I felt a definite commitment, however brief.

I didn't think sixty-five-year-old ex-priests could come the way he came, bucking and breathing hard with animal grunts. His cock swelled up like a mortar shell, and then, like good ammunition, exploded in vibrations that made me come double. My vagina was soaking wet with sweat, sperm, lubricant, pussy juice. I smelled like a fish. We both did. We smelled like a man and a woman who had just made passionate, near-violent love. There is no other smell like it anywhere; we treasured the pungent proof of our shared flesh. But, as they say, we had little time left to us. Our love affair was fast becoming our mutual, most bittersweet tragedy. Our tide had come in, crested, and was now on its way out. The randy bishop, it seemed, had other fish to fry. And there were dark, husky men waiting patiently in line outside my cabana on Copacabana Beach.

My bishop kissed me in my damp, intimate places, under my arms, in the nape of my neck, on my clitoris, nuzzling me for one last time. 'Dearest, dearest,' he whispered, 'we live in a tragic age. My life has led up to you, and now I must leave you, because absolute commitments are no longer possible for me. Nothing makes any sense.'

Well, it *was* tragic, because he was the one who didn't make any sense to me, but I decided to make the best of it. As Picasso says, 'When you run out of blue, use red.' 'Maybe you'll come to New York,' I said, hoping for a miracle, fantasizing abut a three-way with Vanni, the bishop, and me.

'No, no,' he answered, plaintively, 'there's no point in pursuing a fantasy. Tonight was the height of every fantasy I've ever had. It was the splendor in the grass. And now it's gone, I must return to earth.' He looked so sad, so full of darkness and mystery. He was beyond my reach. He left my cabana without turning around. It was a moment of such despair, however brief, it seemed almost religious. The world stood still and held its breath. I felt alone to the point of abandonment. Totally alone, I had no choice but to get up and greet the men waiting in line. I could smell their cigarettes and hear their gutteral remarks, which sounded suggestive and loud.

What can I say? In a word, the dam burst. Those poor boys had been waiting so long, drinking rum and smoking hashish, I guess you could say they had moved to another level of consciousness. The slow lapping of the warm waves of the outgoing tide had an intoxicating effect on all of us. We were seduced by the most beautiful beach on earth. We were drugged by

Carnival and the sounds of samba. The steel drums and shuffling feet stomping out the magical rhythms of blood and pulse hypnotized the civilized surfaces of our overeducated brains. I, for one, no longer cared about my so-called dignity, my so-called sense of self, my so-called ego. If one thing had gotten me into trouble and dragged me into misery every day of my life, it was my preoccupation with myself, my ego, my boundaries, my sense of control. That night in Brazil, it all went, all of it.

Those boys on the beach staggered into my tent and fucked me into nirvana. 'Ecstasy' doesn't begin to describe what happened to me. 'Orgasm' certainly doesn't do it. It was beyond all appeal to reason. Yes, I know that certain members of my grandmother's religion, the Tabernacle Witnesses, if they had seen my activity in that Copacabana cabana, would have become violently ill on the spot. But God would have loved it because God is Love, right, and the author-inventor of cocks, cunts, bushes, tits, and asses, not to mention human emotion, including lust and the so-called carnal appetite.

Having invoked the Deity and his wondrous imagination, let me now describe what a divine time I had with the boys from Brazil. I guess blondes were a rarity in the Southern Hemisphere. The boys literally went wild. In no time, I was surrounded by a forest of cock-spears jutting out from hairy, muscular groins above dark, down-covered sacks of testicles. I did not know who to grab first. No matter. They grabbed me like ten starving men face-to-face with their last meal on earth. It was everything psychiatrists and ministers hate. They call it depersonalized sex, but I don't know what they are talking about. I never felt more like a person in my life. I never felt so cared for, so touched. Wonderful, warm mouths were all over me, kissing, sucking, licking, rimming, biting, – God, mouths are wonderful! There was a tongue in my ass tracing tiny circles around the rim of my anus; in front, some man was lingering on my clitoris with a mouth that contained all his physical energy and half his immortal soul. The athletic studs took my tits, one to a customer; one Olympian used his mouth, the other, his well-practiced fingers to massage and suck my semiprecious nipples, which are first cousins to flesh-jewel clits, connected as they are through a microscopic skein of delicate nerve endings both to the brain and to that special, secondary brain between the legs, namely, the all-knowing, all-seeing cunt. One African god was sucking my armpits and stroking the avenue of skin and muscle between my underarms and the sides of my breasts. My stable of studs were everywhere, nuzzling my neck with the sand-paper beards, kissing me between my toes, tickling the soles of my feet, running lengths of hot cock up and down in my inner thighs, which, on a golden-skinned blonde like me, are pale gold, champagne gold, all the way up to my hot pink labia, where they were taking turns nibbling my raw fish. In all this rampant sex play, there was no evident order. These men had not decided in advance who would concentrate on what part of my anatomy. If there had been twice as many men, I'm afraid there might have been a problem. But, thank God, there were only ten. I pointed to the activity between my legs and, speaking in a universal sign language, announced, 'Get in line for fucking.' Which is not to say I didn't suck every single bronze, black, and olive cock for at least five minutes. And I'm here to tell you there wasn't one wimp in the lot. What a treat! Ten rock-hard erections, bulging with veins, pulsating in my grip and between my lips, their hot Brazilian blood pumping as rhythmically as the waves, as fast as the samba drums! They could not speak English, but boy, did they speak sex! Each stud squealed as I slipped my wet lips over his glans.

What is a glans, anyway? A muscle? Can a muscle have a brain? Nothing in the male human being is as responsive to a woman, not even his face. I can always tell how extreme a man's desire for me is by the state of his glans, that dear little tip of the cock, which, circumcised or not, is normally such a soft, insignificant feature of his anatomy. By the time a hot-blooded member of my opposite sex is standing naked across from my plump pussy with its thick, golden fur, his eyes fixed on my tits, fully-packed with their chewy, caramel nipples, the glans has changed both in appearance and intent to a large, willful creature with a tight, shiny skin which seems stretched beyond its limits. The hole, which, in its flaccid state, seems almost invisible, now looms in front of me like the eye of the All-Seeing One. In some men, that eye is round; in others, it's more of a slit. In each case, there is an eternal message, and that message is clear. Let me put it this way: as the precome ooze glistens and occasionally drips onto my face, as the man in question gets closer and closer, the enveloping skin threatens to burst, until I can finally no longer resist an immutable law of nature; namely, that cock must be sucked; it must be kissed with a woman's lips and tongue; the glans must be cherished; after all, it is where the eternal seed of human life makes its initial appearance – and more; the glans is the most sensitive spot on the man's body. It offers the possibility of extreme physical pleasure, which, once the organ has ceased to function properly, no amount of money can buy or repair. Yes, I probably should discuss the entire cock, and I will, in a subsequent account, but have always believed in first things first.

When I think of that night on Copacabana Beach, I think of ten plum-sized glandes taking turns cleaving into me, forcing their way between my lips, into my mouth, then pressing themselves into my labial slit until it opened wide to receive one hard cock after another. What more could a girl ask for? And how dare the psychiatric profession imply someone like me is suffering a loss of identity, labeling me 'promiscuous'! Those sniveling mind-fuckers, those jealous Mama's boys (excuse my anger)! For an hour and a-half, I had one continuous orgasm; I was one golden-skinned spasm of pleasure, shaking, quivering, vibrating. All fear was released from my body, all negative emotions left me; all anger subsided. Finally, I felt personally wanted in Brazil. I knew that world revolution was insignificant compared to sexual well-being. Once the radical Marxists, along with their friends, the radical clergy, have succeeded in cutting off the cocks of the rich and middle classes in the name of the poor, the poor should be warned that, once they are fed by the Marxist government, they will be expected to join its armies and its secret police, and then, they, too, will be expected to hand over their cocks for amputation. In the Communist state of the future, even more than the puritanical world of today, the free cock will be hunted down and destroyed as an enemy of the state. At least, this is the considered point of view of my Italian lover, Monseigneur Vanni Caro. Vanni has no use for either Communists or the radical Church, but he stays in the Vatican because he says that in Rome, at the heart of things, there is a certain wisdom about Man. After two thousand years of history, 'Mother' Church has accepted all varieties of human passion – lust, greed, envy, gluttony, even madness, as the fabric of life. She knows that only so much outside control is possible, only so much idealism can be imposed. So, Vanni strokes his cock daily and meets with girls like me with loving pussy lips and terrific asses, and he makes love to them and speaks of eternal love.

Am I really talking about my Vanni? Of course not. I'm still striking out at the fucking radical, Che Miranda, and the revolution which drove me onto Copacabana Beach in the middle of Carnival. Later, in New York, I discovered that Mr Macho Miranda really does like pussy, especially mine, which makes me wonder who he was really trying to impress in Brazil with his great revolution. Am I really a right-wing fascist? Am I really power mad, caring only for the rich? The truth is, I am too stupid to understand history. My late husband Adolfo Adoro was the poor son of a Sicilian fisherman. In his middle age, after long years as a hard-working dressmaker who loved women, he began a fashion house, which grew into an international empire. Adoro created thousands of jobs in industries all over the world. And now, in Brazil, revolutionaries who cared little for fashion or for beautiful women were accusing me of oppressing the poor. I cannot overstate how upset I was and why I felt I had to offer myself to the common men of Brazil, the everyday, ordinary men who wandered the beaches looking for a little human attention.

So, when all the boys had come in all possible ways inside my cunt – on my stomach, on my bush, between my breasts, on my inner thighs, inside and outside of my sunny globes, and I was streaked and clotted with globs of sperm; thick, white come, *crème fraiche*, viscous egg white, cooked and uncooked, vanilla ice cream, spittle, salty, sweet, running and thick – and I was caked in my pubic hairs and shining slickly on my stomach and still wet between my tits, I burst into tears of gratitude, crying out in a language I knew none of the boys could understand, 'I love you, my Brazilian boys! I will always love you!'

Somehow, they understood, and suddenly, we were all of one mind, and we ran naked, all eleven of us, from our cabana tent and rushed headlong into the sea, where we chased one another in the warm, salty surf as the ocean washed us clean and calmed us, its maternal rhythms in counterpoint to the ongoing samba. I lay on top of three of my new-found friends, their brown bodies gleaming wet under the moon. I wished that everyone I knew and loved would some day be lucky enough to be, well, gang-banged in Rio on Copacabana Beach. For another hour, we cavorted like dolphins. Occasionally, someone fucked me in the surf, their sperm running out to sea in the outgoing tide.

Eventually, I grew heavy with fatigue. I needed sleep. I needed to be alone between clean, white sheets. I needed to dream. In the morning, I had a special errand. I was to visit the Da Silvas. I dared not arrive there exhausted. An inner voice warned me I would need all the energy available to me. Little did I suspect, as I lay among my lovers in the surf, the bloodshed of the following day.

Dare I describe how I got back to my hotel? Thank God, it was Carnival and three o'clock in the morning and some of my bucks were off-duty policemen, or we all would have ended up in a Brazilian torture cell.

Imagine, if you will, ten strong Afro-Hispanic studs between the ages of twenty-five and thirty-five, all built like brick shithouses with barrel chests and big balls, not to mention all varieties of cocks, dangling, strutting, jutting, swinging, swaying, carrying me wrapped in a beach towel across Avenida Atlantica back to the Hotel Rio Palace. Passers-by, late-night revelers, most of them in string bikinis, looked stunned. If I had been a Skinny Minnie, and my bold companions a bunch of Nervous Nellies, nobody would have cared. But with all due modesty, I have to say we carried in our persons all the self-evident powers of sexuality at its height. We were absolutely sensational. People stopped dead in their tracks. When we walked into the gold-leafed lobby of my hotel, the night clerk, a little fellow, bald, with thick, wire-rimmed glasses, almost lost his dentures. Needless to say, he refused to believe I was Senhora Adoro. I had to have Lulu Touché rung up. She literally ran off the elevator wrapped in her pink satin bed quilt, half-hysterical, imagining I'd been stabbed, couldn't believe what she saw, verified my identity, and then, apparently, after I kissed my men good night and good-bye, took two of the men back to bed with her. Apparently, her all-time favorite lover, the blue-black Hugo Battista, the Emperor of Love, caught up in his 'career' in Room Service, had told her he expected to be paid for his favors. That devastated her. Lulu confided to me that she was too Italian Catholic to pay for sex.

'That's-a the price you pay for your basic principles,' she told me.

'What is your basic principle?' I inquired.

'My principle is, sex, she free or forget it. When you start-a pay for the sex, then you commit the sin. As long as sex, she free, that's okay.'

I'm glad Lulu felt that way, because, as things turned out, I would run into Hugo the following night at the height of Carnival, with no Lulu in sight. I was grateful she had, in a manner of speaking, given me permission to let him fuck me. And, strangely enough, I never paid him a cent. I stuck to Lulu's rules.

Back in my room, I stood under my warm shower washing off the salt sea. In the next room, I could hear the cooing sounds of my irrepressible Lulu with two of my Copacabana studs; they would continue to coo and gurgle the rest of the night, but none of that activity bothered me. I was full up with love. I couldn't take another cock. I crawled between clean, white sheets and immediately sank into a bottomless sleep that carried me to places I had never known in my present life to people I had never seen before, to thoughts I had never entertained in Beavertown.

Chapter Six

My dream bears retelling. It explained to me my karmic connection with Brazil, why I had to travel there, and why I would always return. Karma refers to the law of the spiritual universe, the law of universal return, which means that I bear responsibility for all my actions, good and bad, in all my many lives; in other words, 'as you give, so you get.'

My dream explained to me something I have known about myself for a long time; that my soul or spiritual entity was created from eternity as a servant of the Goddess of Love, known to the ancient Romans as Venus, to the Mesopotamians as Astarte, to the Brazilians as Yemanjá. To me, she will always be Isis, as I knew her in my Egyptian experience; at least, according to what the psychics have told me. According to the laws of karma, until one learns to do good to others, for which charity there are always rewards in subsequent lives, such as being born beautiful or handsome, with many natural talents such as the ability to sing or to understand the stock market, or even, yes, the ability to enjoy good sex, one must experience the consequences of one's bad actions. Physical handicaps and personal deprivations are believed to be Karmic challenges to shape up.

Several psychics had told me that, in several of my past lives, I had misinterpreted my destiny as a slave of love, and had been very cruel to others. It seems that I was once a Spanish nun. In that life experience, I decided love was basically obedience to the laws of the Church, and so I informed on other women I was told were witches or women who had what were considered loose morals. The punishment I brought upon my self for my Spanish experience was my subsequent Brazilian experience as Rosita Morales, in what was roughly the early nineteenth century in colonial Brazil. As Rosita, I was exceptionally beautiful. In truth, I was exceptionally 'hot to trot', as we say, but, because colonial Brazil was so sexually repressed, I had no way to express my sexuality.

But because of events that my dream revealed to me, Rosita Morales died understanding, at last, how being a servant of the Goddess of Love is connected to sexual love. Apparently, my suffering in my Brazilian experience helped liberate mankind from its rigidly puritanical outlook about sex. In this life, I am being rewarded, it would seem, with the infinite blessing of great sex wherever and whenever I want it.

This was my dream. Dom Joao was regent. I could hear the slave girls talking about him. He had fled Napoleon's army and had established Rio as the center of the Portuguese Empire. (My studies tell me this was around 1810). The streets were filled with soldiers in blue uniforms, wearing high, plumed helmets. I know, because I used to spy on them through closed shutters. My dream, in fact, began with my spying through the second-story window. If my father, a Captain of the Guard, saw me, I would be severely beaten. The Hussar in the familiar blue uniform who caught my attention was handsome, with eyes the color of the sea. When I looked into the mirror, I was always taken aback to see my dark eyes, my wavy, black hair and my dusky complexion. I looked like a Hindu princess. Then, I remembered my grandmother was a mestiço, of mixed blood. I was the darkest one in my family. They called me 'morena,' meaning a 'dark white.' The women in my family, as blonde as they were, envied me, however, because, unlike them, I had not grown fat and lazy. I was only seventeen; I still believed there was hope. I still believed that someday I would be allowed to run free like the black slave girls. They would laugh if they heard me speak this way, but girls of my class were usually forbidden to leave the house, except to go to confession. We were married off at fifteen, usually to a man of fifty or sixty. I was, too, except that my husband died of a heart attack before the wedding ceremony. My father grew angry at me when this happened. I was severely beaten. It was then, two years ago, that I decided I would find a better life, even if I became a whore. I certainly had the body for it; my breasts were ripe and full, without sagging. My nipples were dark, irresistible to Portuguese men. Unlike my mother and sisters, who were addicted to honey custards and fried bread slathered with mango preserves, I did not express my sorrows in overeating. Instead, I concentrated on my Hussar officer in the blue uniform, and dreamed that one day he, too, would notice me. But how could he? As I said, like all the women of my class, I was confined in a cloister situation, a trick the Portuguese learned from their hundreds of years under Moorish rule. The Moors, Moslems, were superior to Christians in all the arts and sciences, being particularly renowned for their skills in mathematics and astronomy. If they kept their women in bondage, then, obviously, that was what superior people did. A good excuse, I thought, for one-half of the human race to keep the other half in bondage.

I hit upon a plan. The Hussar officer passed by my bedroom, on the street side of the house, at the same time every day, when I was supposed to be taking a siesta, and he, being German, was out for a bit of exercise, while his Portuguese superior officers were fast asleep (or fast-fucking some lucky African slave girl). I decided there was only one way. I stripped completely naked and anointed my body with all the jasmine perfume I could find. I waited behind the closed shutters, open a half-inch so that I could peek down into the nearly deserted street below. A split second before he reached my house, I opened one shutter six inches and tossed a red rose at his feet. He looked up just in time to catch my naked arm withdrawing into the window. He stared for a minute, smelled the rose, tossed it aside, and continued on. The very next day, I repeated my action, except this time I let him see my shoulder, too. On the third day, I made sure he saw the tip of one naked breast. I'm talking about a matter of five seconds. Every day for two weeks, I repeated what had become a ritual, except that on the fourteenth day I let him see my entire naked body, full frontal nudity, my breasts bobbing in front of me. Again, it was a matter of five seconds. I dreaded that someone from the dePalma family across the street might have the same idea as I, or that one of their servants might forgo siesta to clean the front shutters. Equally disastrous would be someone in my household looking out a front window at exactly the wrong time, at the very second my Hussar was looking up. I had to work fast.

My fifteenth rose bore the note, 'I want to meet you, but I am trapped.' It was a miracle I even knew how to write. My mother insisted my father teach me so that I could read the prayer book in church. Of course, she needed an excuse; ninety percent of the women of my social class were illiterate.

On the sixteenth day, when I opened the shutters, I spread my legs, pushed my pelvis forward, and opened my vaginal lips with the thumb and forefinger of one hand while I finger-fucked myself. I wanted my Hussar to be absolutely clear that I was sexually attracted to him. I guess that I was ahead of my time by at least five hundred years. I knew that, being an officer and a gentleman, he would figure something out. I was correct about that. The very next day, as I opened my shutters, he tossed a rock into my room. It landed on my bed with a thud.

The rock was wrapped with a note that read, 'Go to

confession, Church of Sao Ignacio, Tomorrow, Saturday at four P.M. Go to Father Rao.' He had included a crude pornographic drawing of a man fucking a woman. I guess he wanted me to be absolutely clear about his intentions, too. The figures he drew were drawn in profile, naked, facing each other. The man's cock looked like a drawbridge connecting the two of them; Siamese twins joined at the crotch. Her tits, drawn with big black nipples, were humongous. I was particularly glad he noticed my dark African inheritance. Through some kind of primitive instinct, I decided to eat his note lest my mother or my dueña (my guardian nurse) find it. I quickly chewed and swallowed it, none too soon. My mother came running into my room without knocking, shrieking that she had seen a Hussar officer throw a rock into my room. I denied everything, a denial which did me no good whatsoever, since the fat, half-pound rock in question lay like a dead weight in the middle of my bed.

'Here is the rock!' my mother screamed, 'and you have not lain in your bed! You were standing naked in the window!'

With that, I realized that my mother and I had similar imaginations, except that I applied mine on the practical plane, whereas she was the master of repression. My dark blood, you see, had come from my father's mother. My own mother was pure Portuguese, with blue eyes and a cold, exacting temperament. She was more Catholic than the Pope, and she always said that, if she had known beforehand that my father had African ancestors, she never would have married him. But, of course, the bottom line was that she adored my father any way he came, and probably loved me, too. She was more shackled by convention than any woman I knew, and, not having had the advantage of African genes, she had no inner voice calling her to a more direct relationship with people, especially men. She saw everything African as lower class, and feared for me that I would end up on the streets, unmarriageable because I was neither virgin nor Christian.

It was no good; my heart, you see, was set on my Hussar's cock. I had the perfect strategem. I sank to my knees. 'Mother, it's true. I have sinned. I enticed the officer, but he was repelled by my vulgarity, so he threw a rock at me. Oh, Mother, I must go to confession tomorrow, at Sao Ingancio and confess my sins. Surely, God will forgive me.'

'Why tomorrow? Why not today?' my mother, still furious, demanded to know.

'Because I need a day to prepare,' I insisted.

'Prepare what?' she screamed. 'What else have you done?'

Nothing, Mother!' I lied.

'And why Sao Ignacio?' she continued. 'Sao Ignacio is the next parish over; we're Sao Paolo, here.'

My brain raced to find a suitable answer. 'Sao Ignacio is the Jesuit church, *Mamà*. I feel the Jesuits will give me better advice.'

'Better advice!' she shrieked; 'Do you go to confession for good advice or to beg God's forgiveness!'

'Oh, *Mamá*, please be patient with me,' I sobbed. I could see I had chosen the right strategy. As long as I bowed before Church tradition and religious solutions, *Mamá* would go along.

The next afternoon, dressed in my darkest dress, I left my father's house accompanied by Phillipa, my dueña or guardian. I had no choice. Every unmarried woman had to be accompanied by her dueña. Again, my brain raced. Before we reached the church, I cautioned Phillipa that I might spend as long as a half hour talking with the priest, and that she might as well wait outside. I gave her fifty *dinheiros* for tea and honeycake at a local teahouse less than a stone's throw (oops!) from the church. Phillipa was delighted. The money was more than she made in a week working for my mother. It also sealed the bargain between us. If she ever informed on me, I could say that she left me to go eat honeycakes. Of course, she hadn't the vaguest inkling of what I was really planning to go eat!

99

Once inside the dark, cut-stone church with its faint odor of incense, its flickering votive lights, its ornate, carved marble altar, its statues painted silver and gold with sunburst halos behind their heads, I felt enclosed in a special world of strange sensuality, unlike any other in Rio. I soon found Father Rao's name above one of the confessionals. I waited until I heard the clock in the bell tower ring four times before entering the confessional. I found myself climbing past red velvet draperies into the penitent's side of the ornately carved, mahogany booth. I knelt down on the kneeler, and peered past the grill in front of me into an empty chair.

No one was there! I was in a state of shock! Suddenly, in the back wall of my confessional booth, a door opened. A small dwarf in a black cassock whispered, 'Rosita?' I nodded. The dwarf took my hand, closed and locked the secret door, and led me down a narrow, stone passageway, at the end of which was a flight of stairs leading down to a dungeon of sorts. There were chambers there; perhaps they had once been jail cells, but no longer. Now, they were mahogany and fruitwood rooms, splendid rooms with oriental rugs and polished brass chandeliers. I smelled incense, too, no doubt burning to counteract the dank smell of the stone. The dwarf pointed at one particular door, telling me to go into that room. I noticed that his teeth were black, and his breath smelled of garlic sausage. I could not wait to get away from him.

The door to the room in question was ajar. I pushed on it; it opened effortlessly. I found myself alone in an ornate bower of ebony and silver, with candelabra burning perfumed candles, and with birds of paradise stuffed and mounted on the ebony walls. A silver bed dominated the room, a bed piled high with cushions upholstered in satin brocade in every color of the rainbow. The door shut behind me with a slam. I was not alone.

'Rosita?' The voice was a man's voice, deep, with a

100

German accent. I whirled around to see the man who was in the room with me. It was my Hussar; yes, I recognized him instantly; the same noble head, the same chiseled nose, the same hooded, blue eyes, the thinning blonde hair, the overshot Hapsburg jaw, yes, yes. But now there was no blue uniform in sight, only the body of a Greek statue, and the first erection I had ever seen – long, straight, and white, with a bulb at the end, glistening with a thick, clear fluid. His bush was thick and blonde, his legs were sinewy, his chest and arms hard-looking, without an ounce of fat. It was unlike any body I had ever seen in Rio, and it hit me with the impact of an electrical lightning bolt. I was blinking with embarrassment, but inwardly I desired whatever it was that happened between men and women. 'Rosita?' he asked again.

'How did you know my name?' I asked, as he answered me and undressed me at the same time, unbuttoning my buttons as fast as he could.

'I make it my business to find out, ask servants to ask servants who was the dark, beautiful woman in the Morales house. The answer was always the same: 'There is only one beautiful woman in the Morales house, the dark Rosita, the desire of every man.'

In no time, this godlike presence had stripped me of every piece of clothing; I stood there in front of him breathing deeply as the bulb on the end of his cock grew red, then purple, and he began to tenderly nuzzle me between my breasts, murmuring, 'Rosita, Rosita, my name is Karl; here, in Rio, they call me Carlo. You call me Carlo.'

At that moment, Jesus disappeared; Dom Joao disappeared; my father disappeared. There was only Carlo. His hands cupped my round little ass and stroked the front of my thighs. Inside of me, a lifetime of repression broke through; my hands were all over his hard, masculine frame as he knelt in front of me kissing my dark belly with its fine line of down which ran down the middle of my stomach to my bellybutton, below which was a forest of dark silk, an inverted triangle twice as thick and deep as any woman's I'd ever seen. Until that minute, I had always been embarrassed by my copious pubic hair, but now I realized that it turned men on. I began to tremble. His lips were everywhere – under my arms, along the sides of my breasts, inside my thighs, up and down the backs of my calves, until, finally, he took my hands and placed them around his erection and moved closer to me.

I couldn't imagine what would happen next. My Carlo was a genius at caring, a prince of tenderness. He drew me over to the bed. Then, he sat down on the side of the bed, opened his legs, and pulled me towards him, invading my mouth with his sweet tongue, while his hands began to delicately, sensitively stroke my juicy little cunt, which, up to that moment, had never been touched by a man, not even my mother's doctor. I could smell his desire. He stank like an animal in heat, a brute overcome by erotic desire. Yes, I was wet down there; worse, my juices were beginning to run down my legs.

Since I did not completely understand my sexual organs, I was not sure if I had lost control of my bladder. I was no longer able to focus. The room was a blur of incense. My man's sky blue eyes penetrated to my dark Latin core like the bright sky being let into a sunless cave. Then, he did a wonderful thing, a miracle. He grasped me around the waist with two strong hands and lifted me up over his staunch pole of a cock. Then, he lowered me slowly onto it. 'Help me,' he murmured. And so I did, guiding him into me. My heart was full, my passion hypnotic in its effect. I felt warm all over. Suddenly, with a start, I realized I had reached a place where he could go no further. The laws of nature had decreed a barrier within my very being. I felt afraid, resistant, alone.

Carlo had no patience with scared little girls. He pulled me down hard on top of him. I felt a sharp, stinging pain, a searing flash like I was being ripped apart. I could tell there was blood. I wanted to run, to escape, to cry out that I had been mutilated, but the stronger part of me wanted to remain forever impaled on my German officer.

'You are wonderful and exciting to me,' he whispered, as he laid me on my back. It was as if God himself had granted me permission to live a life as full as the Devil's. While we were changing positions, his hot pole slipped out of me. As sore as I was, I craved him, and so I eagerly pulled him onto me again. He was slippery with my fresh blood. Back and forth, back and forth he moved. Instinctively, I clasped his organ with my pussy lips; what a strong muscle I possessed, I thought, even stronger than my mouth! I was amazed. I moved with him; it was like dancing; he led, and I followed. We were possessed with a rhythm all our own, an intoxicating swaying which became a violent pounding as fast as my heartbeat, a pounding that carried me away into an ocean of music, music I had never heard before, a roaring sound rich and deep and overpowering.

'Rosita, Rosita,' were the only words he spoke, over and over like the chanting of a celestial visitor. During my hour with him, I experienced my first orgasm. I felt as if my very soul had been pierced, as if God himself had touched me with light and power and endless energy. When it was over, we lay drenched in sweat, smelling both sour and sweet from the mingling of incense and our body smells.

'You must hurry back,' he announced, ever mindful of my good name.

'Can't you take me with you?' I pleaded.

'No, no, that is not possible,' he answered.

'When will I see you again?' I implored.

'At the same time next week,' he answered, dressing quickly, stuffing his long cock into his trousers, the white liquid still dripping from the end of it, staining the bright blue of his uniform pants.

When I arrived back on the street, my dueña, Phillipa, was in tears. She was insisting to a policeman that I had been kidnapped by pirates. When she caught sight of me, she turned white from shock, and then immediately launched into a purple rage, screeching, 'Where have you been?'

'I was talking to my confessor,' I announced, for the first time in my life extremely confident. But Phillipa was no fool; she knew that I was not the same Rosita who had entered the church an hour before. Somehow I had changed. She did not dare admit, however, that, in so short a time, I had become a woman.

At home, my mother, thank God, had not been watching the clock. We arrived just in time for supper, with the excuse that we had offered a rosary for my mother's health. My mother could see that I was remarkably at peace. She was certain that the priest had put me in my place, and that abject servitude was what I really desired as penance for my sins.

As my dream progressed, time speeded up and so did my sexual liaisons with my Hussar officer. It seemed that my very existence revolved around my new-found sexual life. At home, I thought about nothing else but Carlo – his cock, his face between my legs, his tongue lingering on my clitoris, his hands stroking the curve of my breasts, making me shiver with arousal. It was sheer sexual passion, and it consumed my brain. It was the closest I had ever come to feeling fully alive. I did not care for any other aspect of what normally passed for reality, and certainly cared nothing for the daily activities within my mother's house. My body tingled. My muscles felt supple and strong. My hair grew sleek. My skin glowed.

In time, by the end of the first six months, I realized I was expecting a child. I had not menstruated in at least three months. Or was it four? My tummy had begun to grow, and the morning I realized that my life would never be the same again, I noticed my mother looking strangely at me.

'Rosita, are you putting on weight?' she asked, certainly an odd question in view of the fact that, compared to my sisters, I was positively a wraith. I decided to dance around her.

'I've been eating too many honeycakes,' I replied, hoping my response would satisfy her curiosity. It seemed to, but the following Saturday, it was announced that Phillipa was sick in bed, and that she, my mother, would accompany me to Sao Ignacio while I made my confession. Unlike Phillipa, my devout mother would be only too happy to remain in church, piously whispering her beads. I had no choice but to pretend that I would be honored by my mother's companionship.

On schedule, the two of us walked to Sao Ignacio. Once into Father Rao's confessional, I bolted past the dwarf, ran down the dank stone corridor to my Carlo, explained that my mother was my companion that day, and that I dare not dally. Carlo looked crushed. 'What's more,' I announced casually, 'I think I'm pregnant.' Then, almost as an afterthought, I said, 'Do you think we could ever be married?'

'But my dearest,' he whispered, nuzzling my lower lip, 'I thought you knew.'

'Know what?' I asked, not wanting to know anything but that he and I were together in each other's arms.

I was not to escape my fate so easily. 'I thought you knew that I may be recalled to Alsace Lorraine any time within the next month, and that I am engaged to be married once I arrive home.'

My mind went blank. It flashed black and white. There was ringing in my ears. I ran from our love nest back down the stone corridor and opened the door to Father Rao's confessional box. My mother was inside, kneeling, facing the empty chair of Father Rao. I heard not a sound. Then, she turned to me, her blue eyes as cold as ice.

'I thought perhaps you had fainted,' she said. 'Where have you been?'

The force of my anger was overpowering. I pushed my mother over with all the strength I could muster, shutting and locking the door to the dungeon behind me. She ran out after me into the street.

'Who is this Father Rao?' she cried.

'He is my confessor,' I replied, 'and it's none of your business.'

'Oh?' she inquired waspishly, just as we were rounding the place where an outdoor barber was cropping the black, lamb's-wool head of a burly slave. 'Is it my business that Father Rao's been dead for four years? Who have you been confessing to, a ghost?'

I didn't know what to reply. She still hadn't mentioned the confessional door, or the stone corridor leading down to hidden basement rooms. Apparently, she had no intention of bringing dishonor to our family name in public. But, when we were within a block of our house, she could not longer contain herself and went berserk, shrieking that I was a whore and that my life was ruined, all because she had married the son of a *mestiço* woman! Such public accusations were common to mothers of our class. If a girl left the house without permission, she was a whore; if she smiled at a strange man in the marketplace, presuming she ever got to the marketplace in the first place, she was a whore. If she wore too tight a bodice or one crinoline too few in hundred-degree weather, she was a whore. In truth, if a middle-class girl lost her virginity, she became unmarriageable to any man worth marrying, unless he was desperate, or a saint. Once inside the house, within the confines of my bedroom, she adopted a cooler tone.

'Are you pregnant?' she demanded to know.

'Pregnant?' I replied, feigning shock.

'Because I know about the basement corridors in the Church of Sao Ignacio,' she replied, looking at me with pitiless blue eyes, which gave no clue as to how she could know, but I guessed she had met my father there. 'There are two kinds of men,' she said, 'those

106

who marry you, and those who don't. If you are pregnant and your man will not marry you, your life is over. You will end up a kitchen slave, especially you, Rosita, with your dark complexion. However, there is still time. If I were you, I would find your amorous young man and ask what his intentions are. If your father discovers what has happened, that will be the end of you.'

With that, I ran straightway to the Hussar Barracks on Avenida De Maio. I had never been to the barracks before, but I had long since memorized the exact address. The men, originally Hungarian mercenary troops, were a motley crew, soldiers of fortune from all corners of the civilized world. I knew that whatever his ambivalence about marrying me, Carlo would be overjoyed to see me. Obviously, I knew next to nothing about soldiers of fortune. Obviously, I knew next to nothing about men. What happened that afternoon was the end of me.

Not one block from his address, I came across Carlo, wedged in an alleyway kissing Phillipa, my dueña, his big, blonde hands under her skirt, exploring her genitals as his lips savoured hers. He devoured her kisses like she was the only woman in the world. I felt like I had been knifed in the heart.

'Carlo!' I wailed.

He looked up at me. His surprise was not overwhelming, to say the least. He looked almost amused. 'Rosita!' he called out. 'My little Rosita!'

That's when the bitter truth struck home. I was taken for granted. Carlo knew he could have me any time and anywhere, no matter what he said or did. And he was right. 'Carlo, I'm pregnant,' I whimpered, ignoring Phillipa and adding my mother's phrase, 'What are your intentions?'

'I already told you,' he answered, 'I cannot possibly marry you.' I saw Phillipa smiling. The revenge of the servant girl. Her mistress was ruined. Now, Rosita would have to climb down off her pedestal and join the human race.

I experienced this dream as if I had actually lived it. The ending seemed familiar to me. Too familiar. It was an event I kept playing over and over again in my mind.

I went home, and found a kitchen knife, stabbed myself in the heart, missed, cut an artery instead, and lay soaked in my blood as it ran out of me until I was no longer conscious. As the dream continued, I fell into a gold light, which became dazzling white, incandescent, a light that illuminated all things and did not burn. A woman, very dark like myself, and wrapped in a cocoon of gold, a black-eyed woman wearing the gold sun which rested between two animal horns on her head, held me in her arms. It was my Egyptian goddess, Isis, the goddess of fertility and love. She promised me that because I had suffered for the sake of love, I would return again to earth, but not until there were laws to protect women who loved to make love and not until there were safe potions to control fertility. She promised me further that when I returned to earth I would be so voluptuous no man could resist me, but that I would belong to no man permanently. I would spend my life making love to one and all, even to women, in celebration of the eternal mystery of sex. With that, I evaporated into the white light, where I experienced absolute peace of mind and a stillness of soul, a place where there was no pain, no suffering, only the sound of the celestial choir and the caress of the heavenly wind.

I woke up from my sleep totally refreshed, even though it was only eight o'clock. In Lulu's room, on the other side of our common bathroom, not a peep. I figured she had fucked all night until she collapsed from exhaustion. In the streets outside my window the samba had begun again. 'One, two, three, four – one two! One, two, three, four – one two!' The beat was already louder than the day before. And why not? It was already Shrove Tuesday, to the French, 'Mardi Gras,' the last day before sin and repentance, the last day, alas, before Lent. Mardi Gras was the culmination of Carnival.

My day held many promises, especially my visit to the world's most notorious brother and sister, the Da Silvas, old friends of Maxey's. Little did I suspect, as I stood in my window looking down into the busy avenue below, where ordinary men and women celebrated their national holiday with such innocence, such childlike enthusiasm, that before the sun set, the Da Silvas would push me over the edge of depravity, and bring me face-to-face with the possibility of my own damnation.

Chapter Seven

Hermano 'Putzi' Da Silva was and is a living legend because of his unusual ancestry, his incredible wealth, and his outrageous life style as an international playboy. Sylvia, his sister, was just plain notorious, because, in a country completely given over to the sexual mysteries of male and female, she was a public lesbian. I say 'was' because during my short stay in Brazil, Sylvia, at the comparatively early age of twenty-eight, came to a violent end, a death not unrelated to her sexual appetite.

The Da Silvas, as they came to be known, were born into the top echelon of the Brazilian aristocracy, a group descended from the Portuguese minor nobility, who were the original land investors and pioneer entrepreneurs in colonial Brazil. This select group intermarried with the sons and daughters of military officers and, occasionally, it seems, with beautiful women of mixed blood. Even today, three centuries later, what pass for Nordic faces below the equator, the fairest blondes, like Sylvia, sport perpetual, burnished tans, their yellow hair curls tightly on steamy days until it resembles golden wire, their upper lips are sensuously full, their nostrils flare, and their nipples are often the color of burnt sugar instead of the expected *crème* caramel. Below their waists, the prepuces on their clitorises are folds of thick, dark, delicious flesh cradling, no, not a little tab of erogenous flesh, but a plump wad, which, when aroused, is often an inch or more long. Africa, the mother of erotic mystery, is ever-present in the city of white skyscrapers which always seem to be making a stand between the constant incursions of savage jungle and ocean waves.

After Brazil declared its independence from Portugal in 1822, wealthy land-owning families like the Da Silvas continued to educate their sons and daughters abroad, where their plantation wealth, their exotic beauty, and their liberated sexual habits in the puritanical wastelands of the Christian north brought them many a titled husband or wife. With the Industrial Revolution and the growth of the twentieth century technological state, the family connections in Germany, France, and Switzerland meant that the upper classes of Brazil acquired an international identity. The Da Silvas were no exception. Their mother had been a French princess of the old Bourbon aristocracy, the daughter of an aerospace-inventor prince. Their father had financed a series of shopping malls in the American South, notably Mississippi. There were investments everywhere, including South African gold mines. It goes without saying that the Da Silva family fortune was secure. Tragically, in the mid-seventies, however, the senior Da Silvas had been massacred by Amazon Indians when they were inspecting a pulp mill they had invested in. Their shrunken heads, stuffed into the Gucci plastic shopping bag Senhora Da Silva had been carrying when she was hit from behind by a poison dart, were dropped on the doorstep of the president of the pulp mill, an American who left for the States that very day and never returned.

All in all, however, the two Da Silva offspring managed their affairs well. Putzi spent a good deal of time traveling, overseeing his fortune; Sylvia often went with him, overseeing her brother's personal life. Over the years, they both developed insatiable appetites for beautiful women. Indeed, the rumors, never substantiated, were that Putzi and a certain well-stacked European princess had been living it up in a Corsican retreat. Other rumors had it that Putzi and Sylvia were sometime lovers themselves. The obvious fact that Putzi at thirty-two and Sylvia at twenty-eight were both at the height of their beauty and energy made them constant targets for gossip.

Maxey had been the source of all my information about the Da Silvas; it was he who gave me my letter of introduction. He assured me that Sylvia would be a treasure house of information about current leisure wear south of the border, and that Putzi would invest his money in a swimsuit factory if we decided to build our own plant in Rio. Maxey thought the labor costs would be even cheaper if we owned our own sewing machines instead of leasing our work to the infamous sweatshops that were the target of Che Miranda's socialist wrath. Of course, Maxey, capitalist pig that he was, had no intention of raising salaries. I could see I was going to spend the rest of my life having to deal with superserious conversations. Like I always say, travel can be broadening, especially for a traveling broad like me.

Senhor Rudnicki, the Polish manager of the Hotel Rio Palace, arranged an English-speaking driver for me, a red-faced Carioca named Paolo Vieira. Paolo told me his mother had been an English manicurist who blew her life savings on a cruise to South America, and never went back. So that was the danger of Rio, I thought; people never want to leave. I wondered if I would. I wondered if I'd fall in love with a Carioca and never go back. I seemed to have a special thing in my heart for Latins who were peasant types. After all, who was, but a girl of the Beavertown working classes? The last time I'd completely given my heart away, it was to my beloved Adolfo Adoro, who was stocky and swarthy, with a barrel-chested, big-cocked peasant body, and who, only by accident, it seemed, had run an international fashion empire. But how many Latin peasants had done as well? If, the first time, I had ended up in the Jet Set, the next time, I could just as easily end up in the gutter. I had to be careful.

Paolo's cab, an old New York yellow cab, was about thirty years old. He said his father had bought it at the end of World War Two. Who knows how it got to Brazil? The windows rattled, the motor rumbled, and he had to rope the doors shut. I gave him the Da Silva's address, apparently a well-known mansion on its own private beach which was west of the city. Paolo looked at the address, nodded his head, handed it back to me, and said nothing until we were well out of the main traffic. I didn't question his silence. Rio traffic is the worst in the world, which is no great surprise, considering that Brazilian men are, in general, God's most macho creations, and Cariocan males are the bantam roosters of Brazil. In Berlin, the German males, however sexually oriented, do not brag to visitors about German sexuality; and the French, who have made a reputation for themselves as the world's greatest lovers, do not greet tourists with invitations to sample French cunt. They are far more subtle, and, of course, the more subtle one is about sex, the more artful one is, the more the characteristic known as 'macho' begins to fade out of the picture. Texans would seem to be among the most forceful and the most masculine men on earth, yet who ever heard of a Texan saying, 'Man, Texan women are the greatest pussy in the world; we ought to turn this whole blame state into a whorehouse.'

Well, the Brazilians are different, and Paolo Vieira was definitely a Brazilian of the first order. Macho driving and God knows what else. There we were, in the old jalopylike yellow cab on this big turnpike heading west. The Atlantic ocean was on one side, the lush, tropical rain forest on the other.

'How far to the Da Silva's?' I asked. By this time, I had made the mistake of relaxing. I was caught off-guard. I had underestimated the ever-present power of sex.

'You know, lady,' Paolo began, 'my mother's sister

113

became an American, so I understand American women.'

'That's good,' I answered, trying to be polite.

'The real reason you have come to Brazil, in case you don't know it,' he continued, 'is because you ain't never had a good fuck from American men.'

'That could be true,' I answered, as calmly as possible, trying to sound a little bored. The truth was, I was beginning to feel queasy; my stomach juices were churning from root instinct that told me I should have walked.

Paolo was not finished. 'But your problem, lady, is that Brazilian men, we don't need American vagina. Brazilian vagina, she the best in the world. The reason Brazilian vagina, she the best in the world is because Brazilian cock, we the best cock, the biggest cock, the hottest cock.'

'So what's your problem?' I said. I was beginning to be a little annoyed. What exactly did Senhor Vieira want me to do, like down on the floor of his taxicab, spread my legs, and beg him to service me?

'Problem?' he answered. 'What problem, lady? I ain't got no problem. You're the one with the problem.'

'What's my problem?' I asked. That's when I noticed that the reason Paolo was having trouble driving a straight line was that both his hands were clasped about a stout, purple erection which was sticking up in his lap. His glans was dark and meaty, and precome ooze was glistening around the little slit at the top. That's when I opened my purse, took out the sterling silver pen knife on my key chain, opened it, and began to quietly cut through the clothesline rope that tied my door shut. I had a feeling that I might have to make a quick getaway. Nothing like a woman's instinct!

Within minutes, Senhor Vieiri had swung right off the main highway onto a narrow, rambling dirt road that led up a hill into the tropical rain forest. As soon as we made the turn, I blurted out, 'Where are we going? The Da Silvas live on the ocean!'

'No, lady, you don't want to see the ocean,' he replied, without turning around, 'you want to see Paolo. I can show you things you never knew exist.'

That line of dialogue was all I needed. I slipped out of my shoes, held one of them in my right hand, leaned forward, and smashed Paolo in the face, right in his eyes, a surprise move which confused him enough to make him take his foot off the accelerator. That's when I opened my door and rolled out, just like they do in the movies. It was the smartest move of my life. We were still only a couple of hundred yards from the turnpike. I was astonished and grateful to discover that I had no broken bones, only a few bruises from the spiky swamp grass by the side of the road. I immediately picked myself up and ran for the highway. By the time I reached it, there were few cars in sight; Paolo had turned his cab around and was coming after me. My gut instinct told me to cross the highway and make for the beach.

Somehow, miraculously, I was able to cross the highway without getting hit. The beach was white, shining, gleaming white, and it stretched for miles in either direction. Rio was to the left, about five miles down the beach. I couldn't chance it. Paolo somehow would catch up with me. The man was hot with rage and desire. To the right, the beach seemed to stretch toward infinity with not a soul in sight. Still, I knew the Da Silva mansion had to be closer than five miles away. And, yes, there seemed to be a dark spot on the beach about a mile down. I knew the spot might be a rock or a piece of driftwood – or a person! I decided to chance it!

Paolo was still on the other side of the highway, trying to decide on a course of action. I could see the top of his cab, a yellow spot bolting to one side and then to the other. If I was to save my life, I had only one way out. I quickly stripped down to my underwear and left my dress lying in the sand behind me. I bolted down the beach. It was not until I was a good hundred yards down that I realized with a start that I had forgotten my underwear! I couldn't believe my stupidity! My breasts were knocking up and down; I had to put my hands on them to hold them steady. Running without a bra is not the greatest idea for the musculature supporting the breast tissue. The ocean breezes blew their balmy air against my thick blonde bush. I didn't have to put my free hand between my legs to confirm what I already knew – I was stark naked!

Looking behind me, over my shoulder, I saw Paolo had driven his yellow cab clear across the highway and down onto the beach. He was now getting out of his car. He had just discovered my dress lying in the sand, and had looked up to see me in the distance. I could see that he had decided to chase after me. No doubt I was an enticing quarry for a sex maniac. I knew that, eventually, Paolo would outdistance me. Eventually, if I did not find a friend on the beach or in a nearby house, I knew I would find myself lying naked on my back as the half-Anglo brute drove his purple passion stick into my unwilling cunt. The word in question was rape, something that a party girl like me fears more than anything. No matter how many men I make love to in the course of a year, much of my pleasure comes from the experience of being a free agent, a woman who freely chooses the man, the place, the time. Now, I was little better than a rabbit being chased by a dog.

The spot on the horizon grew larger as Paolo came closer. I felt sharp pains in my sides. My stomach felt like a cement mixer. I kept hoping that, at some magic spot on the beach, the highway would rise up, affording drivers a view of my naked plight. But, to tell the truth, somehow it never once occurred to me to run along the highway. I found it impossible to disassociate any given Brazilian driver from my would-be assailant, Paolo.

The spot on the beach grew closer and closer. And then I knew. Yes, it was a person – a woman. Yes, I

116

could see her clearly now. A naked woman sunning herself on the beach. She was covered with oil, and glistening. There was something else. Was I imagining things, or was she masturbating? Was her hand really in her vagina or was she only stroking her clitoris with sleek, oily fingers? Was that really a moan I heard escape her lips?

'Help!' I screamed. She didn't hear me. No wonder. I was unable to project my voice. I tried a second time. 'Help!' Now, I was less than a hundred yards away from her, and the madman Paolo was less than half that distance behind me. I could see his cock, still erect, sticking out through his still-open fly. I could not formulate words. I just screamed.

I guess she heard my pitiful wail. She opened her eyes and looked up, frankly astonished to see me. I was equally astonished to see how gorgeous she was, a Latin Venus, dark gold with sun-streaked hair.

'Help!' I said. 'Please, do you speak English? I'm looking for the Da Silvas. That man! That man wants to rape me.'

'I am Sylvia Da Silva,' she answered matter-of-factly.

'I'm Diana Adoro,' I wailed. 'Did Maxey phone you? He said he was going to phone you. I also have a letter of introduction, but I don't know where it is. My clothes ... '

I had to stop talking. By now, Paolo was almost on top of us. Sylvia Da Silva was not fazed. She reached into her beach bag, pulled out a snub-nosed revolver with a silencer on it, and emptied it into Paolo. The last three bullets entered his once-proud head as he lay twitching on the sand. Almost immediately, he was still, except for his blood, which was forming pools on the beach.

His erection, once so prominent, was slowly shrinking. His wide-open, dead eyes stared into the white glare of the noonday sun.

'Quick!' whispered Sylvia, with scarcely an accent. 'Sometimes the police patrol the beach.' For the moment, however, we were safe. There was no one in sight. She reached into her bag and handed me a one-piece bathing suit. 'Here, put this on.' She had a white terrycloth robe for herself. She was a stunner in white. I could have sat on the beach all afternoon admiring her physical form, but we had no time.

Within the space of two minutes, Sylvia had led me back into the dunes where there was a semiunderground concrete shelter, much like a storm cellar. The large underground room contained several pleasure boats, sailboats, rowboats, and a whaling boat. Then, she spied an aluminium rowboat.

'That one!' she announced. 'We'll take that one.' She also picked up a large iron anchor, with a heavy chain attached to it, that was almost too much for the two of us to manage. But manage we did. We had no choice. Our procedure, with Sylvia directing, was out of a war movie. First, we scampered out onto the beach with the anchor. She quickly wrapped the chain around Paolo's neck, and locked it with a padlock she had picked up in the tool chest in the boat room. Then, we ran back for the aluminium rowboat. That was easy. Within the space of another minute, we were lifting Paolo's body into the boat. First, the anchor, then Paolo himself. A dead body is a dead weight. We almost didn't make it.

But Sylvia came from hardier stock than I. 'Come on, Diana Adoro,' Sylvia announced. 'We're going for a boat ride. I hope you can swim.'

'I can swim,' I answered, grateful I was able to do something. The truth is, if it hadn't been for Sylvia, I'd probably be dead.

We each took an oar and rowed the boat into choppy blue-black water out about half a mile. Despite all the attendant horror, I have to admit that I was mightily distracted. Sylvia was one of the most luscious women I had ever seen. As I described before, she had pale green eyes set in dark-gold skin with yellow hair that curled tightly around her temples at the least suggestion of humidity. Her teeth were perfect. Her breasts were small and round and tight, just like her ass. Naïve little me. I found out later that upper-class Brazilian women maintain the best dentists and the best plastic surgeons in the world. Nevertheless, I was dazzled by Sylvia's teeth. Obviously, it was easier for me to fantasize about her than to have to deal with the body on the floor of the aluminium boat.

Once we were out on the open sea, Sylvia told me to turn around. The view of the shoreline was a glimpse of Eden. There was nothing like it in Beavertown. At that moment, I wished that my whole family could have been in the boat with us, except for Paolo, of course. On a promontory, or small peninsula, around the bend from where Sylvia had been sunning, was what looked like a series of interlocking glass boxes. It was the Da Silva estate.

'We had a German architect,' Sylvia explained. 'My grandparents lived in a copy of an Austrian castle in the mountains, but today's generation want to do things our own way, which reminds me – let's dump this boy's body.'

'What if the boat tips over?' I asked.

'Then we paddle back to shore,' she said. Sylvia showed me how to steady the boat while she pushed and shoved Paolo, an inch at a time, over the edge of the boat. Once she had managed to get the anchor into the water, the rest of him followed it right to the bottom.

'The sharks will get him. By tomorrow, there will be nothing left of him.' I could not help but notice, however, that there was blood in the bottom of the boat. 'Don't wory, darling,' Sylvia admonished me. 'There's an old Brazilian saying, 'Don't leave any blood in the bottom of the boat.' We'll tip the boat over before we get to shore.'

At first, the trip back was uneventful. Her terrycloth robe was open. His slit was mouth-watering. I was dying to explore it, which should tell you how ripe and juicy it looked, since I'm not a lesbian. Then, about

119

halfway back to the shore, I noticed what looked like a police car by Paolo's taxicab on the beach.

'Quick!' Sylvia instructed. 'Jump into the water! Immediately! And don't stand up when you jump!'

I did as she instructed. I rolled off the edge of the rowboat into the water. 'Now, give me your swimsuit! Quick! Hurry up! Take it off!' she said.

I did as she ordered, understanding nothing, still in a daze from the most recent hour of my time on earth. Sylvia slipped into the bathing suit, trying hard not to attract the attention of the two policemen who were now looking in our direction.

She said, 'Our story is that the man drove you to the beach to rape you, dragged you out of the car, and stripped you. You ran into the ocean calling for help. He followed you and was caught in the undertow. I was out in my rowboat, heard your cries for help, and picked you up. You got back into the water when you saw the police. One other thing: As I row into shore, I will stand up to attract the attention of the police. That way, the boat will tip over and we'll get rid of the blood.'

The only flaw in Sylvia's story was that she could have let me keep my suit on. She could have explained to the police that she'd taken off her suit and let me wear hers, instead of the other way around. I couldn't quite figure out why, in the midst of so much bloodshed and tragedy, the only thing she was thinking about was that she wanted to see me naked. Or did she want me to see her climbing into her bathing suit? It all seemed so perverse and so predictable. Was there really any truth to the vicious rumors that she was Brazil's best-known lesbian? I also had to wonder if she had liked killing Paolo. She certainly didn't seem very upset by it. I had a strange feeling that this was going to be one of the more interesting days of my life.

As it turned out, my premonition was correct. Before the day was out, I would personally witness a perversity Beavertown never imagined existed, even in the movies. And I would see more murder, I won't say how much more; there's no point in spoiling the story.

Sylvia Da Silva was not heiress to three centuries of aristocracy for nothing. As we pulled into shore, she stood up in the boat and screamed to the police in Portuguese. As she had predicted, the boat tipped over. Globules of Paolo's blood floated away. Schools of minnows followed the blood as it dissolved in the rushing ocean currents. I wondered if the police saw the reddish sheen on the water. Not a chance. Their eyes were glued to the two of us. As she explained to me later, Sylvia, who was well-known to them, told the police what she had witnessed and asked them to please contact her when the cab-driver's body surfaced, so that her guest, the American, could make a statement. Then she picked up my white dress which I had left lying on the beach by the taxicab and threw it to me, saying, 'Here, senhorita, you'll have to put this dress on in the water.'

I did as she instructed, but it was a near-impossible task. My beautiful white gauze dress was ruined! The weight of the water dragged the neckline down to reveal the edges of my aureolas. There was no way I could preserve my modesty. My nipples were clearly visible through the gauze, and, as I climbed out of the water, I could see that my pubic hair was visible, too.

I was absolutely mortified. I needn't have been. The local constabulary's eyes, all four of them, were glued to my tits. One man, a very attractive athletic type, started fingering his crotch.

'What is wrong with the men in this town?' I thought. 'They are sex-crazed.' Part of me wanted to take the policeman by his cock, I mean his hand, and walk down the beach with him discussing his sexual problems. I knew he needed a woman who understood.

I understood. Then I noticed Sylvia staring at me

staring at him. She turned to the policeman and spoke in Portuguese again. I don't know what she said exactly, but the attractive policeman stopped fingering his crotch. She explained to me later that she told them she intended to have one of her employees return the car to Paolo Vieira's wife with her official account of what happened, adding that her victimized American guest was heavily sedated, under psychiatric care; and trying to decide whether to press charges against the entire Vieira family.

As luck would have it, Paolo Vieira was well-known for his sexual rampages. I wanted to send the family some money, but Sylvia said, 'No, what do we have to feel guilty about? Do you want to go to the police and describe how we shot him?' Brazil, after all, was the country where men who murdered adulterous wives got away scot-free.

The policeman seemed satisfied. I got the definite impression that they were both on the Da Silva take. After much nodding, nervous smiling, and more crotch-squeezing, they climbed back into their car and continued toward the city on their beach inspection tour. Once they were safely out of sight, Sylvia turned to me and said, 'Take off your wet dress, my beauty. I'll show you what smart Brazilian women are wearing on the beach this year.' She stripped, too, laughing as she did. 'I tricked you again,' she said.

'Tricked me?' I asked.

'Yes, I love to see you naked. Your body has a certain strength mine lacks. Like they say, opposites attract,' she said, stroking my firm little ass with the palm of her hand. 'Here, the women tend to be either too fat or tiny, like European ballet dancers. But you, Diana, you have the great American body, the Marilyn Monroe body, bit tits that do not sag, rounded tummy, and tight high ass. Bend over, I want to see.'

I did as she instructed, not quite sure what she had in mind.

But she had saved my life, after all. She certainly

must have respected me. I never imagined that her basic respect for me was engendered by pure, animal lust. As I bent over, her hand was instantly between my thighs, stroking my vulva, her hand cupping my fuckflesh, her fingers searching for my labia, exploring the meaty delights of what even I recognize as an extraordinary cunt.

'You and I will go back to the main house, take a nice bath and have lunch,' she suddenly announced.

'But what will I wear?' I asked.

'Wear where?' she replied. 'In the bath? I don't understand.'

'No,' I said, 'what will I wear from the beach to the house?' I really did not want to meet Putzi stark naked.

'Oh, don't worry,' Sylvia said. 'I've got a couple of bikinis in my beachbag.'

Damn it if she didn't too. She was so brilliant; Sylvia thought of everything. When we were dressed in our 'bikinis', both fire-engine red shoelaces, ha ha, with material the size of postage stamps covering my nipples and my labia but not my pubic hair, she finally stopped fingering me, took my hand in hers and walked back to her house. It was a brief moment of innocence.

We walked back hand in hand like two little schoolgirls, with Sylvia every now and then sucking on our intertwined fingers.

The Da Silva house and grounds outrivaled anything I had ever seen in the movies or in my mother's *Architectural Digests*. The grounds were a carefully controlled tropical rain forest broken up by wide lawns and punctuated with formal English boxwoods and Italian walkways of cut marble. Brazilians generally hate even the suggestion of jungle in their ultra-modern cities. To people who are surrounded by millions of square miles of tropical greenery, with all its poisonous snakes, insects, and predatory animals, there is little beauty in plants; they have the same appeal to most Cariocas as dandelions and ragweed have to most Americans. But I grew up in Beavertown where our only foliage was a privet hedge alongside our sidewalk and a rubber tree in the living room.

When I first walked onto the Da Silva grounds, I felt like Eve, the mother of us all. It was truly a Garden of Paradise. The lawns were swaths of emerald velvet; orchids crawled up every bare tree trunk, and yes, as I sat on a fifteenth century carved marble bench from the Villa d'Este, the Medici Palace in Florence, there was something else – the most ravishing young women I'd ever seen, three of them, Indian-looking, with shining, black hair, were weeding the garden. They were bare-breasted, their tits pointing straight down in front of them as they knelt in the flower beds.

'You use women gardeners?' I gasped, more out of sheer delight at their unsurpassed beauty than from the surprise at seeing females doing traditional men's work.

'Why can't women take care of gardens as well as men?' Sylvia remarked, before getting around to the real reason they were there. 'Maybe it's my German blood,' she said off-handedly, 'but I have this passion for black-eyed jungle maidens.' Then she looked at me hard. 'Which is not to say, Diana, that occasionally I don't fall for a blue-eyed blonde.'

I didn't know what to say. I've never been particularly fond of what I call 'predatory lesbians.' Her green eyes *were* riveting. I wondered how much German blood she really had. She moved like she was part jungle cat. Even her head movements were quick, responding instantaneously to the tiniest strange noise in the background, or to the smallest object out of place.

'You do know I'm a lesbian?' she finally asked.

'Well, I'd heard that,' I said, playing dumb.

'Do you have prejudices against lesbians?' she continued.

'Prejudices?' I asked. 'What kind of prejudices?'

'Well, when Putzi gets drunk, which is getting to be a regular activity, he tells me I am a poor excuse for a woman. He calls me a bull dyke. He says I should be put in jail; I'm a scandal to the Da Silva family, and I'm never going to have any children, which is the worst thing for a nice Catholic girl.' With that, she burst into tears.

She looked so fragile, so forlorn, I had no choice but to take her into my arms and begin to kiss her on her soft cheeks, her perfect little ears, and all the frizzy, blonde hair around her temples. I guess that unwittingly I must have aroused her or something. She ripped off my string bikini and began to finger-fuck me again.

'Sylvia!' I cried.

'What?' she asked, nuzzling me.

'Sylvia, I'll do anything for you,' I said. 'You saved my life; you're a wonderful woman. But Sylvia, I'm just not a lesbian.'

'Then why are you wet?' she said, without skipping a beat, her index finger searching for the choice nub of my clitoris.

'Sylvia, please! I cried, breaking away, completely out of breath, my juices running down my legs. 'Sylvia, I want to explain something to you.'

'Explain,' she said, astounded.

'Sylvia, I really need a shower or something to drink, and I'd really like to keep my private life, well, like private.'

'Oh,' she said. 'I forgot.' I mean, there we were, the two of us, standing naked from the waist down on the large central lawn right in back of the house. At least three faces, probably servants, were peeking at us from the upstairs windows.

'You're right,' she said. 'You just never know when some of these lovely employees will win a scholarship somewhere, and the next thing you know, they've written a tell-all book about our family. Come, let me show you the house.'

'But Sylvia,' I stammered, 'I'm naked below the waist.'

Sylvia's response was typical; she ran over to a broad-leafed tree planted against a back wall of her house, and returned with two large green leaves. 'Try a fig leaf,' she chortled. 'Surely, you've heard of them.' They worked perfectly. Now I was Eve, absolutely.

And that's how I entered the world's most glamorous private dwelling, between two fig leaves. Two steps inside, a perfect Victorian ladies' maid in a black dress with a white lace collar handed me a magnificent yellow silk robe embroidered with gold flowers. The maid in question was another black-eyed beauty, a pure Latin type with skin like gardenias.

'Isn't she a proper little ladies' maid?' teased Sylvia, as she lifted the girl's dress. 'I took Branca out of a favela — that's what we call a slum.' Sylvia lifted her maid's skirt way above the tops of her white stockings, revealing garters attached to a garter belt. There was no underwear. Somehow, I had expected that. I have developed sixth sense about such things. The maid's silky black thatch was shining in the midday light.

'Sit on the sofa, Branca, and show Senhora Adoro your sweetmeat.'

Branca did as ordered, smiling like a well-trained little girl. She sat on the ruby-red sofa, leaned backward, and spread her legs. The red brocade of the sofa cast a reflected rosy light onto this girl's labia, which glistened like a pale pink morning rose. She spread open the folded prepuce over her slit and showed us her clitoris, a little jewel of flesh prominent with a desire that did not show in her face.

'Branca is my favorite servant, and she knows it,' Sylvia remarked, kissing her maid on her forehead. 'I save her till three in the morning when I can't sleep. It's my convent school upbringing, I guess, I save the best till last.'

I cannot go on to discuss my incredible shower with Sylvia until I describe the house. Most of the rooms were two stories high and constructed of white marble panels cut so thin they let in the outside light. The floors were white marble, too; they were covered with blonde oriental carpets, pale, muted tones of terra cotta and faded blue. Most of the furniture was recognizably Milanese, oversized white linen modules and banquettes. The accent color was ruby-red; even the lighting seemed rosy; every lighting fixture was fitted with a red filter; it made everyone look healthier, sexier, more voluptuous. Aside from the expected greenhouse, stables, kennels, and an underground garage big enough for fifteen cars, the Da Silva's house boasted a projection room, a recording studio, a small television studio, an indoor pool, and a small gymnasium.

Since the brother and sister had been brought up all over the world, they had picked up a variety of sports and diversions. They invented their own brand of 'fox hunt,' which saw them riding into the jungle chasing down a black panther instead of a fox. They made their own home movies, mostly porno. Putzi had his own TV commercials for companies of which he was the principal stockholder. Sylvia had written and recorded at least fifty of her own songs, several of which had reached the top forty of Brazil. She admitted she hadn't figured out a way to become popular with anyone but the Brazilians.

'I'm a good-natured, how you say, "slut"; they understand that. In North America, they would consider me insane. What female singer do you know in North America who remove her brassiere while she sing? In Brazil, we love naked tit. We must be more progressive than North America.'

The kitchen was all black and silver and mirrors. Smells of roasting pork and fresh homemade sausage wafted through the house. I could smell black beans simmering with ham bones, and rice was boiling in big black iron pots. There must have been six people working full-time in the kitchen.

Mostly women.

'I believe in hiring women,' Sylvia explained. 'They make more desirable employees.' I could see the smile playing around the corners of her lips. The kitchen staff were blonde and 'zaftig,' meaning 'just a little bit of extra flesh.' 'These women, they belong to Putzi,' Sylvia explained. 'We like different types. I prefer black-eyed little women; Putzi, he like big blondes. Very rarely do we both want the same person. That's the one good reason we can remain brother and sister.'

'Where is Putzi?' I asked.

'Don't you worry, you will meet Putzi later,' Sylvia replied. 'Now it is time we take a shower. You must be covered with salt water and sand from the beach, no?'

What could I say? I had spent a hot, tense morning doing all sorts of running and heavy lifting, hadn't I? Enough already. It was time to put on civilization.

Sylvia's bedroom was done entirely in greens – fifty different shades of green, just like the jungle. Wall-to-wall grass-green carpeting covered with grey-green oriental rugs made to order in India, antique Italian furniture, actually Venetian, with the subtle green pigment rubbed into the fruitwood. The draperies were emerald-green brocade, also Italian; so was the canopy bed upholstered in the same green cloth. There were green leather sofas with brass studs at either end of the room. Well, it sure beat Beavertown.

Sylvia's clothes were in a separate dressing room almost as big as her bedroom. There must have been a thousand outfits.

'Don't worry, darling,' Sylvia explained, 'I'm having our costumes made in Rio.'

'What costumes?' I asked, not understanding.

'Carnival, darling! Where have you been? Tonight! All sorts of surprises! All sorts of, well, things!'

'But how did you know my size?' I asked, feeling so stupid. Of course, I'd forgotten. I still couldn't get the image of Paolo Vieira out of my middle-class mind.

Sylvia was more concerned about Carnival and about my costume than she was about dispatching a corpse to its watery grave. My basic problem had always been that I was much too sensitive, much too aware of other people's feelings, especially the feelings of people who had just died. How could I possibly take part in Carnival after the morning I'd had?

'Of course I know your size,' Sylvia prattled on. 'I've seen your picture in *Women's Wear Daily* many, many times. You are the most exciting blue-eyed woman I've ever met. Naturally, when Maxey wrote me to say you were coming, I called him for your measurements. I would not let you come to Rio during Carnival and not give you a good time, no?'

Sylvia looked so beguiling, like a naughty schoolgirl, I almost forgot about Paolo chasing me down the beach. She had vixenish eyes and she was always running her tongue around her lips in the most naive kind of sexual come-on since some of my fellow waitresses at the Beavertown Howard Johnson's got drunk one night when I was working as the hostess there and tried to seduce a table full of seminarians.

But Sylvia, after all, was not as innocent as she pretended. In the short time I had known her, she had killed a man in cold blood and effectively disposed of his body; she had finger-fucked me without asking permission; and she had admitted in so many words that her many female employees performed sexual favors on demand.

Still, I never guessed that she was in any sense depraved. Little did I realize, as I toured the palatial Da Silva estate, that before Carnival was out, I would be witness to varieties of love-making that I had only guessed at, and to the further spilling of blood. Yes, before I saw the last of Sylvia and Putzi Da Silva, I would finally understand the meaning of tragedy.

But, for the moment, I was, in my own mind, at least, just an American career girl seeing how the other half lived. (It would take years before it sunk in that Diana

Adora was a millionaire.) Sylvia's bedroom continued to intrigue me. She pushed a button on a bedside console; instantly, soft-playing classical music wafted into the room; Chopin, I think, and Brahms. In the distance, I could hear the sound of running water.

'Do I hear water running?' I asked, remembering the time I forgot to turn off a faucet in my grandmother's bathroom and wrecked the ceiling of the couple in the apartment below. Sylvia untied her bikini and beckoned me to follow her.

Let's stop right here. There's an issue here that has to be discussed. I had already seen Sylvia naked. I've seen a lot of naked women, gorgeous women, changing clothes backstage at my fashion shows. But something happens when two people are naked together behind closed doors. It's a different experience of seeing someone naked. There is an enforced intimacy in the situation itself. When I first saw Sylvia naked, masturbating on the beach, I guess I was so shocked, small-time girl that I am, that I guarded myself from feeling aroused by the sight of her. A doctor dealing with a naked patient has a similar way of protecting himself from sexual involvement, although our family dentist in Beavertown was not successful in that regard with me; but that's another story.

Sylvia, naked behind locked doors, was ravishing to me, and I'm not even a lesbian. Undoubtedly, when she was first maturing, she must have aroused so many older women that it was only a matter of time before they initiated her into the Sapphic arts. The fact that she'd lost her mother undoubtedly left an emotional void and a heart aching for maternal care.

She had small, pointed tits with dark nipples almost an inch long that stuck straight out. Her musculature was tight, almost unisexual, with a high, tight ass like mine, except that hers was higher and tighter and smaller. Everything about her body seemed to invite my ravenous mouth. In my defense, as an avowed heterosexual, there was something almost boyish about her body, not masculine, exactly, but tight and firm and resilient. There was no age on her. Nothing excessive. Nothing wrinkled or hanging down. She had a ballerina's body. I can't imagine anyone who wouldn't have loved looking at her.

I followed her into her marble and glass bathroom, where an artificial waterfall had been constructed in the middle of an orchid garden. 'This is your shower?' I exclaimed, thinking the river of rushing water would effectively disguise the river of come juice beginning to gush down my leg. I really was not emotionally prepared for another go-round with anyone about anything. I needed time off from passion, and my cunt, as usual, was betraying me.

Then Sylvia climbed into the shower. She bent over to pick up a bar of soap. I was unprepared to see that mass of sweet, dark meat between her thighs. I felt a familiar jab of hunger in my crotch and a delicious warmth spread throughout my body. Of course, none of this made any real sense to me. Like I say, I have never considered myself even bisexual, but there are some women, like Tia Maria, the blue-black chambermaid, and like Sylvia, whose effect on other women is more emotional than sexual. That had to be the case with me and Sylvia. Sex had little to do with it. My feelings were strictly emotional. One hundred percent. Emotional in the sense that I recognized her deep need for some maternal consideration. Granted, she was five years older than I, but I still felt like she was a sweet little girl with a deep wound that needed immediate attention. If I chose to express myself sexually, that was only because there was no other outlet available to me at the time.

Showers, after all, can be an entrapment. We were, of course, only taking a shower together to save water. Even the richest Brazilians have trouble getting enough good water. The shower stall was not very large. It was impossible not to keep bumping into

Sylvia. And, because of some oversight, there was only one bar of soap. We decided to wash one another. To save time. Since Sylvia was my hostess, she went first, using her free hand to spread the perfumed lather all over my back and between my legs. She was very thorough.

'I don't want you to be sweaty in my house, darling,' Sylvia cooed. She was so solicitous. Then she spread lather on my nipples with her tongue, telling me, 'I want you to have the best.'

The best what? The best tongue? I found that I didn't really care about questions and answers. I just wanted her to continue. I couldn't help myself. The day my mother stopped giving me a bath when I was eleven was the day I started resenting her. Every child needs a little parental attention, don't you think? That's what Sylvia was so good at – parental-type attention. And, since she herself was so obviously in need of maternal consideration, her self-sacrifice ennobled her, and made every second spent in her presence almost religious.

I found myself becoming turned on in a big way. When she began to wash my labia with her tongue, working her way up to the clitoris, my whole body began to scream in pleasure. I wanted her to lock her lips around my blood-stiffened clit and suck me till I shook and screamed. She was making such an extreme sacrifice for me; few things in this life are more unpleasant than soapsuds in one's mouth.

'Sylvia, baby, eat me. Please eat me,' I begged. Her hot lips were so close to my soul, I couldn't stand it. The heat rose up inside me. The tip of her tongue was teasing the head of my clit; my ass buckled into her face to meet her sucking lips. I began to lose all sense of reality. I found myself touching her, lathering her; we cooed and caressed, and waves of hot passion swept over me. My heart was pounding as she exposed her clitoris to me. It glistened under the shower like a tiny rosebud in the spring rain. How I got there I don't know, but I found myself on my knees, my face in her pussy, my tongue wandering into her cunt, her inner muscles swelling and contracting around every bit of my mouth I was able to get inside her.

'Oh God, oh God,' she moaned, as my lips swept back and forth over the hot head of her clit. She was choice meat, and I was devouring her. I wanted her to come in my mouth, so I practically wedged my face into her, my arms wrapped around her legs, my hands holding her tight little buttocks as she bucked and heaved and her body became spasmodic.

She let out a howl. She was losing muscular control. During her sustained orgasm, she started to collapse on top of me. I was drowned in her pussymeat. It engulfed my face, my nose, my lips, my tongue, as rivulets of cunt-juice washed me clean. I did not let go. I scraped and gnawed her clit between my teeth so that pleasure ripped through her like a grenade. I spread her ass cheeks and shoved my finger up the tight hole in her ass. It was already wet. I shoved my finger in and out, in and out, as I continued to tear at her clit with my teeth. Her orgasm was so intense I thought she was having an epileptic spasm. She was unable to control a single muscle of her body; strange, infantile sounds issued from her mouth. Primal sounds. Animal sounds. And then, we were both lying on the marble floor in a catch basin of water under her warm, waterfall, kissing and fondling each other, our tongues entwining like snakes in a garden.

'Oh, Diana,' she crooned. 'You are the perfect house guest.'

'Thank you for saving my life,' I said, my eyes filled with tears of gratitude.

'Listen, darling,' she said, 'I never did like rapists on my beach.'

I saw her point. I let go of my small-town guilt about killing Paolo Vieira. There was something so wonderfully matter-of-fact about Sylvia. She made so much sense, in her own way.

'I could stay here forever with you under your magic waterfall,' I said, hoping against hope our tropical idyll would never end.

'I know, darling,' Sylvia said, biting my lower lip, 'but too much water will wreck the skin. Besides, I have a surprise for you.'

'A surprise?' I said, already surprised. 'Sylvia, this whole day has been a surprise. How many more surprises can I take?'

'Wait and see, darling,' she said, as she let go of her embrace, stood up, and turned off the water. Her bush was drying in dark, blonde tendrils. Her drop of African blood made her so unique to me, I regretted not knowing her mother, who I supposed was even more African-looking, but I found out later that it was the Da Silva side who arrived in Brazil on the first colonial ship and who made a little headway with both Indians and West African slaves until they got rich and started bleaching themselves out.

In any event, Sylvia made me realize how much I missed not having any African blood, myself. That's what attracted her to me. Really, it was the attraction of opposites. Sylvia had a passion for life that, in all my experience, I have found only among people of mixed blood, especially in Third World countries. I realized that the Da Silvas don't think of themselves as having mixed blood, but in Beavertown, where I grew up, they wouldn't have been able to open their mouths about their African ancestry without getting themselves kicked out of the local country club. I'm not prejudiced, mind you. My family was too poor to belong to any club. I was just never educated well enough to deal with people like the Da Silvas. They confused all my categories. They overwhelmed me. Putzi and Sylvia each had a level of personal power I had never before experienced in anyone, except maybe my beloved Adolfo.

As we dried each other off with turkish towels as big as bedsheets, Sylvia said, 'Don't worry, darling. I know

134

you have not had your orgasm, but do not worry. You will have everything.'

'Sylvia,' I began, but a tear choked in my throat. I never finished my sentence. I was so awestruck by her concern, I felt like I was back in second grade. She was my teacher and I was completely dependent on her. She began to massage the warm oil into my back, a marvelous unguent smelling of cloves and mint and tropical fruit. My skin, which had been exposed to so much sun earlier in the day when we dumped Paolo Vieira's body into the ocean, absorbed every bit of oil. Sylvia had wonderfully strong hands, not what you'd expect in a rich girl with twenty-five servants. When she reached down between my legs to rub oil into my labia, I squealed from hours of pent-up desire. Yes, I was still on fire down there; my labia were still swollen with the blood of desire. I just hadn't had a really good orgasm; it wasn't her fault. Besides, like she said, there was a surprise waiting for me.

In the meantime, my clitoris ached for the touch of her pointed tongue, anybody's pointed tongue.

'No, no, I must stop now,' she announced. 'I want to save you for my big surprise. Come with me, my precious.' She took me by the hand and led me back into the bedroom. Nothing had changed. What was my surprise? Then, she casually pressed a couple of buttons on the console. Instantly, the canopied bed withdrew into the ceiling, taking with it the bedposts, which folded under it like the legs of a collapsible coffee table. The bottom part of the bed, the mattress and frame, lowered into the floor until it was about six inches off the ground. Sylvia then removed the fitted green brocade covering from the mattress, folded it, and put it over the back of one of her sofas. 'Alas,' she commented, 'some things we must still do by hand.'

The bed, I must say, looked inviting enough. It was about ten feet square, large enough for several people. The sheets were pure Brazilian cotton, woven on a hand loom. I remarked on how wonderful they looked.

135

'We like to keep in touch with our heritage,' Sylvia explained. 'Today, only the very rich can afford one-hundred-percent cotton – but enough of politics and economics! Here is your surprise!' With that, she pressed another button.

I looked up at the ceiling, expecting Jesus to come floating down. It was better than that. A panel opened in the wall connecting Sylvia's bedroom to a bedroom next to it. Out stepped one of this world's all-time hunks, a Zeus of a man, about thirty, a little under six feet, with a well-muscled barrel chest thick with dark red hair, his scholar's face alert to my every nuance. Don't let me forget the most interesting part. He was buck naked, his uncircumcised cock hanging like a banana over a sack of balls that swung as he walked toward the bed.

'Hello, Diana,' he said in even better English than Sylvia's, 'I am Putzi Da Silva.'

'Oh my God,' I said. 'I think I'm going to like you better than Sylvia.'

But in truth, I was still a little confused by him. I couldn't put his face and body together. His face was that of a priest's. He was prematurely balding, with clear blue eyes. His eyes, in fact, were almost cold, almost ascetic. His body, on the other hand, belonged to the devil. When he saw me, the flesh between his legs immediately began to swell and lengthen under its thick red bush, until it stood at attention like the thick branch of a tree.

'Fuck me,' I said, quietly. What else was there to say? 'Diana,' he began, 'I have been with many women all over the world, but never have I seen such a woman as you.'

'Just fuck me,' I repeated. I was telling the truth, my truth. I just wanted Putzi on top of me. I wanted the golden wires of his chest hairs rubbing against my nipples which were already so distended and longing to be touched that the electrical shocks drove me crazy.

'Putzi can fuck all night without coming,' said Sylvia,

still in the bedroom, her fingers in her cunt.

'Skip the kissing; skip the oral sex, just fuck me, Putzi,' I ordered. 'I've been waiting for you since I came to Brazil.'

The bulb on the end of his cock grew red. Precome ooze glistened. I couldn't wait for my cunt to connect with his cock. He was angel and animal. No wonder so many of the world's most beautiful women stepped out of their panties for him. It was even rumored that a certain European queen had rendezvoused with Putzi when her prince consort was off on one of his Hollywood jaunts. As the story goes, this queen, in public, is a carefully calculated vaudeville act, much like the Pope's. She deliberately appears dowdy and frumpy, so as not to give the impression of enjoying her money, a state of affairs which would clearly cause so much resentment among the masses of her poor subjects that eventually her monarchy, one of the world's two or three richest families, would become a scapegoat for the widespread poverty and loss of Empire.

As the story goes (I heard this account from Maxey), the queen keeps a small apartment in the name of one of her ladies-in-waiting in a flat off Hyde Park in London. When the queen is having a fling, she's supposedly such an expert at disguise that no one has ever detected her coming or going. According to the story, she had given Putzi a key to the apartment, and had made plans to meet him there one evening. But, with the world in the mess it's in, she had several emergency meetings, press conferences, and whatnot in her own country. The assignation was changed around several times, until she wasn't sure what time she was supposed to meet him, and couldn't reach him. She decided to fly to England anyway, and wait until Putzi showed up. Apparently, she arrived to discover Putzi fucking both her sister and the young woman who was engaged to her son, the crown prince. The queen was absolutely aghast, became imperious, threatened to have them all executed, searched in her purse for a pistol, which, thank God, was not loaded, and finally broke down in a flood of tears, screaming at the girl who was engaged to her son, 'I know my sister's a slut, but I never expected that you of all people would cheat on my son!'

The girl apparently announced that the crown prince had introduced her to Putzi.

'What was my son doing with Putzi?' the queen allegedly shrieked, now thinking that Putzi must be making it with every one of her relations, both male and female. The girl, in particular, was livid.

'You old fuddy-duddy, you're so pure, aren't you? You think sex has to be between two people who are absolutely in love with each other, and nobody else? Well, I've got news for you, your son and I have three-ways with other men and women. It's absolutely wonderful! That's how we expect to keep our royal marriage royally alive!'

'Three-ways?' sputtered the queen. 'Is there no decency left in the world?'

Well, according to the story, the queen was, after all, the Queen, and had final say on royal allowances; so, at her order, the other women had to leave. Period. Putzi had to spend the rest of the afternoon bringing her to orgasm after orgasm, as the monarch, still mightily upset, kept repeating, 'First the Empire goes down the tube, and now we've got three-ways!'

Putzi was magnificent. Without question, he deserved his reputation. He knelt in front of me, put his hands under my thighs, and pulled me into him, his hands on my buttocks as his plum-sized glans cleaved in through my hot, dripping cunt lips and rammed me all the way to its hilt. We fit together perfectly; his large balls in their downy sack thudded against my lower cheeks; his wiry bush, thick as steel wool, ground into my pubic flesh, driving me absolutely insane as his battering ram thudded back and forth into my moist, dark interior, already engulfed in spasms. Then, he lay

138

on top of me and smothered me half to death with his perfect body. His chest hairs, just as I had hoped and prayed, entangled themselves in my taut nipples, sending shock waves in all directions.

'Oh, Putzi, Putzi, Putzi!' I gasped, and then became incoherent with ecstasy. A seizure took hold of me. I had no will. My brain could not connect with the rest of me. It was plugged into some electrical socket; I saw bright light, blinding light; random energy coursed through me. I flailed about as the great tool bore me away. My head thrashed from one side to the other.

'Diana! Diana!' he shouted triumphantly. He rode me like a gaucho; I was a wild horse and he stayed in the saddle. He tamed me. He controlled me. For the kind of pleasure Putzi gave, I would have stayed in Brazil forever, picking weeds in their garden. I came in waves of ecstasy, my inner muscles heaving me forward into an oblivion of pleasure. When he put his mouth on mine, I forgot Sylvia completely. His muscular lips took control of mine, his tongue invaded me, searching for the vulnerable meat in the back of my mouth, as soft and yielding as the insides of my cunt.

He came inside me in great shuddering spasms, spurting soft globules of sperm against the wall of my cervix.

And there was poor Sylvia on the green leather couch finger-fucking herself, her fingers drenched in come-juice. 'I don't believe in incest and neither does Putzi,' she explained. 'I guess we're basically old-fashioned that way. But I love to masturbate while he's fucking a magnificent woman like you.'

Putzi and I made love twice more during the early afternoon, and Sylvia stayed on her couch with her fingers working away like there was no tomorrow. Finally, a bell rang.

'Oh my God!' Sylvia said as she jumped up. 'Putzi, come on! We're acting like animals!' Then she said, 'Diana, we have fifteen minutes before we eat lunch.

Everybody get dressed, pronto!' She slapped her hands and shouted something in Portuguese. Putzi and I were in the middle of a mutual sixty-nine oral job.

At his sister's command, he stopped on the dime, or should I say, 'stopped on the clit' and kissed my fingers, saying, 'See you at lunch.'

Sylvia was suddenly very organised. 'We have no time for shower.' She handed me a damp, scented towel. 'Rub yourself with this. You clean yourself.'

While I washed up, unbeknownst to me, she brought out a rack of designer sports clothes she had picked out especially for me. One dress, of pleated white silk with a halter top, was perfect. It was practically see-through, and was worn with nothing underneath.

'I never wear underwear,' Sylvia explained, as if that said it all, Now, I, personally, love underwear, especially black bikini briefs, and simple brassieres that point my tits in the right direction, but I do have to admit that I am always forgetting to wear what underwear I have, so I couldn't complain too much. The ocean breeze was so balmy, and the 'natives' so friendly, I decided, what the heck, 'When in Rome, fuck like the Romans.'

Sylvia pushed another button. Out of a dumbwaiter came a tray of perfumes and the most expensive makeup, all my favorite brands. Within minutes, my eyes were lined in a subtle shade of gray, my cheeks were blushed, my lips glossed. I was once again a proper lady.

The late lunch was served on the back patio. We feasted on grilled shrimp and fresh fruit with hot Brazilian breads and an icy wine punch. Just what the doctor ordered. (The doctor and the sex therapist.) Putzi wore white – white linen pants and a white tuxedo shirt with the sleeves rolled up. He had a wonderful simplicity. Actually, he wasn't simple at all; he was frightfully complex. Frightfully. So was Sylvia. Before I returned to Manhattan, a week later, I would find myself educated to realities I never knew existed in Beavertown. They probably don't even exist in New York.

There are two sides to every coin. Where there is joy, there is sadness. Where there is kindness, there is cruelty. Where there is love, there is lust. And where there is life, there is also death. When I think of how trusting and naive I was as I sat on that back patio of the southern hemisphere's most spectacular house, sipping wine punch and smiling innocently into the gorgeous eyes of two professional love-machines, I have to laugh. They turned out to be more wicked than anyone could possibly imagine. Oh why, oh why is it so hard for me to find the perfect love I am always looking for?

Chapter Eight

That afternoon, like every afternoon at the Da Silvas, was tightly scheduled. In all fairness, the two demi-gods did not spend every morning lying on the beach waiting for rapists to come running along. Putzi, in fact, had worked that entire morning with his investment counselors, and Sylvia, who normally traveled around the world checking up on their various companies, was resting up for Carnival, which, strictly speaking, was only the three days immediately preceding Ash Wednesday; although, for the life of me, I could not imagine how she, Catholic as she claimed to be, could abruptly change her life style on Wednesday morning and give up girls for the forty days of Lent!

I took an hour-long nap after lunch. Surprisingly, no one disturbed me. I lay in a second-story room overlooking the sea. The pounding of the waves lulled me to sleep. Sleep came easily. My stomach was full. My sexual tension had been attended to. My rapist had been delivered to the sharks. Lulu was taking care of Adoro business. As the Bible says somewhere, I slept the sleep of the just. But I dreamed the dream of the damned.

I dreamed I was upriver in the Amazon with Putzi beside me. In the dream, it was as if I went to the Amazon to pay homage to the god I worship, the Anaconda, the world's biggest snake, with a head like a dog and a body so thick it could swallow a pig, or a small deer, or a small child, or, in some cases, a beautiful maiden – yours truly. At least, that's what happened in the dream. Putzi, in a pith helmet, stood by my side laughing as this humongous reptile coiled around me, squeezing the life out of me; finally, swallowing me, until, at last, my entire being had melted into liquid in its undulating stomach. Finally, I had melted away. Yet I remained. My mind remained. My awareness remained. The truth was, *I* remained. I could not be destroyed. I was the snake. I was the Anaconda. I was great coils of limitless energy, great muscles able to move anywhere. Hands were not needed. Speech was not necessary. The arts of civilization were useless to me. I was Anaconda, god and goddess of the jungle. And, when I finally realized who I really was, I took off after Putzi, who ran from me, screaming for his life. By moving in galloping coils, six and seven lengths of my body, I propelled myself along the jungle floor, pushing away from it with enormous strength. In no time, Putzi was in my coils. He did not have a chance. I was eighteen feet long. I weighed seven hundred pounds. I unhinged my jaw muscles, and, in great galvanic spasms, swallowed him whole. It was the opposite of giving birth. Once inside me, he, screaming for his life, hammered away. But I was filled with special chemicals that dissolved everything that came into my stomach. Soon, as with me, his screaming stopped, and then his heart.

But the mind of Putzi remained behind. He and I were one, in the same serpent flesh. Our brains had melted into the Anaconda brain. Our hearts were taken over by the Anaconda heart. We were now the serpent god. We were one. We were pure animal energy. We were the dwelling place of the spirits of the Amazon, dispensing justice to all who prayed to us, and to many who did not know us but who ventured inside our jungle territory.

I awoke with a terrible headache, convinced that my dream made no sense. Silly girl. In any case, as strange as the dream appeared to be, it gave me the courage to get through the rest of my visit with the Da Silvas.

That afternoon, it all began. The surreal part. The

unreal part. The real part. If there is a God, how come he constructed the human race in such a way that all the lunatics have the power to destroy the peace of mind of everybody else? Enough theology. Let me just explain what happened.

I awoke with Sylvia's fingers in my cunt.

'Wake up, wake up, whoever you are,' she whispered into my ear. 'I have a big surprise for you.'

'What?' I asked, opening one eye.

'Here,' she said. 'I brought you a new pants outfit to wear.'

Well, it looked like a pair of white satin pajamas. I opened my other eye, sat up on the edge of the bed and got dressed. This time, there was actually underwear, a pair of white cotton panties. Very puritanical. Only the points of my nipples visible through the satin jacket made me look the slightest bit sexy, although Sylvia explained to me that the pants were cut very tight in back. So they were. In front, too. My cunt lips bulged in the crotch. My slit was pronounced. Sylvia said she wanted me to know I looked sexy even when I didn't feel sexy. I responded that I can take only three or four hours of sex a day, and I was tired of apologizing for my inadequacy in that department.

'That's okay,' she said. 'We understand American guilt. We are used to it.' Then, she showed me how to wrap a length of white satin around my head to make a turban.

'Very Brazilian,' she said.

I decided I looked like Lana Turner in *The Postman Always Rings Twice*. I always adored Lana. The characters she played made me think that any middle-class American girl with a good pair of tits could fuck her way to the top with the best-looking men. But it was just a fantasy. I never really could separate sex from love. I only fuck men I am emotionally attracted to. Naturally, I fantasized that I could be different. But I couldn't. Anyway, by the time Sylvia had finished with me, I had gold loop earrings in my ears, dark glasses, and a cigarette in a cigarette holder. It made me wonder just how original Brazilian styles really were. Was the whole world copying old Hollywood movies?

I am avoiding the rest of this account. I find it hard to tell everything. I can only tell what I personally witnessed. Okay, here goes.

It seems that Putzi, with his multimillion-dollar business interests, had bought about a million acres of land in the upper Amazon, and was trying to establish citrus groves there, figuring that, by the time Florida and California had converted its best land to condominiums, he would have planted and harvested enough oranges, grapefruits, lemons, and limes to more than supply the world's markets with fresh, frozen, canned, and freeze-dried citrus products. Naturally, he needed workers. In time, he had built a planned city on the banks of the Amazon. Everything was there. Schools. Stores. Churches. A hospital. Several banks. Recreation areas. Skilled workers came from all over South America. Some of the technicians came from Europe and the Far East. The town of Sylvia, as it was called, was a true melting pot, with its own newspaper and its own television station. In time, there were fifty thousand people living there.

Well, for every action there is a reaction. Across the river from Sylvia, another town grew up, this one unplanned, this one a river slum called Cosa Nostra, a place for drug dealing, gambling, prostitutes of both sexes, and occasional murder. It seems that there were three brothers, the Gambino triplets, no relation to the distinguished American crime family, and not really triplets, not even really brothers, although two of them were cousins, who ran most of the rackets in Cosa Nostra. One day, they went too far. They caught some Amazon Indians, about fifty of them, and every afternoon, from a boat in the middle of the river, they dropped them into the water, after taking bets on how many the piranha would devour. It was a kind of Amazon roulette. Every twenty minutes, they'd fish out the remaining Indians and take another round of bets. Piranha, in case somebody doesn't know it, are little fish with razor sharp teeth that travel in large schools and can strip a person of his or her flesh in one minute's time. Or not. 'One never knows, does one?'

By the time Putzi got wind of the Gambinos, about half of the Indians had gone to their eternal reward, and the Gambinos had made a small fortune, even though, to give them the benefit of the doubt, they had no control over the piranha.

Well, two days after Putzi had heard about Amazon roulette, he had the Gambino triplets locked up in his basement, in one of the several maximum-security jail cells he maintained there; cells which, needless to say, had not been part of my house tour. The Gambinos were subjected to a most strange and unusual punishment. They were stripped naked. They were fed regularly with a high protein diet, spoon-fed, that is, because their hands were manacled behind their backs, the manacles attached to a short chain on the wall. Then they were forced to watch a full week's worth of dirty movies. The point was, they couldn't jerk off to save their lives. By the end of the week, which was the day I happened to be visiting, they were hosed off, and brought by armed guards into an adjoining room to await their fate.

Now, it seems that among certain of the oldest, most aristocratic families of Brazil, there was a patriarch, a multi-millionaire, a friend of Putzi's, who wanted his three, ugly, super-Catholic teen-age daughters to have the benefit of 'real men' as soon as possible. He was afraid that if they were left to their own devices, they would marry late and marry wimps, and worse, marry as perfect virgins, so they'd never know what they were missing. He was determined to spare them a fate he considered worse than death. So this man, whose name was Cerminara, and Putzi worked out an arrangement between friends whereby the girls would be initiated into the mysteries of adult sex. Well, of course, there was more to it than that. I have to take this one step at a time.

146

Sylvia and I were led down into the subbasement of the Da Silva mansion. We sat in a room adjoining the one where the initiation was to take place. There was a two-way mirror so we could observe the proceedings without being seen. The room was upholstered, floor and ceiling, with thick, red wool carpeting, and piled high with huge pillows and mattresses. The pillows were covered in different shades of red, coral, orange, and pink. The mattresses seemed to be covered in what looked like oriental rugs. As we watched, three incredibly ugly girls were led in. The Cerminara sisters, aged sixteen, seventeen, and eighteen. They wore, or rather, were dressed in navy-blue blazers with plaid skirts and oxfords with knee socks, and they were carrying schoolbooks. I never did find out where they went to school.

The next part was not to be believed. Into the room marched three 'nuns'; I recognized them as Sylvia's gardeners. These women were in absolutely official Catholic nun's habits. They told the girls, who believed them to be real nuns, that there was a virulent disease going around Rio, and that, before they could meet the Cardinal, they must be examined and deloused. Amidst giggling and high-pitched laughing, the nuns helped the three girls undress. All traces of clothing were removed, including eyeglasses and religious medals and chains around their necks. Then the nuns informed the girls that 'the doctors' would be there in a few minutes and to please, for the sake of Our Lord, to cooperate with the doctors in every possible way.

'The doctors,' the Gambino triplets, of course, had been told that they had been picked by these girls from other prisoners to give them their first fuck. So, just before they were let into the room where the Cerminara sisters were, the Gambinos had their manacles removed. Then they were let into the room, and the doors were locked and bolted shut behind them.

Imagine, if you will, fat, white legs with black hair running rampant over all of them, eyebrows that met in the middle of their noses, squinty little pig eyes, cheeks peppered with zits, and little crooked teeth with double braces – but, to be fair, the breasts, or rather, the breastlets were incredible. Little, swollen, super-sensitive glandular things needing to be licked and sucked on, in a word, paid attention to. Their cunts were something else – black bushes, thatches, really, growing practically to their navels, under which were hot pink slashes of ripe flesh hanging like some new tropical species, half flower, half animal. Senhor Cerminara must have sensed how ripe his daughters were. He must have smelled them. He must have gone half mad from suppressed desires.

Like I said, in a flash the doors closed behind the Gambino triplets. There was no way out. The three Cerminaras screamed bloody murder as if on cue. There were decibels in those screams that only a dog could have appreciated. The Gambinos, for their part, couldn't believe their good fortune. They never looked at girls' faces, anyway. They never saw the hair on their legs, or, if they did, it was something they had waited for all their lives.

The Da Silvas and I sat there on the other side of the two-way mirror like we were attending some great work of theatre. We didn't utter a sound. We didn't dare. We couldn't wait to see what would happen. The truth, the ugly truth, was that I was as depraved as my hosts. Travel certainly can be broadening.

Have I adequately described the Gambinos? Theirs were Mediterranean bodies with huge chests and shoulders, hair on their backs, overdeveloped biceps, balding, big-eared, scar faced, no-necked thugs, their beards gray black stubble. From the stomach down, there were beer bellies and tough little legs, all sinewy, roped with veins, varicose or otherwise. The cocks, needless to say, were almost red, and were sticking straight out. In a word, there wasn't a boy amongst them. These men were definitely fucking-machines. They wanted those red cocks pumping away inside

148

those freshly grown virginal cunts, period. No psychologizing here. No niceties, no begging for permission. This was raw sex, nonpersonal sex, sex with few compliments exchanged. The girls ran to the door and beat on it relentlessly, but, alas, to no avail. Three pairs of hairy arms were around them in no time. Three pairs of lips were sucking the flesh on the backs of their necks as they screamed and cried. Then, three pairs of hands were fondling their big, bushy nests of coal-black hair.

Two of the Gambinos entered the girls from behind; with blood squirting, their cherries popped. The girls' tears did not dissuade the men in the least. I never heard such grunting. These men were truly pigs, truly animals. The third Gambino spread out the third Cerminara girl, brought her cunt up to his mouth and stuck his tongue in her. It was probably a first for him, probably something he'd seen in one of his fuck films. She put her hands on his head and fondled him, guiding him. In a flash, he was on top of her, missionary position, screaming at her in Portuguese to pick up his cock and put it inside her.

Sylvia translated the girl's reply for me in a whisper, 'No, senhor, I am a virgin. I cannot touch you. My religion does not allow it.'

The man screamed at her again and made her cry. By now, Putzi and Sylvia both had their hands on me, but we were all glued to the screen – I mean, the two-way mirror.

Despite her protests, or maybe because of them, the brute entered the Cerminara girl. In general, all the men were grunting and grinding away. They all had their rough hands planted under the girls' thighs; they were guiding them, showing them how to fuck, how one pelvis follows the movements of another in a ritual dance, how the woman must rise to meet the man, how she must yield to the man without letting go, how her vaginal muscles must learn to grasp onto the man's staff, sucking on it, secreting her juices onto it so that it

149

will glide into her dark recesses and trigger her where she least suspects, catching her in her orgasm unawares; because, if she cannot yield to him, she will never yield to her own dark mystery, she will never drown in ecstasy, she will never be carried out on the tide of orgasm to the deep ocean's floor where all the mysteries of the universe wait for the diver who dares to descend into the black unknown.

I found it strange how those hairy, grunting animals, the Gambinos, the professional underclass, seduced me into a kind of reverie. I sat in that dark Da Silva room on a silk pillow, staring ahead, absolutely fascinated by the carnal lust in front of me. The Cerminara girls, all three of them, were weeping; they were embracing the men; they were fathers and daughters; they were hugging them, whispering, '*Et tu amo*' – 'I love you,' in Portuguese. They had completely forgotten about the mythical Cardinal they had once been waiting to meet.

I began to come right there on my pillow, something that had never happened to me without stimulation, until I realized that both Da Silvas had their hands in my crotch and had been stroking me. I'd been so absorbed by the scene in the next room, I hadn't even noticed. They each kissed me on either side of my face. And then, each took one of my hands.

'Wait till you see the next part, darling,' whispered Sylvia. 'You will have a true taste of South America.'

On the far side of the Da Silva compound was a small airstrip with a helicopter landing pad they must have bought from the same company that manufactures them for the U.S. Army. Maybe I was wrong, but it seemed to me there was room in the back of the 'copter for about ten soldiers. I wondered if Putzi was planning to take over the country.

We sat there in the helicopter for about twenty minutes, waiting for God knows what, while Putzi regaled me with stories about the tour of the surrounding jungle which he was about to give me,

150

especially the national park to the north, the Tijuca
Forest, which boasted more species of plant life than
any place on earth. Accustomed as I thought I was to
surprises, I was not prepared for our six fellow-
travelers who suddenly rounded the bend. The three
Cerminara sisters, who were again dressed in their
knee socks and plaid skirts, walked alongside the three
Gambinos, who, except for their handcuffs and leg
irons, were buck naked. Their tumescent cocks swung
freely between their legs. Two Da Silva henchmen with
rifles accompanied this crew.

'We have only one hour of daylight left,' announced
Putzi. 'We must hurry.'

House servants slammed the helicopter doors shut.
The pilot turned on the ignition. All told, there were
twelve of us, including the henchmen, crowded onto
that 'copter. Quite a crew. I expected the Cerminaras
to be enraged at having been so ill-treated, but they sat
with their arms around the men, stroking them,
fondling their cocks, and petting them like they were a
new breed of teddy bear with genitals. They had, as the
saying goes, no shame. In no time, the Gambino cocks
were again rampant, and the triplets were ready to
direct their protegées in the fine art of giving head.
Unfortunately, since I cannot understand Portuguese,
I can only describe what I saw. The men showed the
girls how to fondle their nuts in one hand while they
pumped away at the base of their sexual organs with
the other. Then they showed them how to place their
wet lips and an eager tongue over their glans, rimming
the edge of the glans with the tip of their tongues. I
never before understood how truly ugly girls, girls who
will never be beautiful, girls with broad noses and
heavy legs, girls with black stubble under their arms no
matter how often they shave, girls with double chins at
sixteen and triple chins at twenty, girls with beady,
black animal eyes, can become the most ravishing
sexual creatures on God's green earth. But it can
happen. I saw it happen. It seems that, given a little

151

encouragement, it is the ugly girls who learn how to become the best women of the bed, women who can have any man for a night, yes, rough-hewn men who recognize their own animal kind.

In a few minutes, we passed over Serra de Tijuca, the great national forest to the north, a hundred square miles of wilderness. Even from the air, the uncontrolled vegetable effervescence was apparent. Millions of lush plants writhed and crept around each other in a profusion of roots and canopies. At Putzi's order, the pilot descended as low as he could, until the wind from the propellers spread the trees of the forest like vaginal lips. I saw masses of orchids of every conceivable color, huge tree ferns, passion flowers, trumpet trees, palms, spider flower bushes, begonias, wild fruit trees with twenty-pound mangoes, and fruits I'd never seen before.

The Gambinos were coming then. They had no use for tropical scenery, Amazon dwellers that they were. The Cerminara girls were giggling as they swallowed their first sperm. I was absolutely amazed that they showed no embarrassment; their sexual initiation had obviously transformed them.

Then, just as the sun was setting, we headed back to Corcovado, that granite mountain on top of which stands a seven-hundred-ton statue of Christ the Redeemer with outstretched arms. At night it is a wondrous sight. When I first saw it from Putzi's helicopter, the floodlights had just been turned on. The concrete Jesus appeared to be shedding unearthly rays of glory and majesty. My Grandmother Coozer (my mother's mother) would have loved that statue. The Cerminara girls were now slumbering in the arms of their men, who also slept. We kept flying south over the most glittering city in the world.

Sylvia kissed me and said, 'You see, my darling, I could live anywhere in the world, but only here in Rio is there beauty unparalleled. Only here do the rich make love like the poor. Only here do the poor have

fun. Only here does the jungle meet the skyscraper.'
Sylvia was a true believer in her own religion, which
was all about primitive beauty and wild primitive sex
served up on a silver tray. Unfortunately, try as I
might, I would never belong to her church. No matter
how rich the House of Adoro made me, I would always
be strictly from Beavertown, Pennsylvania. The word
'servant' would always be foreign to me.

Copacabana Beach at night looks like a glittering
diamond choker; at least to me it does. The luxury
hotels light up the sands. From the air, I could see the
white surf crashing below me. 'Where are we going?' I
asked.

'We have a rendezvous at sea, ten miles out,' Sylvia
said, 'at a place where the sharks are always awake.'

'Oh my God,' I gasped, 'you don't mean … ' I felt
sick in the pit of my stomach. Nobody had to spell out
to me that the Gambinos were taking their first and last
helicopter ride.

Putzi explained to me that the Gambinos had been
responsible for the deaths of many Amazon Indians,
not to mention a large number of working men who
had disappeared both from Sylvia and from Cosa
Nostra. The Cerminara girls, moreover, could not go
through life, at least not in South American society,
where they would undoubtedly become good Catholic
wives and mothers, with those three criminals telling
tales about them, besmirching their reputations.

'But, but … ' I said, 'don't you have judges and
courts in Brazil?'

'In certain respects,' Putzi explained, 'he who lives by
the law of the jungle must die by the law of the jungle.'

For the next twenty minutes, as we headed out to
sea, I said nothing. The salt air felt wonderful. I could
taste it. I figured the Atlantic Ocean was not far below
the helicopter, but I saw nothing. Darkness covered
the deep. Then, without giving advance notice, Putzi
signaled to the men with the guns, putting his index
finger to his lips as if to say, 'Sh-h-h.' In the back of the

helicopter, it seems, were two fifty-pound weights, relatively small masses of lead, hardly noticeable. Attached to the weights were small chains with clips, which the henchmen attached to the sleeping men's leg irons.

'My God,' I thought, 'the Da Silvas have got this procedure down to a science.'

Sylvia explained to me that I must not make a move until it was all over; I must not turn around and look at the tortured, pleading eyes of the condemned men or they would haunt me all my life. I resolved to follow her advice. She assured me that, at the last minute, Putzi would read to them a list of their crimes. This was so that justice might be served. For the moment, Putzi ordered the henchmen to pull the sisters away from their men. The Gambinos awoke to find gun barrels staring them in the face. One sister, the eldest one, was not about to let go. She had to be forcibly slapped, and the Gambino who was holding her kicked in the teeth. Putzi then very quickly read out a statement in Portuguese, presumably their crimes. The girls began to wail and scream. They were clearly upset. Who could blame them, really?

What happened next was incredibly cold-blooded. I heard the doors pulled open, and from the corner of my eye saw the guards toss the two fifty-pound weights out into the night, and then, with horrible pushing and groaning, shove the manacled men out after them. The Gambinos were cursing and shrieking in the most terrible tones of voice. Sylvia explained to me that by the time they hit the water they'd be absolutely dead, and not to worry.

We had a near-tragedy. One of the Cerminara girls broke loose and bolted for the door to follow her man. Sylvia explained to me that the guard told the girl it was too late, the men were already dead. We were as high up as a tall office building.

'I don't believe you!' she screamed in Portuguese, as the guard clapped his hands to emphasize the force of impact of a body hitting the water. The girls were absolutely stunned. Putzi, who had no legitimate children of his own, spoke to the sisters in as fatherly a manner as he knew how. They seemed to listen to him. They gradually quieted down, and the tears dried on their cheeks.

Sylvia then translated to me the following speech of Putzi's: 'Girls, we are on our way back to the motherland, our beloved Brazil, where your father will be waiting to take you home. You will finish school, marry wonderful boys, and grow up to be wonderful Catholic mothers; nobody but you and I will know what happened today.'

The girls, hearing him, were absolutely shocked and began to cry. Putzi kept at it. Didn't the sisters know that men like the Gambinos always talked, and that a girl had to choose between an active sex life and her reputation? He advised them that they should consider themselves fortunate the Gambinos were mass murderers deserving of the death penalty; otherwise, if they had lived, they would have besmirched the girls' reputations from Belèm to Pôrto Alegre. No honorable gentlemen of any family worth talking about would so much as take them to the opera. The Cerminara sisters listened intently to the wisdom of many centuries. I didn't open my mouth. I was, after all, just your basic plain-Jane, girl-next-door, all-American sweetheart type who liked a roll in the hay once in a while. Otherwise, I was in over my head, and I knew it. I was beginning to get nostalgic for New York, even for Beavertown and those simple middle-class American men for whom happiness was a bottle of Scotch and a good blow job.

We rode the rest of the way back to the Da Silva's in silence. Nobody said a word except the pilot checking the weather at the Santos Dumont airport to the east. In a few hours, all would be changed. Once more, I would be part of a swelling throng at the great night of Carnival on the Avenida Rio Branco in sweltering temperatures of almost a hundred degrees. Now, there was only the silence of death. Putzi and Sylvia held my hands. They knew that I was profoundly confused by the customs of a culture so entirely different from my own.

When we arrived back at the Da Silva airport, Senhor Cerminara, the girls' father, was waiting there. He was a stocky man in a tuxedo, evidently on his way to a social function, possibly a cocktail party. I was surprised he wasn't in Carnival costume. Sylvia explained that even in Brazil, 'we have what you call "the no-nonsense" personality.' Well, I guess by now I was most emphatically in the mood for nonsense; I kept my hands folded in front of my tight crotch and kept my head bowed as low as possible. I had nothing to worry about. The man's whole attention was on his daughters. He beamed broadly as they disembarked. They acted like perfect ladies from their first curtsy to the demure way they allowed themselves to be ushered into their father's limousine. They had nothing to say to Putzi, Sylvia, or me. Not even a final wave. Not even a final smile. I often wondered what happened to them.

Chapter Nine

Sylvia couldn't wait to show me my Carnival costume. Why she went to the trouble of having Maxey send my exact size and measurements was beyond me. The only size involved was the hat size for my enormous headdress, a plastic crescent moon three feet across that lighted up. Otherwise, once we were in her dressing room, she stripped me (so what else is new?), promised me that when the night was over, 'if we get back to this house alive, I will make love to you and to whomever you bring home with you,' and proceeded to create my outfit. First, she sprayed me gold, a light spray so as not to close all my pores. Then, she meticulously glued gold sequins, one by one, around my nipples, in a free-form starburst pattern. If I had not had perfectly molded, firm breasts, I would have looked grotesque, but, at the age of twenty-three, I had nothing to worry about. I looked almost respectable. For my crotch, she had me don a gold G-string, which covered my vagina and pubic hair, period. My ass was absolutely bare.

'Don't worry, Diana darling; in Rio, half the people, they go bare-ass,' she said. She then glued sequins on my G-string and lower abdomen in the same starburst pattern that she had created for my breasts. My shoes were simple, gold-leather, high-heeled pumps with added laces that crisscrossed all the way up my shins. My main prop, aside from the headdress, was a gold-sprayed bow, its quiver filled with arrows, slung on one shoulder. I was supposed to be 'Diana, Goddess of the Moon, Protectress of the Hunt'. Considering my maiden name had been Diana Hunt, the whole thing was astrological. Quite a coincidence, I guess.

Sylvia then informed me that we'd wear white satin coats to cover our costumes, we'd travel by station wagon, and we'd use my hotel room at the Rio Palace for a dressing room. In case we got separated during the Carnival, we'd meet again at my hotel room around five A.M.

'Where is Putzi?' I asked.

'Putzi wants his costume to be a surprise,' she answered. 'He told me to tell you not to worry; he'd find you during the night and bear you away to heaven.' I wasn't sure how to react to that; I'd just seen how Putzi bore people away to heaven. No thank you, Ma'am.

Traffic on the Lagoa-Barra Highway was bumper-to-bumper. Sylvia drove. Young studs, from the country no doubt, were piled into jalopies en route to the final evening of glittering madness. Even though I can't understand a word of Portuguese, catcalls and wolf whistles are the universal language of Boy Meets Girl. At one point, I demurely covered my breasts with my hands, a gesture that gave rise to one man's cock. I felt ridiculous. I was wearing the white satin robe Sylvia had given me, but I guess it was just a little bit open. The wind does funny things with white satin robes. As I looked through our station wagon window at the car next to ours, the stud next to the driver of an old Buick was sitting on top of the seat, looking at me and jerking off. He must have been drunk.

Sylvia was absolutely disgusted. 'Men are such animals,' she commented. 'Masturbating in traffic is so gross; thank God I'm a lesbian.' No sooner had she uttered those words than on the other side of us a car pulled alongside with a little black-eyed mulatta in the front seat. She was eyeing Sylvia and obviously, well, masturbating, as she kept digging down between her legs and then licking her fingers. Then, when the young girl sat up on the top of the seat, Sylvia had second thoughts about masturbating in traffic.

'Ooh, isn't she sweet. Isn't she adorable. She shaved her pussy just for me. Oooh, Diana, please, help me. I can't take my hands off the wheel. I beg you. If I touch myself I'll have an accident. Please put your hand between my legs and, you know, rub me.'

Maybe I forgot to mention that Sylvia's costume consisted of sprayed silver, on her skin, that is, with an ostrich plume over her labia. That was it. And a winged hat. She was supposed to be Mercury, the god of communication or something. She said she didn't mind being the god of communication as long as there was someone to communicate with. In any event, the ostrich plume would not stay in place, so Sylvia was, in effect, telling me to masturbate her. If I had been a lesbian, I would have enjoyed it more. Frankly, metaphorically speaking, I thought the piece of chocolate in the car next to us was more delectable than Sylvia's strawberry cheesecake. I was beginning to tire of Sylvia and Putzi. It's true, he was a fantastic piece of prime pork, and I had hoped to be spending Carnival with his pork prod between my legs, but after the Gambino-Cerminara episode, I wasn't so sure.

In any case, for the moment, there was nothing to do but proceed with my hand job. I found that the only way I could bring Sylvia off with any enthusiasm was to concentrate on the mulatta in the next car. I fantasized about her gash of raspberry jam in between those dark, chocolate cunt lips. I felt terrific. The men on the other side of us were hooting. They thought we were just pretending to be lesbians; that is to say, Sylvia was just pretending to be a lesbian as a ploy to get them more interested in us. As far as I was concerned, I have never liked men who drive dangerously. I tried to ignore them. I was confident that, once I got to Carnival, I would attract the more intelligent members of the opposite sex.

I slid my index finger up and down Sylvia's slit until it became swollen with blood and fat with desire. It was slippery now, and the labia began to open up like the petals of a hot pink begonia.

'Ooh, Diana,' she moaned, as we hit the intersection of the Avenida Niemeyer, which eventually became the Avenida Atlantica, which paralleled the Copacabana Beach. 'Oh, Diana, you are the most wonderful houseguest. I'm so glad that I shot that rapist for you. Oooh, Diana, right there, keep your finger there, ooh, don't let me have no accident!'

That's when I knew for sure that Sylvia Da Silva was a little bit cracked in the head. Either that, or the heat had finally gotten to her. I decided the only way for me to get through the rest of the trip into town was to forget Sylvia and to concentrate on her cunt. By now, our mulatta, the little chocolate angel, had disappeared. Her mother had discovered her masturbating and had slapped her down. The truth was, Sylvia really wanted me. She had just been looking for an excuse, ever since she sprayed my body gold. I could tell by the glazed look in her eyes as she stared at my perfect globes. With all her money, she, like most South Americans have a directness that scares other people. They admire and fear us at the same time, a threshold to love-hate. My adventures with Sylvia in her shower-waterfall had been enough for me, but, apparently, I had just whetted her appetite. She really wanted me to pay more attention to her. All I can say is, I did my best. I tried to think as positively as possible. The one thing my Grandmother Coozer's religion, the Taber-nacle Witnesses, did teach me was that there is no point to negative thinking. On this note, I gave my complete and total concentration to Sylvia's cunt in the hopes of cheering her up.

To tell the truth, her cunt was decidedly better than the rest of her. Her musk smelled like rotting, tropical fruit. The edges of her labia in that heat seemed like a rare species of flesh-eating orchid. She tasted of salt air and jungle. She smelled like a whore and jaguar in heat. Up close, no deodorant in the world could disguise her primal odor. I dove into her pussy, and I found, to my surprise, that the more I had begun to

160

doubt her sanity, the more she appealed to me. She was fragile, vulnerable, in need of so much attention, even though, on the surface, she seemed like a bull, I mean a fullback – or something – as she railroaded her way through the dense traffic near the Rio Palace. Anyway, she really was sensitive, and she tasted great.

As we approached the city proper, revelers everywhere were in costume. Like the night before, the whole city of Rio was taken up with the samba. 'One, two, three, four – one two. One, two, three, four – one two.'

Sylvia came in such shock waves of orgasm, one would have thought she had not had sex in months. She almost lost control just as we were turning into the underground garage of the Rio Palace. The security guard had a strange smile on his face. So did I. So much for the power of positive thinking.

Next scene: my hotel room. Notes from Lulu Touché everywhere. It seems that, according to her, at least, she and Che Miranda, the Communist asshole, had fallen in love. Labor and management in bed together.

She wrote, 'I understand the plight of the working classes. Che and I belong together. We have so much to share. Besides, his mother is half Italian. We speak a common language. And besides, he's terrific in bed.' So that was it. The power of the gonads over the brain. I wrote her a long note back, saying, in effect, that she could fuck whomsoever she pleased, but that, if she wanted to keep her job in New York, I wanted fifteen of the sexiest bodies she could find, male and female, for our summer wear show in two weeks. Period. We would be leaving for New York in a week. There were plane reservations to be made. Plus visas and whatever passports were necessary. Lulu was to make all the arrangements, and if there was any unforeseen problem, she was to call Maxey in New York, especially if I got unnecessarily delayed. There was no telling where the Da Silvas would lead me to.

I felt like a royal bitch, but it couldn't be helped. Could it be that I was just a little bit jealous? Did I, somewhere in my dark libido, have the hots for Che Miranda? Not possible. I don't believe in Communism, and besides, I don't understand it. I can't even afford it. The man closed down my factory and called me names. Just because he wore skin-tight jeans, and seemed to have a bulging crotch, had nothing to do with me. My full concentration was on New York and my summer wear show. I was, above all, a businesswoman. My relationship with the Da Silvas was strictly business, too. I wrote a note to myself reminding me to ask Putzi how Da Silva Industries affected the House of Adoro. I was sure there was a very serious business connection there. But I never mix business with pleasure, you know what I mean?

Sylvia's ostrich plume would not stay up. I suggested she wear a G-string like mine and attach the ostrich plume to it. She said that that was a wonderful idea, but I was wearing the only G-string she owned. At this point, my puritanical tendencies got the better of me. I didn't like the idea of her walking around Carnival with a naked cunt, so I removed the G-string I was wearing, pinned the ostrich plume to it, and handed it to her.

'What am I supposed to do with this?' she asked.

'Put it on,' I said. 'Do you want to be raped?'

She didn't answer that. 'But then *you* are naked,' she said, staring at my mons.

'No,' I said, 'I've decided I'm wearing the white satin robe you gave me, with nothing underneath.'

Sylvia didn't understand. 'You can't do that,' she said, belligerently. 'That don't look like no Carnival costume.'

Something in me snapped. The Da Silvas were beginning to get on my nerves. 'Fuck you, Sylvia!' I screamed. 'I'm an American! I do things my way. I fuck my way! I get angry my way! I dress for Carnival my way! So bug off! And I ain't wearing no fucking plastic moonbeam!' And with that, I threw the headdress to the floor.

The woman flew into a rage. Because I sounded ungrateful to her, she became a volcano of hate. 'You fucking whore! I was jus' going to eat you out to thank you for masturbate – masturbating me, but now, forget it, I won't touch your pussy!'

And with that outburst, the gorgeous Sylvia ran out of my hotel room looking like a naked silver woman wearing a construction worker's hat with little wings attached. That, and a big pink ostrich plume over her cooze. The name of the game was *Mixed Signals*. Unfortunately, I would not see her again till four hours later, when the game would be completely over.

Well, it was time for me to be artsy-craftsy. I sewed my white satin robe together at the crotch so that it wouldn't fly open. With red nail polish, I wrote 'Rio!' on the back. Then, I slipped into it. If someone really wanted to get a good look, my sequin-covered breasts were still in there bobbing along nicely underneath. In my luggage, fortunately, I had brought a platinum-blonde Jean Harlow wig just in case the beach wrecked my hair and I needed a touch of glamor. It looked sensational. Then, I outlined my eyes with jet-black mascara. I looked like a cross between a thirties movie star and a slut. Perfect. There was no one in the entire parade who looked like me. I was the most original get-up in Rio that night. It was pure simplicity and pure class. That's what class is, really – simplicity. I guess I've always had class, because I'm basically a simple girl. I like men who like me, and I like to design sexy clothes and make a fortune. And I like to have a good time. What else is there?

As I walked from my room to the elevator, my legs slid out of the slit in my robe, one after the other. It wasn't clear what I had on under the robe. My perfect globes bobbed. My caramel nipples stuck through the satin and occasionally slipped out of my robe altogether. A bellboy, no, not Hugo Battista, dropped his tray when he saw me. When I walked into the elevator, a woman sprayed lime green and wearing a gold bikini with sequins glued under her eyes and a see-through fishtail wrapped around her legs, breathed big gulps of involuntary air when she saw me; then a great hairy hand, her male companion's, reached under my robe to caress my luxuriant garden of dark blonde fur. He had a lecherous leer on his face. I took that leer as a supreme gesture of good will. In New York, I would have told him I had syphilis and slapped him, but here, I expected a little extra attention and was delighted to get it, regardless of his wife's murderous expression.

As I stepped off the elevator and walked through the gold lobby to the streets, the Carnival costumes I saw were not to be believed. A big brown stud dressed in diapers was being wheeled around in a baby carriage by his 'nanny,' a black woman in white-face wearing only a Mary Poppins hat, an umbrella, and a bikini made out of the British flag!

That's when I first saw, or thought I saw him – the figure of Death. A man dressed in black, with a death's-head mask, a white skull glowing in the dark. No, I couldn't have seen him. I decided it was a fantasy I'd seen in some movie. I resolved to think positively, to relax, to have a good time for once. In the throng, I saw revelers dressed as priests and nuns with bright-red Satan faces and devil's horns.

There were hundreds of men in drag. Redheads and blondes were popular. They wore immense, foam-rubber breasts and garish makeup, and two-inch false eyelashes. 'Dream on, boys and girls,' I thought, 'I hate to sound conceited, but I'm what you're all trying to be. I am the blonde goddess of your dreams. Catch me if you can!'

It was growing dark. The samba drums were getting louder. Hundreds of thousands of naked feet were blocking traffic as the city samba'd. The police had stopped directing traffic. They were dancing with the revelers. It was eight P.M. The parade had just begun. Rio was insane. Down the hillsides from the ramshackle lean-tos of the poor came the underclass of the city, their dark faces smeared with paint; orange, vermilion, pink. The samba penetrated to their bones and mine. Through Maxey's intervention, I had been invited to several of the lavish Carnival balls. The chi-chi Hotel National Ball had been the previous night; I had been advised to dress like an Alpine peasant (a white halter with green hot pants were the instructions), but I said to hell with it. The upper-class balls are mostly all college-graduate types with proper housewives trying to sneak in ten minute extramarital affairs, behind their husband's backs. According to what Sylvia told me, the upper classes believe that what happens sexually on the day before Ash Wednesday doesn't count. It's God's day off, supposedly. The term she used was 'carnival romance.' To be honest, I had turned down all my invitations. I figured Carnival was for everyone, especially the poor who had originally begun it. I wanted more than anything to be with the people in the streets, some of whom had been dancing for sixty and seventy hours.

For the past fifty years, the Cariocas have belonged to what are called Samba Schools. These are not dancing classes, but more like municipal clubs who present carnival extravaganzas, much like the Californian businesses who sponsor floats in the Rose Bowl Parade in Pasadena every January. The Samba Schools have their own composers, dancers, and musicians who occupy themselves all year long with the next Carnival. The purpose of each Samba School is to present a story using combined media of dance, music, and visual display. Rehearsals begin in November. Some costumes cost as much as the average man's yearly wage. Nobody complains. The Cariocas live for Carnival.

Well, I guess Cariocas have a thing for blondes, too. Who am I kidding? They are positively crazy about them – us. I was followed by some very horny men

165

from the minute I stepped out of the Rio Palace and headed for Avenida Rio Branco, which, by the way, I never found.

Then, I saw him again. The figure of Death. The figure in black with the death's-head mask. He was following me. I was sure of it now. The white glowing skull kept popping out of doorways and between parked cars. I decided I was not imagining things. Being more than a little superstitious, I began to wonder if I would leave Rio alive.

The crowds carried me with them. I was caught in the undertow. My white satin robe brushed against too many steel drums and soon began to disintegrate. Before long, I was parading in satin tatters, my spangled breasts pushing out between the slashes, my mascara smeared down my cheeks, my lipstick reaching across my face. I tied the bottom part of my robe around my waist in a big knot at crotch level. I was not about to be stripped completely naked by samba drums accidentally-on-purpose brushing against me. Thank God for my long, perfectly shaped legs. They were my last vestige of beauty. Otherwise, I would have looked like a clown. I wished I were at Copacabana again, lying under the stars, letting the ocean warriors take their pleasure with me. Carnival, by comparison, was frenzied, hypnotic, riveting.

Then, somehow, slowly, irrevocably, without my knowing what was happening, I was more or less dragged back into Babilônia Hill, the great favela, the mother of slums. I guess some part of my destiny lay in Babilônia Hill.

A strange awareness began to creep over me. The official Carnival, sweeping through the center of the city, had begun to reveal an order, a kind of rigid pattern that I had not suspected was there. What I had first imagined were heathens carousing in the dark began to look like half-time at the Sugar Bowl. Too many floats had grade-school historical themes such as Columbus's voyage. Too many costumes looked

166

exactly alike. I actually saw a platoon of Aunt Jemimas, each one wearing the identical gold turban, the identical pink rose over the left ear, the identical blue glass necklace. I felt betrayed.

In reaction, I found myself drawn back into the hidden streets of Babilônia Hill. From far away, I could smell the danger there. I could taste the darkness and the sex. The evil in the heart of me grew. I couldn't help myself. The animal in my flesh invaded my soul and clawed away at me until I was one naked cry in the night. My cunt grew dark and heavy and obsessed. I desperately needed to be met by someone equal to myself. Little did I suspect that before the night was over, I would experience the best sex of my life, and I would come face-to-face with death. Again.

The men followed me. Dark men. Men with gold earrings. Men with glittering jockstraps, hooting at me in strange languages, the languages of sin and degradation, of obscene gesture and maniacal expression.

Nothing in Rio prepared me for what followed in the secret caverns under Babilônia Hill. The scenes there were so extreme, I began to black out. The next morning I remembered practically nothing. I have no intention of distressing readers of this account who are undoubtedly more interested in whanking off than in hearing about the horrors of the Rio nights. On the other hand, scenes of passion and betrayal and even outright horror, often heighten sexual arousal. Even the most sophisticated hanker for the low life now and then. We all wonder what it's like in the gutter; we all wonder what happens after dark in the outlaw dens where the rules of civilization no longer apply, especially in the backwaters of Brazil, where thousands of the Damned live outside the constraints of common decency, far away from governments and money, where it is often necessary to trade whatever one can, even one's own body, in order to survive. Sometimes, these outlaw dens, these backwaters, are right under our very feet.

It seems that under several of the hills in Rio, there are natural limestone caverns, high, cathedral-ceilinged rooms where the thieves and murderers of Brazil, most of them poor buggers on the lam, hide from the police. The entrances to these caves are constantly being changed; the entrances are always through the floors of the back rooms of certain shacks known only to the leaders of local gangs.

There must have been dark faces in the crowds who jostled me, who wanted me pushed in the direction I was being pushed, because, somehow, I found myself steered completely against my will into a certain hovel, where I could see nothing except candles burning like votive lights in red glass globes.

'Who's there?' I shouted out. There was no answer. There was only darkness and silence in front of me, and physical bodies whose faces I could not see were pushing me deeper and deeper into the darkness beyond.

And then, without warning, I found myself falling through the floor into what seemed to be utter nothingness. It was an underground space, a cavernous hall the size of an armory, where, at last, the real Carnival I had always dreamed about was taking place. Here, the revelers really were the heathens carousing in the dark. Here, stark nudity was commonplace, although most of the women had glued glitter onto their aureolas and wore belts of braided cellophane, or ropes of fake pearls, or fake costume jewelry around their undulating waists. The cavern smelled of marijuana and sex. Everywhere, the samba was frenetic, a driving jazz beat echoing hard rock, ten times angrier than its happy cousins in the streets above. The air was close here; close, breathless, and hot. Black bodies like mirrors gleamed in their own sweat. Copacabana and the sweet caress of the equatorial breeze seemed far, far away.

There it was again! The figure of Death, its luminescent, grinning skull mask, its macabre expression! Yes, it was true; deathly look-alikes, each one in a black body stocking, seemed to be everywhere in the streets above, like black cats on Halloween, but in the underground cavern with its rampant nudity, Death was unexpected and certainly uninvited. But why was he following *me*? What did *I* do? I was just a clothes designer from New York.

Unseen hands, speaking in a language I did not know, stripped me of every shred of clothing. There must have been some Americans there, because out of the darkness a voice with a Texas accent cried out, 'There she is, the Queen of Carnival!'

I do have to admit that, in that dark cavern, under the floodlights, I looked particularly ravishing. On a beach, under a bright sun, it is true that my breasts look round, fully packed; they are pink and golden; they seem as mouth-watering as ripe melons. They suggest juice; they cry out summer, they beg for the hands and mouth of a sexually starving man. But in the black shadows, under the glare of harsh white light, it is a different story; there I've got 'knockers'; spellbinding, unsubtle, absolutely obscene. Sometimes I wonder why I never became a professional stripper, but then again, like the Moslems say, 'If Mohammed will not come to the mountain, let the mountain come to Mohammed.'

In the artificial lights of night, my breasts seemed to hang in mid-air, suspended above black shadows that dramatically highlighted the contours of my perfect flesh. I'm not bragging; I was simply astounded at the sight of me. Apparently, I did not go unnoticed by others than myself.

I felt someone staring at me. A dark presence. Could it be Death? I could not see even the outline of the man, but his presence was undeniable; it followed me wherever I went; it invaded my bones.

Then, suddenly, he was face-to-face with me. I let out a gasp. It was Hugo Battista, my new-found Nordic Nubian, my blue-eyed Room Service, his sky-colored pools of light staring at me through the black night of his face.

He didn't have to say anything. He knew. I knew.

I lay back in the dark, and opened my legs to receive him. I knew he would find my cunt hole effortlessly. And so he did. I laughed with the joy of recognition, and cried out with relief. So, he was the dark shadow who had been pursuing me through Carnival, pushing me gently back into the black pit of the Underworld! He never closed his light-bearing eyes as his black column of phallic night connected me with his seemingly endless energy. We both knew there could be no relationship for us but sex, no language but shared body heat; we knew we must make love there and then in the cavern under Babilônia Hill.

There is no way, just by describing the dance of our sexual flesh, that I can communicate how full my heart was. I had fallen into night, and night had embraced me. I was no longer afraid of the dark. My orgasm was not hot waves this time; no, just heat rising up from my cunt, heat that warmed my loneliness, a loneliness the sweltering climate of the summer night had never touched.

Then, finally, Death intervened; more specifically, the figure of Death who had been following me.

He lunged onto Hugo at the very moment that Hugo, with furious intensity, had begun to ejaculate, at the very moment his carved, obsidian flesh had begun to quake in primal waves of orgasmic flow.

As his black phallus was wrenched out of me, a stream of phosphorescent sperm arced in the spangled dark like a rain of freshwater pearls. Hugo, more African than European, registered terror at the sight of the figure of Death. Then, a mounting rage came over him when he realized there was mortal flesh behind the mask. With a single wave of his massive arm, he knocked the figure of Death into a throng of naked revelers, tough-looking creatures of both sexes, guzzled, scarred, whoosing, sodden with too much

170

alcohol, stinking of tobacco and hashish. Their half-numbed, short-lived screams indentified where the victim had fallen. When he had been unmasked, I could hardly believe my eyes. It was Putzi Da Silva, his unconscious priestly face looking absolutely innocent.

'Putzi?' I whispered. 'Putzi?'

Hugo, terrified of Death, was even more afraid of a white man. He knew Putzi Da Silva, he knew him from the Rio Palace and all the other hotels, knew him from the many rooms with their many beds, many of which he had seen Putzi sleeping in with whatever woman he had met that night. Hugo disappeared, vanished. Black on black. We could not find him until six hours before our flight to New York.

Putzi revived. 'I love you, Diana. I've been following you all night.'

'You've been scaring me, Putzi,' I said.

'I'm sorry, Diana, I never do it right.'

'Putzi,' I said, 'it doesn't have to be this way.'

'I'm sorry, Diana.'

And then, the thing happened that made me leave Brazil and go back to New York, to Maxey and to Glorianna, and to whatever else was there, the thing that made me resolve never to be bored again.

It seemed like a scuffle at first. As I said, the cavern was filled with noise; it was, after all, the Carnival of the Damned. What was a scuffle compared to that? What was a minor cry in the night?

Well, a crowd had gathered. Putzi and I, holding hands, went to see for ourselves.

It was the figure of Mercury, a silver-painted woman with a dangling ostrich plume, the silver paint running thin through so much sweat and blood. It was Sylvia.

Her head had been practically severed from the rest of her; severed, not by a knife, but by animal bites – in truth, by the most deadly of animals. There were other bites on her once-perfect flesh. Her nipples were gone. Her cunt was half devoured. They were human bites.

The story was, Sylvia had pursued the wrong woman

all night, a woman from the Underworld, a 'gun moll' we would say, a woman with male companions. In the course of the evening, they all took too many drugs, especially Angel Dust. It was said this woman would never acknowledge publicly that she had once been in love with Sylvia. 'Go away, woman,' she said many times, but Sylvia, apparently, could not stop her pursuit. Then, all reason snapped. The pack of savages attacked with hands and teeth, driven by some primitive appetite, now awakened, for blood, for cunt, for anything soft and sweet and beautiful. Good-bye, my love.

Putzi, crazed with grief, cradled her in his arms and lifted her up, raging, bellowing; then, he disappeared into a bottom-less hole below Babilônia Hill. If he had had access to weapons that night, half the city would have died. It was a full year before Putzi Da Silva made a public appearance, and, when he did, he had aged beyond recognition.

'Take me home!' I screamed. 'Take me home!'

Hugo must have heard my cries. Or maybe not. Nonetheless, someone very black, anonymous, enveloped me, put his hands around my eyes, and, cradling me, his hand on my cunt, bore me through the shrill cacophony of that place to the street across from my hotel. I went straight to bed. It was early, but I fell asleep immediately, as I prayed to whatever god was listening to be good to Sylvia Da Silva. I had known her less than a day.

Chapter Ten

There's a chapter in this account I must keep separate and brief because of current controversy involving sexual relations between an adult and a minor. It is this chapter.

The boy who followed me my first day in the streets, the boy to whom I gave the card that said 'Wednesday' was named Remo. As I explained, I had figured if he cared about me, he'd find someone to translate the card. Well, needless to say, Remo found a translator, and Remo came Wednesday, in more ways than one.

I was half asleep in bed, my face sticky with the half-dried tears of grief for Sylvia Da Silva. Who knows what time it was? I wasn't in the mood to begin another day. When I heard a click, I paid no attention. After all, what is a click to a woman like me? It was minutes before I realized someone was in the room. How Remo got past the front door, how he obtained the key to my room, I'll never know. As with most of my Brazilian acquaintances during my first visit there, we had no common language but sex. Perhaps Remo's mother was a chambermaid, perhaps Hugo Battista was a distant relative. How tragic that I will never know the particulars of Remo's life; simple things like last name, religion, address, name of prep school, and, in later years, his business phone and address, presuming he got out of the ghetto, that is. He will.

That was my next point. Where there is no language between a man and a woman but the direct communication of stark naked flesh, the poetry can be blinding; in our case, embarrassingly so, because, when I gave the boy my card, I certainly did not mean 'Come and let's fuck.' I hope I didn't. Of course, according to *Psychology Today*, we are all possessed of multiple personalities. We are both sane and insane at the same time. I'm the last one who would know where to draw the line between conscious and unconscious; in this case, between boy and man. That's why I follow my feelings. I don't pretend to be an intellectual.

Without warning, he was under the covers, beside me in bed, smelling as clean as only a young man can smell, breathing on me with warm breath, nibbling my ear, whispering, 'Senhora, senhora'.

Do I have to belabor the point that I was still recovering from the tragedy of the night before? I don't want to sound overly melodramatic, or, God forbid, too serious, but I had definitely been traumatized. The image of Sylvia with her cunt literally eaten out would not go away. Just before Remo entered the room. I was contemplating taking drugs or even getting flat-out drunk, so I could return to a few minutes of what I call my 'Beavertown reality.' I guess, in some strange, providential way, Remo saved my life.

Why wouldn't I put my arms around a lonely boy of the streets, a lad who probably had never had a mother; otherwise, why would he be under the covers with me, seeking comfort and affection?

He certainly hadn't come to rob me; otherwise, he would have cleaned me out before I awoke. Well, I certainly wasn't involved in one of those middle-aged-woman-with-the-gigolo situations. I wasn't even middle-aged, and I certainly wasn't buying his favors. See, already, the guilt is creeping in, already the confusion as to what really happened. I can only give my version. I believe that, in some small way, I helped the cause of world peace, and aided Pan-American diplomatic relations. Above all, I probably reassured a frightened boy who probably didn't understand his emerging sexuality, although I can't say we discussed it, because I found Portuguese beyond my capacities.

'Don't be afraid,' I said, myself terrified at the thought of invading him psychosexually and eventually having to appear on *Donahue* or *The David Susskind Show* to admit *everything* to the American public.

Remo snuggled up against me with his skinny, golden limbs. 'What is that?' I thought to myself as I felt a sharp stick of some kind rubbing against my stomach. Then, as I stroked his buttocks, I realized he was completely naked, and he was also probably holding onto a banana, his only food for the day; whereas I, never hungry, for food, that is, had only to order room service for anything I wanted, including Hugo Battista. Having Hugo discover me in bed with a sixteen-year-old boy, however, was not my idea of fun. Then I realized, to my horror, that Remo might be holding a gun. The newspapers in Beavertown were invariably filled with horror stories about children with guns accidentally blasting their playmates' heads off. I could see it now; 'Sixteen-Year-Old Boy Accidentally Shoots and Kills Beavertown Native in Lovers' Nest In Rio De Janeiro!' I had flashes of my bloody body lying unclaimed in the Rio morgue, with a gaping hole in my middle. Most inattractive, to say the least.

We gazed into each other's eyes, Remo and I. His were almost yellow in his dark-honey face, startling to gaze into and possessed of a strangely familiar expression for a boy so young. It looked almost, well, sexual. I had nothing to worry about, though; he was certainly too immature to understand a woman like me.

Then, without warning, he took my hand, which felt so warm under the covers, and drew it down in the direction of his 'gun.' I thought, 'This is it,' and immediately began to fantasize about where I'd be when I was dead. I could not believe my next reaction; the child was holding a weapon fashioned out of human flesh. Oh my God, no, it couldn't be! It was his cock! How could he do that to me? He wasn't old enough to have an erection. He hadn't shaved yet. He seemed so innocent, yet, under the covers, he was making me jerk him off while he murmured, 'Diana, Diana.'

Despite what you may think, I am very straightforward. My first impulse, when I have sex with someone I've just met, is to think I should be properly married to him. Even in my occasional experiences with orgies, I am bothered by the fact I don't always know the name of the person I'm having sex with. My friends have counseled me that I'm entirely too sensitive, that my squeamishness is a reflection of my grandmother's religion. I guess they're correct, because, to be honest, the Tabernacle Witnesses barely approve of sex between married couples. I guess, like most people, I'll have to struggle through my life a little bit crippled, sexually speaking, that is.

So, having acknowledged my guilt in indulging a sixteen-year-old, I decided to do everything I could to prevent him from becoming permanently damaged by anything remotely suggesting disapproval by an older, more experienced woman. I felt I had an obligation toward the next generation, especially the next generation of men.

We kissed like starving animals. All of a sudden, the passion was there. Where did it come from? I, for one, will never know. I only know our lips were on fire, our tongues grappling, exploring with one another the soft, warm flesh inside our mouths. My hands were all over his body. I could not help myself; he was so untouched, without a single defect or sign of age. He was, moreover, rail-thin, most unusual in the athletic men I usually fu—date. I could feel the outline of his collarbone and ribs pressing against my own ripe, golden flesh. And, needless to say, I could feel his man's cock lying against me, rubbing into me, prodding me with its fat knob, looking for a way into me. Did the boy know about sexual intercourse? Was he a virgin? Would the dark beauties of the favela have already initiated him into the sacred mysteries of suck and fuck?

It seemed to me there was nothing to say. Now was the time for action.

I drew Remo over on top of me. He was sweating profusely now, but whether it was from nervousness or passion I could not tell. I stuck a pillow under the small of my back. I decided that the missionary position would be best for us. Yes, I would teach him everything he had to know.

That's when Remo took me by surprise. Without warning, his head was between my thighs, his lips hungrily eating me out. He knew exactly where to go. In fact, he acted like cunt was his favorite food, like he hadn't eaten in a week. He slurped on my bittersweet juices like a man in the desert dying of thirst. His tongue traveled up and down the length of my labia until I could have fucked a horse, I was that hot, and all the while he kept repeating, 'Diana, Diana.'

My fingers tangled in his curly, black hair; I lost control early on. My orgasms came mainly from the turn-on of me fucking a boy my family wouldn't have approved of.

'Diana, Diana.' He wouldn't stop. I wanted to tell Remo I felt like a goddess, someone carved out of alabaster in the Athenian sun, but that if he did not stop, I would be punished by a jealous Zeus. Remo, this boy, was worshipping me. I had done nothing to deserve his adoration except receive the homage of his mouth.

'Diana, Diana.' He was so dear, so sweet, he deserved my constant attention. 'Diana, Diana.' I could not withhold my release a second longer. The barriers between us came crashing down. He moved upwards to kiss me again and, with his cock, he plunged into my most vulnerable spot, the very seat of my sexual soul. My passion-swollen labia closed in on his red-hot rod with a savage, animal life all its own. The sucking sounds down there were so loud I was afraid we would be overheard; today, of all days, the streets were silent. It was Ash Wednesday, a day of penance, the beginning of Lent. The pious worshippers of Jesus the Crucified wore ashes on their foreheads. 'Remember, Man, thou art dust and unto dust thou shalt return.'

'Fuck Death!' I cried out loud, locking my ankles around Remo's back. It felt wonderful! I had finally taken a stand! I wanted the cocks of growing boys to give me new life. Yes, I had my summer show to do, and I would do it, despite the Communists, despite the Workers of the World. Yes, I was evil, I was obscene, I was Diana Adoro, capitalist and sow, the debaucher of boys. Tears came rolling down my face from the turmoil within my poor Beavertown heart. Surely, I had no right to be paid such glorious attention by Latin-American, well, men. Remo's kisses felt so good against my neck. His cock felt even better as it stabbed me into an orgasmic frenzy. I guess if it's true that the boy is the father of the man, Remo was the father of a superstud. He seemed to rotate his cock inside me as he thrust in and out, in and out, like a steel knife cleaving into soft butter. My juicy, inner lips met his violence with the most aggressive cunt-sucking of my life. Sometimes men move in and out of me, and I just like there as their cocks seem, at best, to stroke my vaginal walls. Sometimes, I am invaded by monstrous organs; I hold on to them with my cunt to avoid being completely overwhelmed; in some cases, my body takes over with its own autonomous laws, and I am dragged through orgasm like a swimmer in a hurricane sea.

But with Remo, it was the best of times. With him, I was a woman making choices, choosing freely to take his sexual organ between my thighs, choosing to rub it back and forth in my dense, silky bush, choosing to press it into my vaginal slit, choosing to press that plum glans, shiny and purple, into my sucking cunt hole, choosing to envelop his manhood with hot, juicy sexual flesh.

I was, so to speak, willing to give the boy his money's worth.

With every stroke, however, the boy became less of a boy and more of a man. The expression in his eyes seemed harder and more calculating than I had realized. This was, after all, a boy of the streets, a survivor-prisoner of the Third World. Desire, and desire alone, had brought him into my bed; it was the rock-hard hunger for sexual love that had made him risk being caught by hotel security as he stole the key to my room and my cunt, I mean my heart.

In my bed, Remo was a predator, all sinew and bone. His dark skin lent him an exotic cast; he seemed to embody the sheer force of naked will, and buried in that will was the suggestion of desire. He did not need to say, 'I love you,' or 'I want you.' His hunger was apparent just in the way he moved, in his manner of clutching me. The force of his mouth on mine went beyond shared pleasure. His lips had the vampire's touch. In his desperate attempt to drink my love, he could not help biting into my tongue and gums and the sides of my mouth. Occasionally he broke the skin, causing a wash of pink blood to trickle down his throat and mine, a state which only added to our sexual pitch. I felt like I was grappling with my murderer, a man-boy whose love could easily go too far; he was quick and lethal, like the best street fighter who could plunge a knife between your ribs just as soon as look at you. Remo was that way with his cock. Remo was that way with me.

I didn't want to come. Honestly, I didn't. I fought being intimate with him. I fought unveiling my soul to a youth who presumed too much. I fought coming to that moment of orgasm where my head would thrash involuntarily from one side to the other, and strange, uncontrollable sounds would issue from my mouth. Sometimes, too, my limbs would lose control. I would become spastic, and my brain would fall into a bedazzled night, just like the song says, 'With the

179

rockets' red glare/ The bombs bursting in air.' Ah yes, the dawn's early light. The whole thing seemed much too passionate to waste on a sixteen-year-old. But Remo rode me into the original orgasm of oblivion; yes, he rode me to victory, my Brazilian Napoleon. He never asked anything, made no demands, except to have his own way with me. His sperm gushed everywhere; spurts coated my vaginal canal, the mouth of my cunt, lubricating my outer lips; his white seed streaked across my bush like whipped cream from a dispenser run amuck. Remo shuddered visibly as his orgasm ran its course.

And then, he was still. We both were. I fell asleep with the boy in my arms, and my pussy warm as toast. Yes, I am fully aware that the reader of this account may lack sympathy for my sexual adventures, and judge me some kind of nymphomaniac, since I seem to have such an inexhaustible appetite for strange men and, occasionally, strange women who happen casually to pass in front of my open cunt. But the truth is, I just don't keep score. I live for the present moment. No matter how many men I may have accommodated on Copacabana Beach, when I awoke to find my dear little Remo snuggling beside me after the trauma of the night before, I realized I had awakened to a new life, replete with endless possibilities limited only by the slight soreness in my cunt.

Perhaps Remo was only a dream, or an interlude between the scenes of harsh reality which frequently punctuate my workaday world. Alas, he was all too real. When I awoke a second time, he was gone, and so, unfortunately, were all my jewelry, cash, traveler's checks, keys, and every stick of clothing I owned, including my fabulous collection of open-crotch panties, which I had designed myself. I was absolutely devastated. Then I reminded myself that he had left me physically unharmed, and I was, after all, still head of an international fashion empire. Remo, further-more, had been a great lover. My loss was a small price to pay for an hour with the world's most precocious teenager.

Postscript to Chapter Ten. Lulu kept most of our cash, etc., in the hotel safe. I didn't want to ruin a good story by telling the bottom-line truth. I figured I'd already revealed too much about myself and, for the moment, at least, wanted a little sympathy. Which leads me to my second point. In *Diana's Debut* I detailed the account of my five hours at Mrs. Boothby's whorehouse in Rome with 'Red,' a sexually precocious fourteen-year-old from a socially prominent and deeply religious Baptist family with connections in Louisville and Boston. I promised that when I told the story of my trip to Rio, I would tell the tale of my incredible night with the now fifteen-year-old Red and his industrialist father. I guess I mentioned something about incest or something. Red, in case you've forgotten, was the one, who, when he took off his glasses, and then when he took off his clothes, went through instant puberty. Anyway, my lawyers have advised me that no such person ever existed, so it would be pointless, my telling the story of how he and his father sandwich-fucked me, and then sixty-nined each other, because it never happened. I guess they're right. Besides, where would I have found the time?

Chapter Eleven

In the two days remaining before we left for New York, Lulu and I chased down the greatest bodies in Brazil for our summer wear show.

Hugo Battista, when we were finally able to locate him, agreed to come. And Tia Maria, too, our ebony goddess. For her, it was like signing a movie contract. There were thirteen others, all dark and sinewy and proud, sexual magnets even in Rio, and every one of them excited to be traveling north.

'Can Che come?' asked Lulu.

I wanted to say, 'Che who?' I couldn't believe she was actually asking me if I'd pay for an in-house Communist companion, but I'd been expecting it. 'That's up to you,' I said.

'He really should observe what we do,' insisted Lulu.

'Apparently, he already knows what you do,' I retorted.

'I don't mean in bed,' she replied.

'In bed?' I asked. 'Did someone say something about in bed? Besides, who does it in bed anymore? Are you two planning to give us a demonstration on the floor of the plane?'

Lulu's eyes were filled with tears. 'You know Hugo's the one I want-a. Why do you-a torture me?'

With that, I hugged my dear Lulu. My eyes were also filled with tears. I was thinking of Sylvia, that insanely passionate child I had loved so much. I had so wanted her to see my summer wear show.

Chapter Twelve

Like I said, New York in February has all the charm of a dead eel. Any New Yorker with any sense spends February sitting on a Caribbean beach playing with himself/herself or a new-found companion of either sex, anything to jolt the dead mid-winter brain into some semblance of life. Notice I'm talking about a hypothetical New Yorker. This has nothing to do with me. Wrong. When we flew over the Statue of Liberty, which looked as gray-green as ever, I knew I should have stayed in Brazil for at least another month.

Actually, I looked at Miss Liberty and said, 'Oh, Miss Liberty, why are you dressed in a toga; why can't you take off that cumbersome iron garment and let it sink to the bottom of New York Harbor where it belongs. The whole world is waiting to see your mammoth breasts and feast on the sight of your cunt.' I imagined a new 'immigrant elevator,' a glass tube ascending right up through her huge vulva into a giant sauna just about where her womb would be. There, the new arrivals to the Land of the Free would strip, be massaged by nubile maidens from all over the world, and finally be invited to join in an orgy, where 'the tired, the poor, the huddled masses yearning to breathe free' would suck and fuck themselves into Nirvana. Of course, I have been fantasizing. If I dared to speak these thoughts aloud, I would be sent to Bellevue for observation.

The air that day was like gray paint. I discovered I

had sinuses. I discovered I was capable of migraine. I discovered that a good vacation does not guarantee an easy homecoming.

Glorianna and Maxey were both at Kennedy to meet us. I'm afraid I had not properly forewarned them. I had simply wired, 'Am bringing some models from Rio for summer wear show.' Nobody was prepared for fifteen sex machines off the streets of the world's hottest city.

I didn't even notice them at first, I was so busy looking for the Portuguese-speaking aides Lulu had supposedly hired. I couldn't find Lulu, either, or, for that matter, Che Miranda, our 'labor-management observer,' some half-assed title Lulu had invented to cover the real reason he had come, which I guessed had something to do with his cock and its imperial destiny. He certainly wasn't talking to me, capitalistic sow that I was. In the meantime, the observation deck was jam-packed with well-dressed Latin Americans looking for relatives. I was frantic. My Brazilian entourage, about to disembark, was so sex-obsessed that I have carefully avoided going into details of our flight from Rio to New York. Even *I* draw the line somewhere. I knew it was going to be next to impossible to prevent our 'models' from following come-hither strangers home. I had about a minute left before my Carnival superstars walked off the plane to meet the flash bulbs of the Western World, when I heard a familiar voice.

'So, are you still bored?' The voice was low, gravelly, and full of sex. Moreover, it was German, which is redundant. Maxey, who else?

'Thank you, Maxey,' I replied, as sincerely as I knew how, nibbling the back of his neck. 'Without you, I would have stayed in New York imprisoned in my own neurosis; instead, I got a chance to celebrate the beginning of Lent.'

'Schotzie, you're the greatest,' Maxey exclaimed, trying to be both German and American at the same time.

Then I noticed Glorianna, his constantly constant companion, glaring at me through her practiced smile. I embraced her, too. My two best friends. My feelings were decidedly mixed. Maybe, down deep, I resented our three-ways. Maybe, down deep, I was desperately in love with one of them. The trouble was, I didn't know which one, and, for the moment, I didn't have the time to go into them, I mean 'it.'

Maxey, in true form, was wearing a sheared Persian lamb trenchcoat that probably cost the price of a small Pugeot, and Glorianna, who boasted of her 'simple Midwestern taste,' was wrapped in what looked like a white fox blanket complete with white satin turban. Given her height and partial Cherokee heritage, she stole the show on the airport observation deck. The real show, however, was simply not on the observation deck, and when the Best of Brazil began to disembark, I thought Glorianna's jaw would drop clean off her face. If she thought she had used the color white to its best advantage, she was sorely mistaken. Let me be more specific.

Those Afro-Latin gods were wearing condom-thin, white silk pants, practically see-through, with no underwear whatsoever, pants that were cut off at mid-calf and tied at the waist. Every time one of those specially chosen studs moved, his rump muscles rippled visibly under the silk, and his genital equipment seemed to lob up and down. I had had the men choose from an assortment of white silk shirts that Lulu had bought in Rio. Some chose white silk T-shirts, absolutely skin-tight over their massive pectorals and biceps. Others sported white silk tank tops rolled up in front to reveal hairy, muscular abdomens. Others preferred to wear white silk dress shirts, open at the neck, and then unbuttoned to the navel. As a gimmick, I had them wearing white zinc oxide, the sunscreen so popular at Copacabana and Ipanema, on their noses and chins. Considering how brown most of our studs were to begin with, either

185

from the sun or courtesy of Mother Nature, their white noses in February looked spectacular. don't ask me to explain; you should have been there. Let's just say we successfully trod the thin line between style and exhibitionism.

The women were something else. What I did was so daring, Glorianna practically had a stroke. I had Lulu buy a bolt of see-through silk gauze from which we whipped up sleeveless shifts. Then we sewed on sequins, different colors for different dresses; yellow, red, silver, gold, green, in the shape of birds and fish and flowers. We sewed the sequins onto the crotches to cover the genitals. Only the genitals. We wanted the breasts to peek through, which they did, magnificently; most Brazilian women, with their African bloodlines, can boast of nut-brown nipples and dusky auereolas even on the whitest breasts. As the see-through material was practically invisible, my beauties were practically nude from the waist up, and below the waist there were clearly patches of pubic hair.

We went farther than that. I bought them all white pocketbooks, white pillbox hats, and simple white pump shoes. Then I asked them to sew fragments of their Carnival costumes, especially bits of feathers, tinfoil, spangles, the gaudiest glitter imaginable, onto their prim' n' proper shoes, hats and pocketbooks. The contrast of opposites was sensational. Onlookers couldn't decide if these were Latin-American society women parading a new style of punk, or chorus girls who didn't know style from styrofoam.

Then, while photographers were snapping away, I realized with a start that I had completely forgotten about covering their asses! As my people walked off the 747 into Kennedy Airport, New York photographers got rear and side views of tits and asses that belonged in *Hustler* magazine. What had seemed so innocent in the heat of Rio, where half the people wore bikinis to go shopping, suddenly looked prurient here. I had forgotten that New York preferred its sex completely under control and behind locked doors. Even the most promiscuous businessmen who thought about sex more than they thought about food or taxes demanded that intercourse take place behind closed doors for X number of minutes and for X number of dollars. I say intercourse because that was how the city seemed to define sex. Even on the Broadway stage, which, by reputation, was interested in little else but tits and asses, except for flashes. of nudity intended to shock, body parts were well covered up. North America put its raw sex in the gutter, along with fortune tellers and mental patients. (Ha, ha, I'm just kidding.) The House of Adoro, above all, had a reputation for attracting an upper-class clientele. The very idea of a woman with bare breasts and ass having dinner at '21' with the President of the New York Stock Exchange was unheard of, and likely to remain so. Maxey was absolutely amazed. He didn't know what to think. He was, to say the least, intrigued.

'Diana,' he exclaimed, pressing against me with a noticeable bulge in his crotch, palpable right through the Persian lamb coat. 'Diana, you don't know how glad I am to see you.'

'Maxey,' I countered, 'before we start humping on the Long Island Expressway, please tell me what you think of these models. You know, Maxey, I tried very hard to ...' And then, I couldn't talk anymore. His hungry tongue was in my mouth, exploring crevices that no tongue but his ever gets to.

When he had taken his pleasure, he murmured, 'As usual, you're a genius. If they don't get arrested for indecent exposure, we're the only good news this town has seen for a week.'

Well, House of Adoro aides plus Portuguese-speaking interpreters had been hired to escort our revelers to a certain midtown Manhattan hotel which will have to remain nameless, to wine them and dine them, take them to clubs and to the theatre, to call us if anyone got arrested; but I will have to continue with

Carnival as it impacted on New York in the next chapter.

What happened next deserves immediate comment. The sexiest cop I ever saw tried to scare me and Maxey with some smart-ass comment like, 'Hey, we don't do stuff like that in New York,' meaning our kiss, I guess. I looked up at him to give him a piece of my mind. Our eyes met. We were both shocked at our immediate attraction to one another. Instead of a piece of my mind, now I just wanted to give him a piece of me. His face had high color, and the eyes in question were cornflower blue, the color of a summer sky. The hair was red, blonde, brown, and gray, all of it. The man's appearance bespoke the outdoor life. A certain weariness in his expression told the world that, yes, he had seen it all. Maxey noticed it, too. I noticed Maxey noticing. There was a visible flinch.

Competition loomed on the horizon. Glorianna Bronx, the Polish-Amerindian princess of love-hate, stood there so wrapped up in her white fox that she noticed nothing. She was too busy trying to attract Hugo Battista's attention. Hugo, typically, feigned nonchalance as his open fly, accidentally, of course, offered a good view of his phallic specimen to anyone, male or female, who happened to be checking out crotches. Glorianna was one of a new breed of New York females who checked crotches before they checked credit ratings and bank accounts. Unlike me, Glorianna was never interested in long-range romance. She was strictly a girl of the moment. But, before she had a chance to unbutton her fox blanket and reveal to Hugo the see-through lingerie she was wearing, a female taxicab driver from the other side of the street saw Hugo, made an illegal U-turn, jumped out of her cab, walked boldly over to Hugo, stuck her hand inside his open fly, took hold of his member, and whispered, 'How'd you like to take a ride with me?' Hugo, not understanding a word of English, got the message, followed his ardent admirer as a stud horse follows a trainer, particularly a female trainer who wants to be fucked by a horse.

So, to wrap up this anecdote, Glorianna, because of her passive seduction act with Hugo missed what was happening behind her, between me and one of New York's finest, Officer Myles Muldoon. Maxey had a curious reaction all his own. I had certainly never expected him to be the least bit interested in a cop. Usually, if our orgies involved other men, the men were strictly exotic – Russian dancers, Dominican busboys, Ukrainian cabinetmakers he picked up, as they say, selling ice cream in Central Park. Now, it goes without saying that Maxey was ninety-nine percent male, macho, and Prussian, not about to so much as look at a man he couldn't dominate, couldn't buy and sell ten times over. Consequently, I was more than a bit taken aback to hear Maxey invite Officer Myles Muldoon up to our penthouse 'for a late-night supper.'

Muldoon accepted, crinkling his sky-blue eyes as he smiled, revealing a sexy gap-toothed smile. 'Sure,' he said.

That's when Glorianna turned around. There was something in Muldoon's voice, a come-hither resonance that caught her ear. When she saw the way he looked, I thought she was going to drop her fox. And Officer Muldoon, who, I hoped against hope, would become my hot, new romance, as I was now ready for a real relationship, seemed to be very turned on by my top model.

His opening remark to Glorianna was telling. 'Hey, babe, whatcha hiding under that polar bear?'

Glorianna, the dumb cunt, did her frost-covered come-on. 'Excuse me,' she said, arching an eyebrow, 'did you say something, Officer?'

Officer Muldoon was thereby given notice that, if he wanted her, he'd have to forcibly strip her and drag her to his bed as she screamed 'Rape!' and struggled to dial 911, Emergency Hot Line. Only when he had about three inches of hot cock wedged into her streaming pussy, would she, presuming she'd had a stiff drink, moan, 'Oh, baby, baby, I've been waiting so long.'

Muldoon seemed to enjoy the challenge. Thank God, there are still a few he-men left to penetrate the pathetic disguise of a phony cock-tease like Glorianna Bronx. He took her by her fur-covered elbow, turned back to Maxey, and asked, 'Can the polar bear come with us?'

Maxey, world-weary as he was, sensed an interesting evening. 'She is us!' he answered. 'Bring her! Drag her, if you have to!'

Ten minutes later, the four of us were piled into one of New York's roomy Checker cabs. As I studied his all-American outdoorsman face, Muldoon seemed even handsomer than I had dared imagine. His tough-guy front, which intrigued us all, never changed. He was completely masculine, a rarity in the New York business world, where the most successful men need to cultivate feminine traits, especially instinct and sensitivity to the feelings of the potential buyer, if they plan to survive and prosper. His hands were sinewy, the hard muscles of his fingers roped with thick veins. His Adam's apple stood out in sharp relief to his strong, sculptured neck.

Maxey, that day, seemed pale by comparison. He also seemed every day of fifty-six. Clearly, he was on unfamiliar ground. Glorianna was studying Muldoon like a hawk stalking its prey.

Finally, our honored guest, Himself, spoke. 'What are you having to eat at this late-night supper of yours?' he asked Miss G.

'Warm pussy and hot pork prod,' she answered, without skipping a beat.

'How does that strike you?' asked Maxey, probably hoping that our Irish stud would jump out of the cab at the next stop light and run for his life from the crazies who had picked him up.

'I'll tell you,' answered Muldoon, rubbing one hand up Glorianna's leg, and with the other hand kneading the inside of Maxey's thigh, 'I'll take whatever I can get.'

'If you can get it!' retorted Maxey, not very convincingly. Maxey, who could have easily been a four-star general, was clearly under the spell of Officer Muldoon. We all were.

The rest of the taxi ride was five minutes of unbearable sexual tension, as each of the four of us pretended we couldn't care less about the 'late-night supper' that was to come.

New York was its usual mid-winter self; gray buildings and formal brownstones fronting untold, unseen passions. The east Sixties, where the House of Adoro maintained its world headquarters, seemed almost British upper-class with its row of four gray townhouses, their brass carriage lights gleaming, their small front yards of gray-green English ivy appropriately fenced in by black wrought-iron railings.

Maxey pumped me about Brazil and the Da Silvas. I wanted to forget Brazil for the time being. I didn't even want to go through with my summer wear show, but I never let on. I was heartsick about Sylvia. I had tried to offer her a certain amount of human affection, but apparently it wasn't enough. Or maybe she was ahead of her time. Maybe, in another hundred years, there would be 'affection machines' where women like Sylvia could be plugged in, for several hours a day if necessary, to artificial cocks and cunts and hands with perfect body temperatures, skin surfaces, heartbeats and calm, soothing voices, who would make love to them for hours at a time until they felt calmed down and at peace.

Yes, of course, I informed Maxey that I had been questioned by the Brazilian police, but, in truth, what did I know? They combed Babilônia Hill for days looking for clues to what was, in the end, a mystery at the heart of the world, namely death. Please! My imagination was making me depressed. Stop already. Turn yourself around, Diana Adoro. Life is now!

Even though I had left New York in a state of almost catatonic boredom, unsatisfied with Maxey von Fuchs, one of the all-time studs, Carnival had roused me from my stupor. I was back to my old self, wasn't I? I had no time for negative thinking, even negative memories, isn't that right? I was determined to attack New York with zest and enthusiasm and all my old naive childlike wonder; everything was perfect. The English ivy looked great. The wrought-iron fence never looked more wrought. I mean, more black. Look, let's get something straight right now, I take life as it comes, and right at this moment, Officer Muldoon was my best bet. The Brazilians were tucked away for the night, I hope, and nothing looked better than a great American cop, who happened to have my hand in his crotch as we pulled up to the House of Adoro. That crotch was either begging for attention, or he had a couple of grenades stuffed down his pants. I decided to hedge my bets.

The cabdriver, a little runt of a fellow with an appropriate gray face and big bulging eyes, had overheard Glorianna's remark about warm pussy and hot pork prod. He wanted to come, too, in more ways than one.

'I'm really great in bed,' he whispered to Maxey.

'I'm sure you are,' said Maxey, overtipping him by at least ten dollars to make up for the poor man's loss of face, 'but, unfortunately, we are very kinky here.'

'Kinky?' The self-proclaimed Lothario suddenly developed a slight nervous twitch.

'Yes,' continued Maxey with his customary aplomb, 'you see, these people are my two sisters and my brother.'

The driver's face understandably fell, but he did not look desperate. After all, he was ten bucks richer. My Max, always so considerate, had figured out a way to salvage the poor man's dignity, and save us from what was, at root, a case of sexual greed.

Upstairs, Maxey had an exciting surprise for me.

While I was cavorting at Carnival, he had completely redecorated my private quarters! What a change! What had been rosewood and mahogany and cherry with polished brass sconce lights and red damask draperies was now the most unusual decor in Manhattan. The walls were panels of shining ebony, the blackest wood imaginable, with flat strips of sterling silver covering the seams. Who would have dared decorate an apartment suite in black and silver but my Prussian prince? The floor, formerly dressed with oriental rugs, was now wall-to-wall bone-white carpeting of the finest virgin wool (the only virgin in town at this point). Everything else, and I mean *everything*, was *red*. I kid you not. All the furniture, the double canopied bed, the end tables, had been lacquered in Chinese red, that special orange-red, that hard-surfaced, gleaming red that seems a little bit like blood, a little bit like the sun. The armchairs and sofas had been reupholstered in red silk, each one a slightly different shade; melon, peach, coral, some almost lavender, some almost orange.

The silk draperies were a private joke between Maxey and me. They were the exact color of my labia, a personal touch that absolutely delighted me. The emotional effect of the hot labia color against the black-ass, ebony walls was strikingly sexual in a completely different way than the mahogany had been. Before, any man who visited my quarters might have felt swallowed up in a sea of rosy hues, but now, somehow, against the pink and black and silver, human figures seemed more prominent, and, for that reason alone, the room seemed more sexual. Looking at it, I could not wait to begin a new, more sophisticated phase of my life.

Officer Muldoon didn't say a word. He walked around with his brawny arms folded, surveying my strange and splendid court. He kept a superior little smirk on his face; he was evidently amused.

Glorianna, who had not seen the redecorated rooms,

kept posing against the black ebony walls. She was, by design, a figure out of a thirties movie, but her affectations had precious little to do with the odor of cunt musk and the smells of masculine arousal that pervaded my private suite. No matter. Maxey knew how to deal with Glorianna's spaced-out fantasies. First, he bolted the doors shut; then, he adjusted the lighting; we were instantly bathed in pools of soft, filtered light. What would happen next?

Maxey, ever the commanding officer, made a short speech that informed us that dinner would arrive later by dumb-waiter; the downstairs staff had been put on overtime. Then, without missing a beat, with his right hand he reached out and pulled Glorianna's white fox wrap off her, exposing her sexy underwear, and causing a noticeable bulge in Officer Muldoon's crotch. Noticeable to me, anyway. Then, Maxey shouted, 'Okay, campers, let's get washed up! No dirty hands for dinner!' Immediately, he began stripping off his pin-stripe business suit, black patent-leather pumps, knee-high socks and BVD's.

Glorianna sulked. 'Oh God, Maxey, do I have to wash my hands?' Reluctantly, like a bad little girl, she pulled down her white lace bikini panties. Her inverted-V snatch was as black and shiny as a fat, healthy beaver pelt. And, when she unloosed her see-through, white lace bra and let it drop to the floor, her tits took my breath away. Glorianna is one of those tall, model-types you'd expect would be flat-chested. Her pendulous, pear-shaped mounds of cream cheese breasts, with big, dark, chocolate aureolas, are the original food of love, delicious to contemplate sucking on.

Muldoon's jaw dropped. His tongue hung out. He uttered one word, 'Jesus!'

Maxey, starkers, with the body of a middle-aged Nordic god, a far more attractive man with his clothes off, was disappearing into my bathroom, where the sounds of the shower started almost immediately.

Muldoon, eyes glued on Glorianna's crotch, was slipping out of his policeman's duds.

'Muldoon,' I said, 'please put the gun away.'

He nodded. The gun landed on top of my bookcase. At this point, mind you, I was well aware of Muldoon's fix on Glorianna. I just wasn't sure how I really felt; I wasn't sure if I wanted to fight for him. Any man who preferred Glorianna to me can't be all good, I decided. But when Muldoon had completely wrestled out of his clothes, I took one look at him, and was ready to fight. He had the face of a cowboy with the body of a professional fullback, huge chest muscles covered with a fine auburn fur, a straight line of dark red hair on his stomach, connecting his bush with the abundant hair on his chest. His splendid cock was long and thick, with a big, purplish glans. It hung down on top of a sack of oversized testicles, which swung between his legs. But mostly, it was Muldoon's easy way about his physique that made me want to compete for him. So I did, in the only way I knew how. Just as he reached out to touch Glorianna's nipple, I peeled my clothes off, leaving them in a heap at my feet. Then, I headed for the shower.

At the doorway to my bathroom, I turned around and smiled at Muldoon over my shoulder, knowing full well that the sight of me nude had instantaneously divided his attention. In about ten seconds, his cock attained a full erection. Glorianna, as could be expected, grabbed it and started to pull him toward her. Unfortunately for her, few men can resist a dairymaid like me, round and fully packed, with handfuls of ripe tit and more than the suggestion of a mouthful of sweet pussy. Needless to say, 'washing up for dinner' promised to be an interesting ritual as we all piled into the shower.

A brief word on my bathroom, which Maxey had also redecorated. White tile and pink wallpaper had given way to chrome and mirrored surfaces, all specially treated not to steam up. Once in the roomy shower, all hell broke loose. There was no shame, absolutely no sense of decorum, and certainly no asking of permission. Officer Muldoon became my obsession, and I, his. In a sense, we first met in the shower. As much as Maxey has always remained my favorite fuck and a dear friend, in that moment – I don't know, he seemed, well, too available or something. Besides, I had real problems to contend with. Muldoon had one finger up Glorianna's cunt and one up mine. He clearly had not made his mind up. As much as I wanted to run my lips around his massive chest and shoulders, I decided to get to his manhood before Glorianna (or Maxey) got there first. The knob on the end of his cock was as big as a baby's fist, and as red as an apple. I decided that now was the time. I sank to my knees in sexual adoration, grasped his cock with both hands and ran my tongue around the rim of his glans. Maxey, for once, lost his single-minded, Prussian sense of authority. he had one hand on my tit and one on Muldoon's arse. Glorianna, for her part, kept running the policeman's head between her boobs, while she fucked the knobby end of his shoulder, her cunt lips sucking his hard muscle like a voracious, predatory fish.

As I drew his hot tool back and forth into the warm-flesh cavern of my mouth, Muldoon started incanting, 'Yes! Yes! Yes!' but, as so often happens, when orgasm is imminent, fate intervened. Maxey had forgotten to install non-skid pads on the bottom of my shower. In a cloud of steam and vapor, the four of us tumbled into a writhing mass of bodies, pieces of erotic flesh, genitals unconnected to personality. In a flash, Western Civilization had given way to a more primitive state, and a more basic need – the need to be one. It seems that Glorianna, Maxey, and I were all madly in love with Officer Muldoon, which is saying something, since Maxey isn't remotely gay.

Muldoon, for his part, wanted all of us. He especially wanted me. He had both hands on my head, and he drew me down on his humongous erection, crying, 'Diana, Diana, please come down on me, please come down, oh, thank you, thank you, I love you, I love you.'

Maxey, for his part, could not contain himself. He buried his face in my cunt, his tongue exploring my inner muscles, his lips sucking my labia. Like a starving man, he crammed as much of my fuckflesh into his mouth as he could manage, while Glorianna jerked him off with both hands. Then, as if some fairy godmother (or some fairy, anyway) had waved the proverbial magic wand, Maxey was on top of Officer Muldoon, planting deep kisses on the man's mouth, fondling his head like a mother strokes a weary child. This burst of homo-erotic love on the part of a great womanizer seemed to give Glorianna permission to start sucking the back of my neck. She reached around and, with her elegant artist's hands, began to squeeze my hardened nipples, causing excruciating pleasure to course through my body; then, since no one else was aggressively interested in her offerings, she began to fondle my cunt, finger-fucking me as mini-orgasms moved in waves outward from the center of my body.

I knew then that Officer Muldoon and I would have to meet later, we would never find love at an orgy. But, for the moment, there were terrible complications, to say the least. With Maxey's tongue buried in my cunt, and Muldoon's cock stuffed inside my mouth, I should have been the happiest girl in the world. Especially since the orgasm I was experiencing kept erupting in shock waves like a world-class volcano. A lava flow of pleasure streamed through the nerve endings of my body, threatening to suffocate me in ecstasy. I tingled. I glowed, but it was misleading. My body was simply betraying me. As far as I was concerned, there were only two magnetic poles in that chrome-plated shower stall, me and Officer Muldoon. I wanted Muldoon. Muldoon wanted me. Glorianna and Maxey, consequently, presented definite complications with respect to etiquette, protocol, and a basic good manners. The question was how to get rid of them. It was my impression that I had acted fairly and diplomatically in 'going along for the ride,' but the time had come to order my life. But first, I wanted to make sure Muldoon knew how deeply I cared. Using a soapy lather, I increased my hand movements up and down his barber pole, intensifying my pressure, especially around the base of the penis. I rubbed the edge of his overswollen glans against the corrugated ridge on my upper palate, causing him to cry out, 'Yes, baby, yes!'

It was just great. All my years of learning the true art of sex had finally begun to pay off. Finally, I knew what I was doing, and I was doing it with a man I deeply cared about. The blood flow in his organ doubled; the penis swelled up like a python that's just swallowed a pig. When he came, his sperm burst into my hungry mouth in soft, sticky globules. White cream ran down the sides of my mouth and down the back of my throat. It was absolutely delicious. Despite the fact that Maxey's tongue was still flickering away on the tip of my pleasure bud, and Glorianna was slobbering kisses on my back, I felt completely at one with my new-found love. In the most unlikely place we had found one another.

He lay on his back under the tropical rainfall of a steamy shower murmuring 'Yes, yes,' as I licked the last drops of come off his cock, wondering how I could bid my Prussian general and my Polish-Cherokee prima donna good night. The two of them were now in each other's arms by default, haphazardly fucking, missionary-style, as if to relieve themselves of genital anxiety.

Officer Muldoon and I were now face-to-face on the floor of the shower stall staring into each other's eyes. 'I found you, babe,' he whispered, grinning, stroking my back with strong hands, bringing his knee up between my thighs all the way to my cunt, so I could rub against him, half-rotating on the bony protuberance. Every angle of this man was sexy to me.

Every hump. Every knob. (Which is why what happened between us before the end of this account is all the more tragic and devastating; I was truly in love for the first time since my beloved Adolfo died.) I pressed against him as hard as I could, trying to get closer, trying to blot out the other two bodies on that white-tiled floor.

I had no choice. If I wanted Officer Muldoon, I decided that, at the risk of injuring my career, I would ask the House of Adoro's financial advisor and my top model to vacate the premises as soon as possible. Having made my decision, I stood up and turned off the shower, just as Maxey and Glorianna shuddered in mutual orgasm. Then, I took Officer Muldoon by the hand and pulled him up to me and kissed him, then led him to the dressing area between the bedroom and bath where I kept piles of fluffy, white turkish towels. We dried each other off, ritually kissing each other's arms and shoulders and necks slowly, deliberately, ravenously.

'Hey, babe,' he kept murmuring in his own understated way.

It was at this moment that I realized that Officer Muldoon was the first real man I'd ever met. He would have fit right in in Beavertown. He wasn't like the New York studs, the Roman gigolos, the Rio macho men. He had a big cock, but he was no porn star. He kept his body taut and lean and muscular, but he certainly was no candidate for Mr. Universe. His face was tanned and lined with sun creases, but he didn't look like a matinee idol. He had a sense of his own limited authority, and a limited sense of what he expected from me, which was sex and only sex. As it turned out, Muldoon had never heard of the House of Adoro; my six-figure income meant little to him; my sumptuous living quarters hardly attracted his attention. He would have been happy in a cold-water flat in the South Bronx, he said, if I were there, too.

I told him that, if worse came to worst, I'd prefer a

mobile home in a trailer park outside of Pittsburgh; he said if that happened, he'd follow me to Pittsburgh, provided he could get a job on the force. The man was a real American, and when I was with him I felt like one, too. Just plain folks.

Well, yes, it was true, as I found out, that once, for five years, he had been married to an automobile heiress, and had lived in Palm Beach in a pink marble Renaissance palace, and had attempted to write a detective novel based in Harlem, but that his wife, who had a thing for working-class men, started carrying on with the pool repairman. Officer Muldoon told me if there's one thing he hated, it was a slut. When I inquired about his marriage, and presumably his divorce, he said that, no, there had been no divorce, he was a widower. It seems that his wife and the pool repairman had gone out fishing on her sailboat. Since neither one of them knew how to sail, they depended on an outboard motor. Well, the motor must have failed, and the shortwave radio must have been broken, too. There might have even been an unforseen leak in the boat. In any case, neither one of them was ever seen again. Muldoon claimed the whole episode had devastated him, and he didn't want to talk about it. As it turned out, his wife had reached the bottom of her bank account; Officer Muldoon inherited nothing.

The pink palazzo was sold for taxes. Whatever was left, according to her will, went to her cats, about thirty, all told. Like he said, he hated sluts. It was the only negative aspect of his character, and, once he had said it, I resolved to put it out of my mind.

By now, Officer Muldoon and I had wrapped ourselves in bath towels. He was kissing my neck, and the inside of my elbows, and nuzzling me with the stubble of his five o'clock shadow.

'Officer Muldoon,' I said. 'Please, there's too much confusion here. You've got to help me get rid of Maxey and Glorianna.'

200

'Sure,' said Muldoon.

With that, he marched into the bathroom, flicked on the lights, and announced that the party was over, it was time to go home.

Maxey was furious. 'What!' he screamed in an unnaturally high octave. 'Nobody has eaten dinner!'

'Maxey,' I said, trying to appear calm, 'take Glorianna to a good restaurant, and charge it to me.'

'Out?' he screamed. 'We have not seen you for three weeks and you are throwing me out!'

'Maxey,' I stammered, 'you take too much for granted.'

'Too much? Too much?' he shouted. 'What is too much?'

'My cunt!' I yelled. 'My cunt can only take so much!' I really didn't know what I was saying. Maxey had always been my Nordic god, my savior, my protector. Even Glorianna and I, when strange circumstances had brought us together in a Roman whorehouse in *Diana's Debut*, had found a way to break through our mutual hostility. She had a spectacular coral gash between her legs that I feasted on; I savored her banquet of raw fish meat. I bathed in the glow she created so effortlessly when she was willing to let down her natural barriers. For the moment, however, I prayed for her instant demise.

Maxey looked ridiculous. He was soaking wet, furious, and sputtering. Glorianna looked like a drowned rat. I didn't care. It was time to put some order in my life: 'Here,' I said, handing them their clothes. 'Use our guest suite at the end of the hall. I'll see you both tomorrow.'

Maxey was not about to be appeased. 'Presuming I'm still with the House of Adoro tomorrow!' he shouted.

'Me, too,' echoed Glorianna, drying herself off.

'Without me, you'd be nobody,' sputtered Maxey.

'Whatever you say,' I answered, adding, 'I'm sick of orgies, I'm sick of sharing my cunt with two and three people at once; I'm sick of promiscuity!'

201

My protest was, of course, all a contrived lie. I just wanted to be alone with Officer Muldoon, who, to make things worse, turned to Maxey and said, 'I think you better do what the lady says.' The line was out of a bad Western.

'The lady? The lady?' bellowed Maxey. 'She is now a lady?'

Muldoon refused to give an inch. 'Did you hear what I said?' he proclaimed.

Glorianna, always a sweetheart, continued to stare at him with hunger in her black eyes. Sex in the shower stall, and a volcanic orgasm had not been nearly enough. His finger in her cunt had not been enough. Her soapy hands on his engorged erection had not been enough. She wanted the man to become infatuated with her, to desire her and her alone. Unfortunately for Glorianna, I wanted the same thing. And I always get what I want. If one year of power and wealth had taught me anything, it was that I wanted more power and wealth, and at any cost. But I never thought I'd ever have to fight for sex. There were few men who did not prefer me to other women, if for no other reason than I asked nothing of them but the warmth of their bodies.

Officer Muldoon proved to be the single obsession of my life. And my single mistake. In my short, tragic time with him, I discovered one overriding truth: never, never, never must anyone be obsessed with anyone else. Try to hold on to a man, and it's like trying to hold a river in the palm of your hand. You can ride the river, but if you build a dam to hold it in, one day that dam will burst; or worse, once the dam is built, the river will cease to exist; instead, there will be a lake, a lake without the torrent, the force, the momentum of the original attraction. Translated into human terms, a rushing river is a phallic force; a lake is a woman. What can a woman who is attracted to men do with a man she has tamed? What's the point of it?

I sound so worldly-wise now. The truth is, the day I

met Officer Muldoon, I was an emotional child. I knew nothing about obsession and its dire effects; already, my all-consuming hunger for him had caused me to fuck up a perfectly decent orgy. I had insulted Maxey, a man with whom I truly loved to have sex; I had come down hard on one of New York's resident goddesses, my bitch queen, Glorianna Bronx. Something terrible was happening to me, and I was too inexperienced to realize the dangers of my mental state.

Ten minutes later, my will had prevailed. Officer Muldoon and I were alone on my bed which Maxey had had made up with black silk sheets and a silver satin, fitted bedspread. In short, we climbed under the black silk sheets and proceeded to devour the dinner we had rescued from the dumbwaiter; champagne and raw Chinoteague oysters, a gallon of them, followed by poached chicken breasts, spring vegetables *al dente*, and, finally, chocolate mousse. We gorged on the mousse, enough for ten.

'Officer Muldoon,' I said, wiping smears of chocolate from around my mouth, 'do you have another name?'

'My first name is Myles,' he answered with a sly smile, 'but my friends just call me "Cop." '

'I'd prefer "Cock" myself,' I said, 'it sounds a little bit harder.'

'Listen, Pussy,' he announced, placing my hand on the eight-inch-length of steel between his legs, 'don't you think I'm hard enough for the two of us? Oh, Pussy,' he pleaded, 'I've never met anyone like you. You're so successful, yet you're as down to earth as any stewardess or waitress.'

'I used to be a waitress,' I answered, 'would you like me to wait on you?'

'Would you?' he said. 'I'd love to order. How about a nice piece of ass?'

'And as far as stewardesses go,' I said, pretending not to hear his tasteless remark, 'fly me.'

There. It was out. I discovered I was tasteless, too. So, there we were, two lousy swells, on black silk sheets in some strange, overdecorated bedroom. All I wanted was for the two of us to be back in Beavertown with no-style furniture from Sears and the stack of unpaid bills, the leftover chili in the icebox, my 'Cop' on the local force, and me a part-time waitress, with the fashion industry just something that popped up on *The Merv Griffin Show* once every three months. In that moment, I thought, 'To hell with Women's Lib and Equal Rights and Sigmund Freud and the Jet Set. All I want is to be safe in my policeman's arms with the door bolted and his big cock home where it belongs, in my hot, steaming pussy.'

For the next hour, I successfully blotted out Maxey, Glorianna, Brazil, and the international fashion empire I had inherited. I forgot about my week in Mrs. Boothby's and the time every available man and woman in a particular African tribe took pleasure with me. You see, where I grew up, nice girls normally didn't fuck three hundred men by the time they were twenty-three. There were names for girls like me.

Where am I? Oh, yes. Officer Muldoon and Beavertown. I wanted to be with him in Beavertown. I wanted the ordinary life that would never be mine.

'Pussy,' he began, 'I know I don't talk much, but I was thinking that maybe I could retire, and you could sell your business, and maybe we'd have enough money to move to a trailer park in Florida, and spend the rest of our lives fucking all day long, ha, ha. I'm just kidding.'

'What makes me so different, Cop?' I asked, testing him.

Then, he grew serious and his blue eyes narrowed, as he took my hand and stroked his balls with it. 'When I first saw you, Pussy,' he began, 'I thought you were just another blonde. You see, my normal appetite is for tall, dark, exotic types like that model Glorianna – that is, until I saw you with your clothes off. Honey, I'm thirty-eight, and I never saw a body like yours anywhere. When I first saw your cunt, you had just

204

turned around and bent over to take off your shoes. It was like a shock wave hitting me. Pussy, I mean, you should never have taken your shoes off. You've changed the direction of my life. Jesus, Pussy, it's like coming home.'

'What are you telling me?' I said. 'That I remind you of your mother?'

'No, no, hell, my home's not where my mother is, my home's where I am, except, since my wife's death, I don't know where I've been or who I am. Your bush is pure spun gold, Pussy,' he continued, 'and that cunt of yours, I'll never be able to get enough of it.'

For a man who had been silent all night, my Cop, or 'Coppo' as I decided to call him, sure turned out to be a gabber, but I figured that as long as the subject was me and my cunt, I'd listen to whatever he had to say.

Then he shut up and made love to me the way a tough New York cop should. He just got on top of me, pushed my legs apart, and stuck his stout rod straight into me, cleaving my cunt lips like a butcher knife, cutting through raw filet of beef. Needless to say, the man's mere presence made me lubricate. I was hot. He pulled my legs up over his shoulders. I locked my feet around his neck. We stuck a pillow under my ass and got down to the business of a good, solid, middle-class fuck, something I'd been missing. There were to be no 'golden showers' with Officer Muldoon. No sado-masochism. No tying me to the bed and whipping me. What turned me on about this guy was that he treated me like a regular middle-class broad. He acted like I was the one he needed to service his need for sexual release. If I hadn't been available, he would have found somebody else.

That's what I liked about him. There was no big romance, no discussion of 'the relationship,' no trying to dominate me, but, let's face it, where regular, down-to-earth intercourse is concerned, the guy is in the driver's seat, so he better be the one to drive, right? Well, to put it mildly, Coppo drove. At first, slowly, then he increased his speed, cradling my ass in his hands. He seemed to be steering me. I felt the force of him. I rubbed his forearms furiously. I hit him. I couldn't get away from him. He had an overpowering will. He just kept ramming into me. I felt trapped. I felt suffocated. I felt like I was close to the edge of darkness.

I normally liked to maintain a sense of control, at least for myself, but he did not let up. I could not stop him. 'No! No!' I cried. 'No! No! Stay away from me! You're getting too close!' I clung to him, digging my nails into the sides of his biceps. He did not stop, until finally I gave in. I let him crash into the black space I had kept all to myself. He just kept coming. I felt the black space grow larger and larger, spreading outward from my crotch until my whole body was drowning in the blackness, until, finally, my brain was drowned in it. There was nothing but darkness and the pounding of his cock, until everything exploded. Fireworks. Just like they say. Spangled lights in the nighttime sky. In a word, Officer Muldoon, my Coppo, definitely of the 'Slam Bam, Thank You, Ma'am' School of Fucking, was absolutely great in bed.

Yet, something else was also true. The man had eyes of blue ice. There was a mystery about him I could not understand. To a certain extent, he was beyond me. But, if he felt the same way about me, it did not seem to bother him.

Chapter Thirteen

Three days later, Coppo Muldoon and I got married at City Hall. He wore his uniform, complete with service revolver. He looked smashing. There is nothing like a man in uniform in a society that's falling to pieces. I wore my white turban with diamond stud earrings, a white satin blouse with leg-of-mutton sleeves, and white satin pantaloons with a chain of diamonds for a belt. That, and white, glove-leather boots. I carried a bouquet of one red rose. There was more. I had a surprise for my groom. I had left the crotch of my pantaloons with an open slit. No zipper. No buttons. Open. It was meant to be a surprise at the ceremony.

After the clerk said, 'I now pronounce you man and wife,' and then, with a wink at Coppo, said 'Sergeant, you may now kiss the bride,' I whispered to Coppo, 'While you kiss me, give me your hand.'

Well, I guided him right to my muff. Coppo couldn't believe what was happening. 'Hey, Diana, what are you doing? I can't fuck you on the fucking floor of City Hall!'

'I just wanted you to have something special,' I said.

'Diana, you don't understand, putting my hand on your muff is like lighting a forest fire. Quick, stand in front of me, I've got an erection!'

'So, who hasn't seen an erection?' I said. 'Most men would be proud to have an erection like yours.'

So, that's the story of how Coppo Muldoon and I left City Hall, me with no underwear, and he with a bulging crotch. It's how every marriage should start.

We had decided to postpone our honeymoon to Tahiti until after my fashion show. For the moment, we rented a suite at the Helmsley Palace, a new hotel on Madison Avenue. Very luxurious. Well, I'm afraid we consummated the marriage in the taxicab. Once we sat down, Coppo couldn't keep his hand out of my open crotch. And I didn't have the heart to stop him. I could feel his big, meaty Irish hand feeling me up, stroking the underside of my thighs, his strong thumb running under my pubic bone, driving me to squeals of arousal. The driver kept his sight fixed on the traffic, which, unfortunately, did not prevent Coppo from sliding open the glass partition, brandishing his service revolver in front of the driver's nose, and threatening to shoot him in the face if he turned around during the next ten minutes.

By now, Coppo's thumb, wet with my vaginal juices, was flicking my clitoris. I just couldn't stop what happened next. I lay back on the seat and spread open my legs, keeping his hand pressed down firmly on top of my cunt, squeezing my warm fuckflesh around his fingers as they hungrily explored me. With his left hand and my right hand, we managed to unbuckle his belt and unzip his trousers. His enlarged cock was strangling in a pair of jockey shorts. His glans was trapped, the top of the cock bent around it was neither in nor out. We managed to extricate his glans by pulling his jockey shorts around the top of it. Finally, thanks be to God, his jockey shorts were down around his thighs, his cock arced out in front of him, long and thick, with his sack of balls swinging freely between his legs. I grabbed his balls with one hand, to squeeze them and stroke them and fondle them, knowing this gesture of appreciation aroused him. With my other hand, I guided him through the slit in my satin pantaloons, gliding the shimmering satin against his cock as he entered me, causing him excruciating pleasure.

208

I must say that all my wedding day sexual encounters have been magic, no matter how many men I've made love to, no matter how many times I have 'known' my new husband before the wedding. When I put on my new dress, or, in this case, pantaloons, and stand before the City Clerk or the Justice of the Peace, God's representatives on earth, I feel clean all over. I feel virginal again. Don't ask me to explain. I can't. I just know that getting married is the best way to start all over again. A clean slate. A new life.

Coppo came right through me, a nuclear missile cleaving into the side of a tramp steamer. I exploded. I burst into incandescent particles. I became the Milky Way. As far as I was concerned, it was The First Time.

'Yes, baby, yes, you pussy cunt, pussy cunt, let me fuck you. Baby, Jesus fucking Christ.' Coppo kept coming, ramming me. He squealed with delight, squealed like a greased pig as we used to say back home. He turned his cock into a roto-rooter, a pile driver, a hammer, a crowbar. The tool did not stop. It kept on coming. It bore into me, turning, twisting, pummeling my soft inner muscles. I yielded to him as I continued to grip that fucking tool.

It dug deeper and deeper, eating at my reserve until I screamed out, 'Aiiiiii!!!!' I could feel myself coming. I could feel my vaginal muscles in spasm. I began to thrash like a freshwater fish on the end of an angler's line, as a delicious glow spread out from my genitals to every area of my body, making me feel warm and tingling and glad to be alive.

Tragedy followed. Violent tragedy that threatened to send me back to Beavertown in a pine box.

I didn't mean to cause a commotion. I love to squeal when I come. But the driver, poor man, fearing the worst, turned around to see what was causing the noise. This happened three blocks from our honeymoon hotel, right in the middle of rush hour. Coppo made good on his word. He drew out his revolver and pulled the trigger. The bullet went clear through the glass divider, and nicked the driver's ear before smashing into the front windshield and out the other side, hitting a professional dog walker in his hand, a hand holding the leash to sixteen dogs. The driver's ear was gushing high spurts of blood which rained red splotches on the glass divider. Dogs ran shrieking into the rush-hour traffic. The driver, hysterical, thinking he'd lost half his ear, lost control of the car, then fainted. We crashed into the show window of a leading department store, no names mentioned, just as Coppo came.

Nothing I've just detailed had been enough to make him stop the sexual act, or me either. To hell with rush hour traffic! It was my wedding day, and my white satin gown, I mean my pantaloons, were wrapped around my man! My heels locked into the small of his back; My hands cradled the back of his legs. I should know. My picture was on the front of *The Daily News* the next day.

The driver, who was, in fact, an out-of-work actor, also turned out to be a Harvard graduate. His brother was a Harvard lawyer. His brother-in-law was a Yale lawyer. Maxey got Coppo out on appeal.

I played dumb. I had no choice. I just kept saying, 'I don't know what happened. We had just been married. My husband, Officer Muldoon, was showing me his gun and it accidentally discharged.' Muldoon, unfortunately, was not so apologetic. He said New York was full of anarchists, particularly anarchistic cabdrivers who had to be controlled.

Chapter Fourteen

Why do I attract so many nuts? Why do so many sexually uninhibited people, men, that is, have so many serious problems dealing with ordinary day-to-day activities? Why is having sex in the back seat of a limousine such a big deal? So what, if the cabdriver saw Coppo pumping away at me? What was there to see, really? Don't we all know what sex looks like and feels like? Don't we all know how we got here? What is the crime in biological function?

The problem was Coppo's. That's what shocked me. I thought he was beyond worrying about what people thought. I couldn't believe it; my brand-new husband had mental problems! Coppo Muldoon, the 'real man' most women are dying to meet, turned out to be living in a Western movie. I was absolutely destroyed. How could my marriage survive?

I wanted to run to Maxey and pour out my troubles, but I was too ashamed of how I had banished him from my bed, and I was too proud to admit I had been wrong. Furthermore, I was livid that Maxey was regularly being seen in the company of Glorianna Bronx, that intense rival of mine. In short, I was upset, confused, and desperate. There was no telling what I would do next. I had to do something to regain my poise, in order to get through my summer wear show. I could not afford to let an erratic husband affect my equilibrium. I didn't know who to turn to. Hugo Battista, my Brazilian stud? Out of the question. He couldn't speak English. What to do, what to do?

I decided to visit St. Patrick's Cathedral on Fifth Avenue, where my beloved Adolfo had had his funeral, and light a candle. I hoped that the answer, somehow, would come to me. Where in New York, city of eight million, half of them male, was there the man strong enough, responsible enough, caring enough, to help me through the night?

St. Patrick's was its usual impressive self, a most unusual space, huge, dark, with strange islands of light and statues of dead people, called 'saints' by the Catholics, lining the walls. St. Patrick's was so different from my grandmother's meeting hall, which she considered the only honest, sensible place to worship 'in the plain light of a General Electric light bulb,' that I'd come to prize St. Patrick's as my special discovery in the heart of Manhattan. Even with the hordes of tourists coming and going, St. Patrick's seemed like my special place to light a candle.

Well, what can I say? It happened. As I was kneeling there, the answer came loud and clear. There was one man I had neglected, ridiculed, abused. He was the only man with a sense of social responsibility I knew, the only one who cared about the future of the human race. Che Miranda. All right, so he was a Communist. No, I don't particularly like Communists, but that doesn't mean I'd throw one out of bed.

I made sure Lulu was overworked, running around the city on various errands relating to our upcoming show, at all costs far away from telephones. When I was sure she was out of the picture, I had a special messenger go to Che's hotel room, tell him he was wanted at the House of Adoro immediately. When he arrived, he was to be brought to my special elevator, and then to my private apartments. Coppo Muldoon? Directing traffic at Kennedy Airport, where else? He wasn't quitting his job on my account. Give him too much time off, and the next thing you know, he'd be firing guns at my seamstresses.

For my meeting with Che, I wore a peach-colored robe of see-through organdy. Although the garment was full-skirted with a high, tight neckline and long, flowing sleeves with fitted cuffs, my full breasts were clearly visible underneath. And anyone who looked closely enough could see my ripe cunt, with its splendid golden fur and its gash of watermelon pink, lingering in my crotch, waiting for special attention to be paid to it. My buns, as I checked my appearance in my full-view mirror, my buns were just that, twin loaves of fresh, mouth-watering bread, with a delectable golden crust awaiting a hungry tongue.

Che had no trouble finding the House of Adoro. The front desk called to say he was coming up. The red light, the elevator signal to announce his arrival, flashed. I pushed the button which opened the elevator door. I couldn't believe it. He stood there looking ten years younger. He had shaved off his beard, retaining only a well-trimmed moustache. He wore a white oxford-cloth shirt, unbuttoned to reveal his hairy chest, and he wore tight-fitted khakis instead of baggy fatigues. True, he kept his work boots and his wire-rimmed glasses, but now they looked almost preppy. I wondered what he was up to. I was surprised at how blonde his hair looked; on the other hand, his blue eyes seemed as cold as ever. I am an expert on blue eyes. Some blue eyes reflect the sky over Pago Pago. Some are Mediterranean blue, mirroring the dark blue-green of the sea that was a mother to us all. Che's eyes were the blue of Arctic shadows on ice. Frightfully cold and frightfully sexy. I felt that he could cut right through me with a single look. But I wasn't sure how much more sado-masochism I could take.

'Yes?' he said, looking beyond me to make sure we were alone.

'I thought maybe we could talk about the revolution,' I said. 'I need you to educate me, Che. I'm just a small-town girl from Beaver ...'

I could no longer speak. His tongue was inside my mouth, driving down deep into the meat in back. His arms squeezed hard around me; his groin pressed close. I could feel his rising excitement.

'What about the revolution?' I asked.

'The revolution can wait,' he replied. 'What about you and me?' he said, taking off his shirt to reveal a hard, muscular chest and shoulders.

I was surprised. I expected a scholar's body. I thought revolutionaries were supposed to be ascetic. I couldn't wait to see the rest of him; his penis bulged right through his khakis. I stood hovering over him as he stripped. The body unveiled was overpowering in its raw sexual statement; the cock was of average length but the broadest I'd ever seen, with a head like an oversized mushroom cap. He was all animal sinew; nothing about him was soft. How mistaken I had been! His hands and arms were wrapped in the veins of a great athlete. His body hair made him vulnerable. It was the soft part of him. That and the eyeglasses.

He took me by the elbow and led me to my gold satin bed. His hairy forearm brushed against my nipples, right through my organdy dressing gown. You see, I was still dressed.

He ripped the gown off of me, took it by the intricately sewn neck, and pulled down with a strong pull of his muscular arm. My body blushed. I could feel my nipples redden and my labia turn bright red from the rush of blood. Che did not speak. He looked like a wild dog ready to pounce. I heard him gulp in air.

'Fucking capitalist!' he said, with a lewd expression. Then he pushed my tits together so hard I cried out. His tongue flickered back and forth onto both nipples. 'Don't tell me who you are; don't tell me what you do!' he cried, 'ours is forbidden love!' He pressed me back on the bed, and moved in on top of me like a surfer catching a wave. He filled my sopping pussy with his cock, pushing his enormous, swollen head in and out

214

of my outer labia until my genitals yawned open, a mouth hungry for the whole length and width of him.

'Fuck me! Fuck me!' I cried, as he plowed deeper and deeper into my gaping hole, the walls of my cunt sucking voraciously on his thick rod. Every one of his thrusts made me moan with agony and pleasure; my throat knew no reticence, the sounds of my orgasmic storm broke involuntarily, matching the driving blows of his cock. I enveloped him with sexual heat and vaginal breath, my juice coating his cock and balls like a second skin. And when I came, it was with unbroken come, a hurricane of orgasm that refused to let go. Somewhere, beyond my mind, beyond my feeling, a strong man was stirring me. Somewhere, we were both spilling over, our inner lava from deep inside our respective mountain peaks had erupted with the force of a nuclear bomb, and gushed molten earth into a common valley, creating a common sea, a sea of liquid rock and earth fire. Diana Adoro had ceased to be. For the moment, there was only the lava sea. The force on top of me was demon sex; it possessed me and carried me away into the only heaven I'd known (excepting, of course, the sex I'd had with my beloved Adolfo Adoro).

'Thank you,' I said, tongue-tied and slightly idiotic. Who was I, after all, in the greater scheme of things? What was a fashion designer to world revolution? What was the House of Adoro to the destiny of a nation larger than the continental United States, with the world's longest river, with a river basin whose plants supply the earth with forty percent of its oxygen? Here Che Miranda was, depending on how one looked at him, an extraordinary political force who had deigned to be an observer at my summer wear show. Here was a stud in spite of himself, a cocksman who had the pick of Copacabana, a man who thought enough of my body to override enormous philosophical differences and commit adultery with me. It was thrilling beyond belief. We had broken the bonds of bourgeois morality. We had traveled beyond our self-importance into the area called Desire, which is, after all, my favorite place.

'Diana, when will I see you again?' he said.

'Che Miranda,' I replied, 'can't we crawl under the covers and rest in each other's arms? Just for a little while,' I begged. 'The doors are locked. Lulu is running errands. My husband is at work.'

'Your husband?' he asked, startled. 'I thought you were a widow.'

'No, no,' I replied, trying to sound casual. 'I got married yesterday afternoon to a New York policeman named Sergeant Muldoon, but before we got back to our honeymoon suite, he exhibited mentally deranged behavior and was given a summons. As far as I'm concerned, the marriage is already over. It was the dumbest thing I ever did.'

'Poor Diana,' intoned Che, as we climbed under the covers. 'Everyone knows American policemen are prone to violence. Even if I were a woman, I would never go to bed with an American policeman.'

'You wouldn't?' I asked, playing dumb, remembering the glorious time I made it with five of New York's finest in one afternoon on only my second day in New York. With one hand, Che was circling my still-taut nipple, while with the other, he was stroking my fuckflesh, stirring it up; his left knee, broad and bony and wonderful, screwed into me like I was an orange-half on a juicer. Farfetched? All I can say is the man definitely wanted juice. Within minutes, I was soaking wet, pussy nectar streaming out of me. We were locked in each other's arms, fast asleep, warm. I was warm. I was contented. I had forgotten the disaster of my marriage to a trigger-happy cop. I had forgotten my fears about my summer wear show. I had forgotten my bitter widowhood, and all the deaths during my week in Brazil. Perhaps, if Che and I had not been enemies, we would never have known how fatally attracted to each other we were. What a wonderfully caring, considerate man!

Have you ever made love to someone, knowing the two of you would probably never see one another again, usually because the other person lives halfway around the world? That's how it was with Che and me. We were worshippers at each other's shrines. The next day would bring a fashion show. Some wealthy women would be there. No doubt, he would be simultaneously so repelled and so attracted to them, his frustration would mount to an overpowering rage, and he would decide he really hated me, and that our sexual interlude was naught but fantasy, nothing but a dream. My question is, what is the greater fantasy, the anger or the love?

I clung to him for the rest of the afternoon, until, finally, knowing my Coppo would be home from work, I had to usher Che down the back stairs. He was still buttoning his shirt as the elevator carrying Coppo rose to my suite. With seconds to go, I ran back into my canopied bed, jumped under the covers, and pretended to be asleep.

Coppo smelled him. I'd forgotten; Coppo had a legendary nose. The only reason he was directing traffic now was because he'd once been a narcotics cop, and he had been caught taking a bribe. According to his own testimony, which I did not entirely believe, he was a great narcotics cop because he could smell heroin, cocaine, and hashish at fifty yards. He said he could tell the difference between Acapulco Gold and Aztec Red.

'Diana,' he said, 'you've had some Spic in this bed. Don't pretend you're asleep, his smell is still warm.' And then, he did the unforgiveable. He slapped me, and slapped me hard. That was the end of Let's Pretend.

'What do you want!' I screamed.

'Hey, baby, don't yell at me. I'm your husband, remember? said 'the husband' in a suddenly easygoing voice, with a do-it-yourself veneer of laid-back charm. I thought about calling the police, but, let's face it, he was the police, and I did not feel like an all-night gang-bang at the fashion show. I decided to lay it on the line.

'I'm divorcing you, immediately,' I cried.

'Not so fast,' he shot back. 'Not so fast.'

'Faster than you think,' I said. 'Faster than you think.'

He seemed genuinely shocked. 'What did I do?' he asked, with tears in his eyes.

'You're pistol-happy, for one thing, and now I see you're slap-happy as well!'

'But – but most broads like a little slapping around,' he said, 'that is, most normal broads. It's part of the normal male-female relationship.'

'Yeah?' I countered. 'Guess what? Abnormal little me didn't like the way you shot the driver, and abnormal little me doesn't like getting slapped in the face!'

'You cunt!' he screamed. 'You castrating cunt! You're lying there naked like you're somebody special, and you're criticizing the way I run my life, and the way I deal with my marriage.'

'*Your* marriage!' I shouted. 'It's my marriage, too. I think I have some say in this.'

'Oh, you think that just because you make so much money, you can wear the pants!' he screeched. 'You're an unnatural woman!'

'Get out of my house!' I cried, buzzing the emergency call button on my bed. 'One one, two three. One one, two three.'

Coppo didn't see me push the button, and by the time my security guards arrived from the downstairs, he was naked, erect, and jerking off in front of my face, his right fist grasping his broad shaft, pumping the elastic flesh over the hard steel core, while his left hand fondled his balls; he was flaunting his manhood in my face, deliberately upsetting me, deliberately throwing me into serious confusion, while he screamed, 'Suck me, suck me, you slut!'

I was repelled, disgusted and, of course, part of me, the nonliberated part, wanted to jump on him, grab him around his hard thighs, run my hands up and down over his marble buttocks, while I deep-throated him with a hot, slippery mouth. The masochistic part of me wanted to run my eager, muscular, nonthinking tongue around and around that vein-wrapped shaft until the white *crème* spurted out in thick globules, coating my mouth and throat. But I restrained myself. I may not be well-educated, but I still have my street smarts, and I aim to survive. My heart was breaking from the strain of this madman I had once loved trying to break my will by wielding the force of his sexual magnificence.

Coppo was still shouting, 'Suck me! Suck me!' as the security guards entered. One of them, a sweet young man named Andrew, much too nice to be a security guard for anyone but me, took Coppo up on his offer. First, the two of them grabbed Coppo from behind and handcuffed him behind his back. While the second guard forcibly restrained his legs, Andrew sank to the carpet in front of Coppo, lifted that weighty sceptre to his lips, while Coppo screamed, 'Faggot! Dirty, rotten faggot! Take my cock out of your filthy faggot mouth!' His rage only seemed to arouse the guard more. He behaved like a starving man at a banquet, occasionally stopping to mouth Coppo's balls, sucking them, first one and then the other into his eager, open mouth, as Coppo moaned, 'I can't stand this! I can't stand this!' Finally, he gave in to the situation. His swelling glans practically broke poor Andrew's jaw. It was lodged between his teeth, and when Coppo finally came, poor Andrew was as relieved as Coppo. My policeman bolted and thrashed in unwilling ecstasy as his gelatinous seed ran down the side of the security guard's mouth.

I gave orders for Coppo to be given a room at a nearby hotel until he was able to return to his former living quarters. If necessary, I was willing to rent him an apartment for a year, just to get him out of my hair. He had to be removed forcibly from my suite, wrapped in a blanket. All the while, he was shrieking that he

219

intended to 'smell out the Spic I was fucking,' and it was going to 'cost me' to divorce the best lay in the United States, namely him. I couldn't believe this was the same steady, self-assured man who had so captivated me less than a week before. I was shaken by the fact that I did not seem to know my own mind. But things were not over yet. By the end of the following day, there was to be further disaster.

Chapter Fifteen

My fashion show. My summer wear show. My swimwear show. Whatever did I originally have in mind? What was my intention? I have thought long and hard about spending some time with a shrink to find out if I was responsible for the disaster. Oh yes. Despite the fact that not one buyer took one order, and some fled screaming from my showrooms, some poetic reporter from *Women's Wear Daily*, plus a drunk journalist from a leading magazine managed to make my show sound like the latest style, something wondrous and inventive and worth looking into. Because of them, the owners of the department stores ordered their buyers to take big orders from me or lose their jobs.

As in Rome, I had a big surprise for everyone. When my Skinny Minnie model types pranced down the runway in my swimwear, some of them looking like Auschwitz inmates on holiday, I would then have one of my gorgeous street people from Brazil follow them in the same suit. Americans had never seen skimpy little bikinis on the bodies of mature, sexually-active women, who had given birth a few times. The American idea had been to switch from bikini to cover-up at the first sign of middle-age bulge; otherwise, a woman risked being called 'disgusting.'

On the other hand, Tia Maria, my jet-black angel, certainly did not have an ounce of fat. She was leanly muscled like a young jungle cat; she glowed with the satisfaction of a gymnast, but when she walked out on the runway following a six-foot-tall German blonde in a black bikini, the audience gasped, and not only because she looked stark naked (blacks wearing *black*?), but because she strutted out there like she *was* stark naked and en route to her lover's bed. She seemed much too self-confident, her hips seemed too relaxed, and when she put one foot in front of the other, her pelvis seemed to arch forward almost imperceptibly with just the suggestion of fucking. She drew attention to herself, something a model is not supposed to do. On the other hand, maybe they should. Movie stars draw attention to themselves, and the public invariably wants to dress like them. As Tia returned to the dressing rooms, her tight, high, black ass wiggled in everyone's faces. I noticed a few society women were not amused.

I also noticed Maxey von Fuchs and Glorianna sitting in the back row, Glorianna with a pair of high-powered binoculars, both equally expressionless. Glorianna, normally my leading model, had, according to her doctors, succumbed to a rare form of noninfectious hepatitis the morning after I had so unceremoniously kicked her and Maxey out of my bedroom. I guessed she was hoping Maxey would marry her, if for no other reason than to enrage me. Maxey, for his part, had been keeping his distance. He had not sent so much as a telegram congratulating me the day I married Officer Muldoon. I was at sixes and sevens (whereas it had once been strictly sixes and nines). I had never before experienced such bitter coldness from him.

Lulu Touché, suspecting nothing of my afternoon with Che Miranda, pretty much kept the show organized and on time. Che, dressed in an English tweed walking suit, no doubt a gift from Lulu, wandered in, looking scholarly and absent-minded. Quite a contrast to the first time I met him, a grimy, bearded revolutionary in faded khakis. I wasn't sure what had happened to Coppo Muldoon; I had asked my lawyers to call him, but he seemed unreachable. Little did I suspect that Muldoon's fiery Irish heart was connected to an inventive brain, a deadly combination when provoked to anger. Little did I realize that I had set the stage for revenge.

The summer wear proceeded apace. Nothing much to be said about the usual runway girls. The Brazilians were another matter; Tia Maria made her second entrance in a white, pleated tennis skirt with a white bandeau top. It looked great till she got to the edge of the runway. For some perverse reason, a sexual one, I'm sure, she had decided not to wear underwear. She insisted on pantomiming a tennis game with an imaginary tennis racket, and her coral gash was clearly evident every time she jumped up to hit the imaginary tennis ball. Every time she did this, there was an audible gasp from the front row.

Then, when the men's wear started, I had Hugo saunter out in khaki shorts, wearing an Inca headdress of hammered gold plates borrowed from the Metropolitan Museum of Art, and brandishing a spear, also borrowed (I think). When he walked out, his fly was unzipped. His big, black sausage flopped up and down, back and forth, half-erect. I was aghast. I even heard a certain leading good-advice columnist (no names mentioned) gasp. Nobody understood, really. They figured I was trying to make a statement about cock display as the latest trend.

Then, I tried a segment called 'Loving Couples,' where men and women in matching 'his and her' swimsuits walked out arm in arm. When it came time for the Brazilian couple, he had his hand down her bikini bottom and was feeling her up, finger-fucking her, while with the other hand he was trying to jerk himself off by rubbing his stainless steel tennis racket back and forth over the hard bulge in his crotch. The Brazilian woman must have been very nervous because of the upper-class, North-American crowd. In any case, she fell to the floor in a stunning orgasm as her companion with the tennis racket struggled to wrestle out of his bathing suit so he could spread open her legs and really sock it to her. In all fairness to me, this moment was not only a theatrical statement, it smacked of real life and real passion. Better yet, it demonstrated how truly flexible my clothes were; they were so easy to move in, the wearer could remain sexually active.

But my audience, the New York chic crowd, which constantly pretended to be 'with it,' were actually a bunch of Judeo-Christian puritans interested mainly in money and profit. They were in no sense ready for live sex in theatre, the Church, or, God forbid, Seventh Avenue. A certain blonde princess, who had been so helpful and supportive when I first came to New York, had to be led from the showrooms, and a gorgeous former First Lady, who I thought approved of nudity and sex, I mean, some people have called her the world's highest-priced hooker, actually was heard to say out loud, 'This is sick,' as she left the room. I was so shocked! Another fantasy destroyed! I reluctantly had to ask my Brazilian lovers to leave the runway.

I wanted to leave them there and have the other models walk around them as they made love, but no, it would have been labeled a 'pornographic fashion show,' and the mid-western buyers would have refused to attend. So my two lovers had to be forcibly dragged off the runway as they were copulating.

My next couples, first two models and then two Brazilians, were all men. The item for sale was a boxer-type, loose-cut bathing suit in preppie colors, pale blues, yellows, pinks, and greens, but made out of material so thin and so clinging it left little to the imagination. This was intended for men who wanted to show off their sexual equipment while pretending they couldn't care less, the bathing suit's at fault, right? The projected market was very active, heterosexual studs and, of course, gays. The two New York models were long, sinewy blondes with dancers' bodies, in other words, a little too tight; and, whereas their cocks were pretty plump, these men did not consider themselves sexually predatory. They were polite. They were on display. Neither gay or straight.

The Brazilians never thought about such things. They seemed to be perpetually half-erect, and looking for cooze, wherever it might be. They actually started out on the runway towering four feet above every female in the room, one eye staring under their dresses, or trying to, the other eye glued to cleavage, which, in New York in February, was not exactly a matter of nipples straining over the edges of constraining boundaries of velvet and tweed. Nor do upper-class women in New York appear in public with their unwrapped jugs bouncing up and down under sheer material, although, to be fair, there are always certain women who understand and appreciate the power of sex; after all, it got them the 'right' husband. Their problem is often that once having married Mr. Moneybags, he's too old or too tired or too bored to jump on them, so they are forever on the prowl, as subtly as possible, looking for hard, young bodies and appreciative men who love women so much they don't ask too many questions, they just take what they get with a smile.

I saw several of these women sitting in my front row, their skirts hiked up, revealing six extra inches of inner or outer thigh, depending on whether her legs were crossed or uncrossed. It wasn't just the legs, either. Certain women have a way of feverishly running their hands through their thick hair, of maintaining moist, slightly parted lips, their tongues resting languidly between their lower teeth, sometimes taking time to lick their lips, glazing them with warm spit, while they inadvertently, almost accidentally, stroke themselves on the outside of their dresses and silk suit jackets almost exactly where their nipples lay waiting to be aroused.

One woman in particular, the wife of a cosmetics

tycoon, young enough to be his daughter, had a seductive pair of thighs, and she knew it. They were not fat, not really. Slightly overflowing, like perfect yogurt, not molded exactly, but self-contained, inviting the mouth or fingers, depending on the state of one's desire; the perfect sexual thighs. She still wore those 1940's stockings that end halfway up the thigh in wide bands of a slightly thicker, slightly darker color, to which garter snaps are connected to a garter belt. This particular fashion is so startling today, in an age of pantyhose and body stockings that the masculine eye, once aware of the top of the stocking, which she seems to inadvertently reveal as she twists her entire body around and thus raises her skirt to supposedly look in the opposite direction, travels past the stockings in the direction of the garter belt, to discover that milady has forgotten to wear her panties! Her bush, which at first seems like a dark shadow, is now clearly a bush. I say clearly, because its dark hair is in startling contrast to the hot pink slit below it, a slit which grows wider and pinker and juicier as Lady Bountiful continues to keep her torso turned completely around. Now, she's checking the exit sign at the back door, you see. Her companions, unless they are sensitive to the smell of fresh cunt, which most of them are not, haven't a clue as to what's going on. They are still so Victorian, if they notice the male model with the bulging eyes, they imagine he's noticed their friend's out-of-date stockings, and they suppose he's staring at an outdated style. The more hip among them, of course, *know* he's lusting after a mouthful of inner thigh.

As I was saying, four male models were modeling conservative-cut swimsuits in the world's thinnest fabric. Just to be cute, and so that the buyers would get the point, I had all four models take a shower in my swimsuits just before stepping on the runway, so they would look like they just stepped out of the ocean. I gave them beach balls as props. There was a gasp from the wife of the tycoon as the four men stepped on the

226

runway. She had not been prepared for such animal haunches and for such visible, or should I say 'obvious' cock meat; it wasn't so much visible, it was more or less a living presence.

My tycoon's wife must have been a repressed nymphomaniac, or else she'd never seen a naked man, or something, because she began to masturbate right there as if no one else was present. The men on stage, seeing this, snapped, too. I'm afraid the whole setup was too explicitly sexual. It was my own fault. The Brazilians' knew I had brought them to New York for their sexual appeal. They knew I considered them to be an almost pure state of sexual energy intended to alert some of my most neurotic customers and fashion critics to the real world of flesh and blood, instead of some idealized spiritual or artistic state of being. What I had not counted on is that opposites attract. The Brazilians found themselves drawn to a new kind of human being, the physically soft, highly strung, supernervous, highly repressed, ruthlessly competitive New Yorker. The two men on stage, seeing the woman, who shall remain nameless, with her finger up her cunt, stroking her own clitoris, ripped off their tissue-thin suits and jumped on top of her.

With that, all hell broke loose. The security guards started blowing whistles and dragging models off to the paddy wagon, by now waiting downstairs. Alarms sounded.

I screamed, 'Refreshments in the dining room!'

Within five minutes, my small theatre was empty. It was just as well. I had only two more outfits to show, including a beach wear bridal gown made out of a canvas beach umbrella worn over a white, Spandex bathing suit with a 'veil' made out of an old-fashioned white rubber bathing cap and a small red rubber tire. A necklace of empty tin cans completed the vision. A joke, of course.

What happened next was no joke, and I don't mean my customers changed their mind and decided to return for an orgy.

That's when the bomb went off. Yes, the bomb. Coppo Muldoon, acting on information from a third cousin in the IRA, had planted plastic explosives under the runway. They were clearly meant to blow the room apart. If I had not run to the bathroom one minute before, to check my mascara, I would have been blown to smithereens, which was precisely Coppo's intention. I normally stood less than three feet from where the bomb had been planted.

The room was destroyed. Pieces of chairs, carpet, the wooden runway, wall plaster, and window panes danced together in the air, a macabre ballet of chaos and destruction. I could not believe that a man could hate me so much. I did not think I inspired such emotion. He said more to me about the depth of his feelings for me with the bomb than he said in person with his cock. I had to be taken to the infirmary, I was shaking so much.

To end this chapter on a happy note, I will add a few words on Che Miranda. It seems that while he was in New York fucking me, buying clothes at Brooks Brothers and keeping an eye out for the well-being of his compatriots, he discovered some of his mother's family, his Brooklyn Irish cousins, the O'Donnells. Several of the O'Donnell men were top New York lawyers; in the course of five generations, they'd gone from organized crime to organized labor to labor law to real estate law to investment counseling. They were rugged, right-wing millionaires, willing and able to help an individual who needed help; they were absolutely opposed to Che's beloved Communist party, whose members they despised as a bunch of mindless thugs. Che, of course, had considered his cousins mindless money-grubbers until he discovered one of them had done his doctoral thesis on the Communist dictator Josef Stalin and the Soviet death camps. It was a revelation, pure and simple. Within a month, Miranda, who was already an American citizen by virtue of his American mother, had been offered the possibility of joining his cousins in real estate. It was their gain. Che exhibited natural leadership abilities and a strong belief in the average working man.

A year later, he had enrolled in Fordham University Law School. Che was well on his way to becoming everything he had despised as a young radical. Like me, he had come from the working classes to the edge of aristocracy. Like me, no matter how much money or power he accumulated, he would never forget his lowly origins when it came to negotiating reasonable salary hikes for his constantly complaining employees. I knew that, as an older man, his radical origins would serve him well in little things, such as the way he addressed his employees on his yacht or the waiters at his beach club, or the way he would carefully cater to his wife, who would undoubtedly be an Irish-Catholic convent girl, a woman who would consider sex one small but necessary element in the complex give-and-take of marriage. I also knew that Che would continue to make a wonderful lover for a select group of women who would appreciate pleasure for its own sake.

Naturally, I had myself in mind. I knew that whether I was single or married, Che and I would always be sexually available to one another. We would be able to enjoy one another because, unlike most people, we knew we were not fucked-up. And he, being a wealthy, self-made stud, would have no reason to compete with my husband, whoever he might be. You see, my beloved Adolfo Adoro had so trained me in the art of the three-way, the four-way, and the 'intimate orgy', as he called it, that I wasn't quite sure what would happen if I married an old-fashioned kind of guy who was great in every department but sexual liberation. Believe it or not, there are still men out there who think marriage means a man and a woman are, with occasional outside affairs, exclusive sexual partners. I decided early on, after my experience with Coppo Muldoon, that if I married again, and if my husband had old-fashioned ideas about marital fidelity, I would keep the truth of my sex life to myself. I realized that meant I would have to find lovers who could keep their mouths shut. Actually, experiencing a great deal of upset about this point, I realized that, if I continued my present pattern of fucking absolute strangers, men and women who had no idea of who I was in the business world; chambermaids, busboys, waiters, cab drivers, lifeguards, chorus girls and men who propositioned me on the streets, thinking I was some kind of hooker, I wouldn't have any trouble. This was pure sex without ulterior motivations. In other words, they weren't fucking me to get back at my husband, they were fucking me because I was a great piece of ass, and I was free.

When some of my Adoro models, who are always having affairs with married men, come to me for personal advice, I always explain my philosophy of pure sex: fuck for the moment, fuck because you like to fuck, fuck because it feels good. Don't get into fucking as a way of making a third party jealous. Don't fuck your way to the top. Likewise, don't fuck your way to the bottom. I tell them, fuck with a glad heart; just make sure you've got an IUD or diaphragm in place. Life is real. Sometimes.

Chapter Sixteen

Finally, the Brazilians were gone. Most went immediately back to Brazil. Some, like Tia Maria, became illegal aliens in the U.S. Let's just say that according to my sources, that delicious piece of chocolate is now working on Park Avenue, learning English and polishing silver and other things. Hugo, like I already reported, disappeared forever into the streets of New York and the deepest recesses of Lulu's fantasies, never to be seen alive again.

All in all, my summer wear collection, the Brazilian models, and the bomb blast generated a great deal of publicity for the House of Adoro. American women, a huge percentage of whom are constantly dieting, when they read articles about my show, began to understand how 'fat can be sexy.' The clothes sold; I can't explain. Like me, Adoro was experiencing constant growth.

Needless to say, Coppo Muldoon and I were divorced, and I got a restraining order barring him from coming within a hundred yards of me.

Of course, I have been leaving out the most important person of my life, namely Maxey von Fuchs, with whom I had been on the 'outs' ever since I took issue with his wanting to share me with Coppo. Maxey and I hadn't spoken since that disastrous night except about strictly business affairs, and then only on the telephone in crisp official tones. I found I couldn't cope with him. His presence was there, always, looming large in my overactive imagination, but I had no desire to look him in the eye. Why bother? He was an arrogant German and, on paper, at least, he was working for me. True, there were nights, after Coppo and I were divorced, when Hugo was gone and Che Miranda was courting his Irish-Catholic convent girl, when Maxey came to me in my dreams, and his sexual presence insinuated itself into my night-time fantasies. Maxey, after all, was my one sexual link to my beloved Adolfo.

I made a profound personal decision, in those dark hours of abject loneliness following my tragic divorce from Coppo, that I would, with respect to Maxey, become a celibate. Oh sure, I planned to go on making it with the occasional delivery boy or traveling salesman, why not? There are a lot of lonely men out there, and sex is really no more than yet another animal appetite, as necessary as food and drink, and definitely not worth all the aggravation that organized religion and male-dominated society has placed on it. I mean, if I've got the hots for a man, and he wants to shove his warm, throbbing member into my cunt, sure I'll take him, and I don't want to be called a whore or slut for doing what nature decrees. Because basically, that kind of casual sex does not affect celibacy. Even cloistered nuns should be allowed to fuck themselves silly if they want. The real issue in male-female sex is what I call 'fucking with the heart.' The open heart. That says it all. That's where the danger lies, and the adventure.

That's how Maxey threatened me. I just couldn't fuck him and forget him. He was too strong a presence. Nor could I ever hope to possess him. He was unattainable. Mostly because he was too neurotic. He'd seen too many wars, I guess, and he'd been with too many women. Like I say, I swore off Maxey. I didn't need the aggravation. I decided he was the perfect financial manager for the House of Adoro, but otherwise, forget it. Life was already complicated enough.

Maxey didn't think so. He began to pursue me. And like I always say, a man's desire is my undoing. When I say 'desire,' I don't mean momentary appetite. I mean the man's all-consuming passion for me, which rises up in his gut like a python who hasn't eaten for a month. He is consumed with thoughts of trapping me and holding me fast in his fatal embrace. When I know I am desired to that extent, I am turned on like never before. In fact, a man's desire is my main aphrodisiac. Desire is something that can't be faked. It arises in the depths of the soul. Its brain is somewhere hidden in the root of every man's cock; in the woman, it lies near the end of the vaginal canal; it permeates the labia; no, I guess in the case of the woman, it permeates everything she is or hopes to be.

When a man like Maxey absolutely desires me from the depths of his groin, I mean his soul, when I know how consumed he is with hunger for me, and, let's face it, even I sometimes get turned on by the sight of my spectacular knockers, which are perfectly ripe and firm, with aureolas like little inverted cones of chocolate mousse – where am I? Yes, of course, Maxey's desire.

It began with the usual – flowers and phone calls. The straw baskets filled with fresh-cut wildflowers, daisies and tiger lilies and irises, whose delicate crepelike petals reminded me of cunt lips, especially the way they seemed to envelop the center of the flower, much like the soft sweet lips in the vagina protect the precious clitoral bud. I told one of my assistants to put the flowers in water, we could use them to decorate our reception rooms.

The phone calls were another matter. Maxey called day and night. They were not business calls. He had no intention of discussing stock portfolios or capital gains taxes. Nor did he invite me to dinner at Lutèce, or to brunch at the Palm Court. He didn't even suggest getting together for a chocolate sundae at Rumpelmayer's. His approach was more one of a communicated ecstasy, or is the word 'lust'?

'Diana, I love you. I want my big, hot cock to take a joy ride at the top of your legs.' Very subtle, right? 'Diana, I want my tongue to take a vacation on your clitoris.' Sometimes it was just 'Diana, I want to eat you,' or 'Diana, I want to fuck you.' Sometimes, he tried the guilt trip, 'Diana, why are you torturing me?'

Usually I said, 'Thank you,' and hung up. I knew it was only a matter of time before I lay down in front of him and spread my cunt lips wide. I could feel the force of his spirit walking ahead of him, a dark sexual presence that I felt certain had invaded my bedroom several times when I was asleep and dreaming, because my dreams too often seemed like real experiences of being fucked by a spirit, Maxey's spirit. I know that sounds like nothing at all, but, after all, the difference between a stud and the corpse of a stud is exactly that, the living, breathing spirit I've just described. In any case, I was not surprised by the idea of it. After all, Maxey and I had not been lovers for over a month, and in real life, he *was* trying to get under the sheets with me.

Real life, however, happened just as I dreamt it. I wouldn't go so far as to call it a rape, since, God knows, way down deep I wanted the man way down and definitely deep, but about a week after the flowers and the phone calls started, after I had said 'Thank you' and hung up for the hundred and fiftieth time, I was fast asleep in my suite. Maxey, true to form, had managed to get ahold of my new keys, and had made copies of them. I had suspected he would try to take me unaware; for that reason, I had been having my casual, relatively unimportant sex, what I call my 'fun' sex, outside the house and during the day, because, God knows, I was not in the mood to have Maxey break into my suite, only to find me with come on my face. I'd like to think I am smarter than that.

There I was, on a cold, rainy night, dead to the world. I woke up in the middle of it, my legs spread apart, Maxey inside me, my labia sucking voraciously on his big German cock as he pumped it in and out.

234

'Diana, forgive me, but it's been too long,' he announced, breathing with deep, labored grunts as his orgasm approached. I realized I had forgotten about the intense passion of the willful Nordic race. Maxey had taken me like a rapacious conqueror. He was a Viking and a Hun, and I was thrilled beyond belief. There was nothing I could do but lie back and enjoy this passionate man who was willing to break the law to force me to resume our relationship.

Outside the window, the late winter night sky was black; inside, I had been desperately lonely. What normal woman wants to sleep in the nude by herself? But I don't want to belabor this account with my emotional problems.

The bristly hairs of his bush ground into my clitoris like a Brillo pad rubbing up against a live oyster. God! Every part of him assaulted me, pushed, prodded, hooked into me. Was there nothing soft in this man? I wrapped my legs around his neck, locking my ankles together as his flesh pole drove deeper and deeper into the hole in my mound. I reached under and squeezed his balls, hard. He helped, and then howled with a loud, angry sound. The harder I squeezed, the angrier he became, I was, of course, only testing him.

'Stop that, you fucking Hun!' I cried. 'Coming in here, with stolen keys, practically raping me because of your fucking sexual needs. Go back to Glorianna, your Comanche princess, if you have sexual needs!'

'You and I belong together,' he said, slapping me hard, hard enough to make my eyes well up with tears.

'What was that for?' I pleaded.

'Stop squeezing my balls!' he cried. But I suddenly found I wouldn't. I wanted to wound him. I'd almost been raped and killed and mangled in Brazil where he'd sent me, and where had he been? He'd set me up with Che Miranda, the Communist radical. I was sure of it. I squeezed his balls harder. Maxey punched me square in the jaw, cutting me on my upper gums. The blood gushed out of my mouth all over my new silk sheets.

235

'You fucking Nazi!' I screamed, digging my fingernails into his never-stopping cock, drawing some blood of my own.

'You nobody!' he whispered. 'You nothing! You cheap little tart!' He took my nipples with his Nazi hands and practically twisted them off. I did the same with his balls, squeezing them with both hands in an attempt to amputate them, to literally castrate the man. But he was held together by steel cables, and his sexual movements did not stop. I began to smash him in the face with my fists, beating on his mouth to no great effect, and then, I tried to gouge out his eyeballs; they were like marbles. I seemed to have little effect on them, although I was able to successfully scratch his cheeks and draw blood, which dripped onto me in slow rivulets as I writhed and twisted, trying to extract my pussy from the driving force of his cock. The more I writhed, the greater was my pleasure. The excruciating pain was punctuated with jabs of satisfaction. The cut on my gums continued to drip blood on me and on my sheets. Maxey and I were a shining, glistening pink, both painted wet with sweat and saliva and blood mixed together and spread over our bodies like a glaze. We shimmered in the light, shimmered through our hatred and our frenzy, shimmered through our exertions, our madness, our refusal to end our passion until we both went up in flames, and were finally reduced to ash.

Then, I could feel him swell up within me, that great insulting tool, that engorged weapon that had invaded me and brought me to a pitch of ecstasy. Again, I felt loss of control as my orgasm began from a point deep in my groin. From where I had been dead and dark came the unexpected waves of warmth, which I knew would grow in size and strength until I drowned in their undertow.

'Maxey, I hate you!' I screamed. 'You sent me to Rio to die!'

'Diana ...' He broke off in mid-sentence. Then he,

236

too, went under. He, too, drowned. He, too, went into death. A moment of nothingness. A moment when there was no air, no space, no human voice, no hope. Then came the resurrection. The light. The warm glow. The gurgling in the throat. In our mutual orgasm, Maxey and I became friends again.

For once, I felt completely happy. To think that such a short time before, Maxey had sent me to Rio de Janeiro because I had been bored out of my mind, not realizing that, in the frenzy of Carnival, in the face of murder, violence, corruption, madness, I would come to grips with my own soul.

'Soul!' What an awesome word! It suggests that, having attained a new spiritual depth, I would lead a life of discipline, if not deprivation. It suggests soup kitchens for the poor, a return to religion, and a kind of sexual monogamy that I have never understood. Frankly, 'soul' suggests I would stop having fun.

Yet, here I was, having fun, my bed filled with the weight of Prussia, my mouth full of Maxey. Below me, in my incredible brownstone, my fashion empire was filled with the classiest clothes in New York, insured to the hilt, and equipped with the latest burglar alarms. I was still twenty-three. My tits did not sag. My face found it easy to smile.

I thought to myself as I lay there among my most cherished genitals, Maxey's and my own, 'Money isn't everything; sex is. Money doesn't buy happiness; happiness comes only to those who take it for themselves, usually by taking off their clothes.'

Thank you, my Maxey. Thank you, Rio de Janeiro. City of samba. City of sin. City of sympathy. City of sex. City of cities. Amen.

The End

She saw . . . she conquered . . . she came . . .

DIANA'S DEBUT

Lytton Sinclair

Travel is meant to be a broadening experience. Even the delicious Diana, who though a simple girl from a little town in Pennsylvania had seen and done a thing or two, discovered that travel can always teach you something. For it was in Rome that, despite an international incident of unforgettable violence and bad taste, she met so many warm-hearted people with fantastic bodies eager to communicate with a sensuous down-home American girl. In Rome that she learned to let go of her small-town hangups about sex and *really* enjoy herself. In Rome that she discovered just what men meant when they said to her, 'Diana, you have so much to give.'

FUTURA PUBLICATIONS
FICTION
0 7088 4028 0

DON'T MISS THE EROTIC ADVENTURES OF SLEEPING BEAUTY

Step beyond the wall of your own imagination to the place where erotic enchantment lies . . .

THE CLAIMING OF SLEEPING BEAUTY

A. N. Roquelaure

When Sleeping Beauty awakes at the Prince's kiss it is the begininng of our story, not the end. Once the prisoner of a spell, locked in the sleep of innocence – now she is the prisoner of sensual love, held fast by the magic of desire. Claimed by the Prince as the slave of his passions, Sleeping Beauty learns that tenderness and cruelty, pleasure and pain, longing and fulfilment are all one in the awesome kingdom of love.

Beauty she is – but she is sleeping no more . . .

FUTURA PUBLICATIONS
FICTION
0 7088 2743 8

BEAUTY'S PUNISHMENT

A. N. Roquelaure

Once the prince's favourite pleasure – once the passionate plaything of his court – Beauty is being punished with banishment from that kingdom of carnal delights. But though Beauty's enchantment is over, her lessons in loving have only begun . . .

FUTURA PUBLICATIONS
FICTION
0 7088 3567 8

BEAUTY'S RELEASE

A. N. Roquelaure

Once pleasure's plaything, Beauty is about to become love's willing slave . . . Beauty has learned her lessons well. There are no pleasures she hasn't given, no delights she hasn't known – but there can be no freedom for her if it means she must deny her body the joys it expects, the excitement it so desperately craves. Now, as our story nears its end, Beauty meets the Prince of her dreams – the one man whose touch can release the torrential passions locked within her. And, as with the best of fairy tales, they are destined to live ecstatically ever after.

FUTURA PULICATIONS
FICTION
0 7088 3663 1

All Futura Books are available at your bookshop or newsagent, or can be ordered from the following address:
Futura Books, Cash Sales Department,
P.O. Box 11, Falmouth, Cornwall TR10 9EN.

Please send cheque or postal order (no currency), and allow 60p for postage and packing for the first book plus 25p for the second book and 15p for each additional book ordered up to a maximum charge of £1.90 in U.K.

B.F.P.O. customers please allow 60p for the first book, 25p for the second book plus 15p per copy for the next 7 books, thereafter 9p per book

Overseas customers, including Eire, please allow £1.25 for postage and packing for the first book, 75p for the second book and 28p for each subsequent title ordered.